"Intricate. Astounding. Suspense woven together with lyrical prose. Characters you hate, others you bleia Ruchti, has done it again with *All My*

—Lauraine Snelling, creator of th
torical series and *Wake the Dawn*

"I was blown away by the beautii   .ll *My Belongings*. Her story was warm, tear-jerking, and beautiful with healing. I want to read more of this novelist's intelligent work."

—Hannah Alexander, author of *Hallowed Halls*

"Loved it. Loved. It. Wonderful characters. Creative story line. Get yourself comfortable because it's a read-at-one-sitting book. Highly recommended."

—Gayle Roper, author of *Lost and Found; An Unlikely Match*

"Cynthia Ruchti has penned another compelling story with a hero and heroine who are both trapped by their pasts and complications in the present that could destroy futures. This is a story that leads you through the pages to a place where light and forgiveness stream. A beautiful story for people who love rich layers of truth mixed into their novels."

—Cara Putman, award-winning author of *Shadowed by Grace*

"Where do you turn when changing your name isn't enough? When putting hundreds of miles between you and your family of origin doesn't distance you from the shame? With achingly real characters facing crises of conscience that challenge even those solid in their convictions, Cynthia Ruchti creates a story of faith, forgiveness, and families who are sometimes called to reinvent themselves to survive. You will not get through this book without some fraying of your heart . . . but it will be tenderly mended by the final page."

—Becky Melby, author of the Lost Sanctuary series

"I couldn't put *All My Belongings* down—I was enraptured and caught up in the words, in the feelings. I loved the romance and the mystery and the beauty of God's grace and love that overarched the story. I know just how Becca felt with Aurelia—and with her dad. This was such a blessing!"

—Deb Haggerty

"I am a dedica*   \ll My *Belongings* is just   FICT RUC   )f her stunning novels.   Ruchti, Cynthia.   it few great ones. Rucht: All my belongings   a tale of a young woman fighting to overcome her father's legacy, Ruchti keeps readers on the edge of their seats even as we are challenged to consider our own faith and courage in the face of overwhelming odds."

—Kathi Macias, author of more than 40 books, including *The Singing Quilt*

"Perhaps the greatest longing of every heart is to find a safe place to belong and be loved. For those feeling lost and shut out of love, Cynthia's powerful story provides a map for the journey to where grace and forgiveness intersect with hope and healing."

—Lisa Abeler, Women's Ministries Director at Camp Lebanon in Minnesota

"The word pictures Cynthia Ruchti paints in my mind's eye are like no other! This book is filled with mystery, intrigue, and love wrapped up in the embrace of God's grace—destined to become a best seller!"

—Shari Radford, Event Planner/Owner, Christian Speakers Bureau

"Ruchti's characters in *All My Belongings* face real problems that have no easy solutions. They struggle with trust, they wrestle with forgiveness. This story captured my attention and held it to the end when the main character at last discovers where she truly belongs."

—Emily Parke Chase, author of *Standing Tall After Falling Short*

"*All My Belongings* is the type of book you would want to have as you curl up in a soft chair with a cup of tea! I loved the plot of this book. The main character is a woman we all could identify with and yet her courage and faith are inspirations. Of course, everyone loves a romance, and the way the author brings it about is done with such taste and thoughtfulness. I was on the edge of my seat as one thing after another happens, but the ending of the story as well as how God is there for us will warm your heart. What a wonderful story!"

—Lane P. Jordan, best-selling author of *12 Steps to Becoming a More Organized Woman*

"Thank you for the chance to read your new book. I absolutely loved it. Your information on medications and the progression of the illness and the care was right on. This story really hit home to me in so many ways. Throughout the book thoughts would take me to my own family experiences and those at my job. I will highly recommend this book to everyone when it is published."

—Cindy Hardrath, hospice caregiver

all my belongings

CYNTHIA RUCHTI

a novel approach to faith

Nashville

Library of Congress Cataloging-in-Publication Data

Ruchti, Cynthia.
  All my belongings / Cynthia Ruchti.
    pages cm
  ISBN 978-1-4267-4972-8 (binding: soft back, pbk., adhesive,
perfect binding : alk. paper) 1. Fathers and daughters—Fiction. 2.
Runaway
teenagers—Fiction. I. Title.
  PS3618.U3255A79 2014
  813'.6—dc23
                                                    2013041874

Printed in the United States of America

1 2 3 4 5 6 7 8 9 10 / 19 18 17 16 15 14

To those who feel homeless when they aren't,
whose journeys take exceptional courage,
whose hearts tell them the love
they seek is possible, present,
and not at all what they imagined.

It's ocean-deep and laced with grace.

Other Books by Cynthia Ruchti

Fiction
They Almost Always Come Home
When the Morning Glory Blooms
Cedar Creek Seasons (contributor)
A Door Country Christmas (contributor)

Nonfiction
Ragged Hope: Surviving the Fallout
of Other People's Choices
Mornings with Jesus, 2014 (contributor)
His Grace Is Sufficient, Decaf Is Not (contributor)

Acknowledgments

My husband pouted, "I haven't read it yet. Your new one." The thought of Bill stealing away with a book I wrote, falling in love with the characters who moved me, tracing the journeys imagination penned but real life inspired stirs my soul. He doesn't just sacrifice my making a "real" income and expecting lasagna and my full attention when characters are wrestling something through in my head. He cares. I'm blessed. Thank you, Wonderhubby.

When even my youngest grandchild talks about "authors like you, Grammie," I'm more grateful than ever to have been given the privilege of telling stories. The legacy of love I hope to leave includes what shows up between the covers of books I write. The support of my family—from my children, grandchildren, siblings and their spouses, and all branches of the family tree—feels like having a personal cheering squad, a cheering squad that prays, for which I'm humbled and grateful.

Readers, you did this! You enabled me to launch this story to the reading world. Your blessed acceptance of other novels and nonfiction from this author with the unpronounceable last name (Helpful hint—the first half rhymes with book. Ruchti = ROOK-tee) opened the door for *All My Belongings*. As you read the story, enjoy the sensation that you helped breathe life into it. I can't wait for you to read what's coming next, too!

Ramona Richards and Jamie Clarke Chavez knew just what the book needed in the editing phase. Thank you, Ramona and Abingdon Press, for trusting me to write this particular story.

So many at the Abingdon offices have become like family to me. My appreciation for you spills over every day. Cover designers, marketing team, sales staff, Cat Hoort, Pamela Clements, Mark and Linda Yeh, Brenda, Susan, Julie, Preston, Bryan . . .

As always, I've leaned heavily on the camaraderie, insights, and grace of kindred spirits like Jackie, Becky, and Michelle. Amazing women, I'm grateful for you.

Wendy Lawton, my agent who accompanies me on this breath-stealing adventure, I so deeply value your friendship and wisdom and the way you call me up higher in my walk through this achingly beautiful world.

My writing friends at ACFW; my author friends who are as faithful to pray as they are to critique; my brainstorming, talk-me-off-a-writing-ledge,   how-can-we-help-spread-the-word community; first readers; and publicists, you bless me to my marrow.

Breath of Life, You who first whispered this idea in my ear and branded it onto the flesh of my heart, thank You for being faithful to the end . . . and beyond. I am forever Yours, my Belonging Place, the Source of all my longing.

Hope delayed makes the heart sick;
longing fulfilled is a tree of life.
—Proverbs 13:12

1

The coffee tasted like burnt marshmallows. The charred bits. Jayne set the vending machine cup on the corner of her advisor's desk.

Patricia smiled over half-glasses. "Don't blame you." She nodded toward her oversized thermal tankard. "I bring my own from home."

Home.

"I'm surprised you wanted to see me today, Jayne. Aren't they—?"

"Yes." She directed her line of sight through Patricia Connor's office window, over the tops of the century-old oaks and maples lining the campus, toward the courthouse in the center of town.

"And you didn't want to be there?" The woman removed her glasses as if they interfered with her understanding.

Oh, I'm there. I've been there every agonizing moment. Several little shards of me are embedded in the hardwood floor in the court-room. What's left of me wants an answer from you. "I need to find out if I can reenter the program where I left off."

Patricia leaned back in her nondescript office chair. "And you have to know today?"

"Yes."

Her advisor's head shook so slightly, Jayne assumed the movement originated in the nervous bounce of the woman's knee, not her neck. "We've had . . . concerns."

"My grades were good."

"It's not that. Most nontraditional students are committed enough to pull decent grades."

Twenty-seven and nontraditional. In every way. Jayne leaned forward and added, "And work two jobs while doing it." She wouldn't look out the window again. Her future lay here, in this decision. "If you're worried about the financial aspect . . ."

"Aren't you? Word is, you're tapped out with what your family's gone through."

She'd shelved the word *family* a year and a half ago, the day she found out her father's middle name was Reprehensible. Bertram Reprehensible Dennagee. Her mother didn't think she could endure the pain one more day. Her father made sure she didn't.

According to the charges against him, it wasn't the first time.

Thanks to Jayne's discovery, though, and her call to the police, it was the first time he'd been caught.

Her eyes burned behind her eyelids. She could feel her sinuses swelling.

"Jayne?"

She repositioned herself in the chair, dropping her shoulders from where they'd crept up near her ears, straightening her spine, breathing two seconds in, two seconds out. "I'll find a way. I need to finish the nursing program. Get on with my life. What's left of it."

Behind her a voice leaned into the room. "Did you hear? Guilty on all charges. They got him!"

Patricia's face blanched and pinched. Her eyes made arrows toward where Jayne sat.

The voice faded as it backed into the hall. The expletive a whisper, it still rattled the window, the bookcases, Jayne's ribs.

Lips pressed together, Jayne waited for her advisor to say something. And for her throat muscles to unclench.

"I'm sorry."

Jayne let the hollow words bounce around the room for a moment. "About the verdict? Not unexpected."

"Have you thought about trying another school of nursing? Someplace a little farther away from—"

From her father's reputation? How far was that?

I.C.E. *In Case of Emergency*. Geneva Larkin's name and code showed on her cell phone screen. Jayne hadn't turned the key in the ignition yet, twenty minutes after leaving Patricia's office. Perfectly safe to use her cell phone even though she was behind the wheel. Safe. If it had been anyone but Geneva— the mentor who'd kept her tethered to reality since Jayne was ten years old and for all practical purposes orphaned—she wouldn't have thought so.

She punched the talk button. Deep breath. "Hello?"

"Where are you?"

"Depths of despair. Where are you?"

Geneva's smile registered through the phone. "Whatever you do, maintain that sense of humor, Jayne. Don't know how you can, but it's going to keep you upright. That and the God of the Universe who holds you in the palm of His—"

"I couldn't go to the courthouse."

"I'm there now. The reporters are going nuts looking for you."

Jayne slid her hand down the side of the seat and flicked the lever to move her farther from the constraints of the steering wheel. "I don't think I can go back to my apartment. They'll be waiting for me."

"It's what they do."

"'So, Ms. Dennegee, how does it *feel* to know your father's headed for prison because of you?' 'Fine. Thanks for asking.'"

"He's going to prison because of his own sins, Jayne, not yours."

"Is that what you tell all the snitches?"

"You did the right thing. You did the only thing you could do. What kind of guilt would you bear right now if you hadn't turned him in?"

The temperature in the car peaked somewhere between preheat and broil. Jayne reached across the seat to roll down the passenger side window of her aging, no-frills Cavalier. Cross ventilation proved a false hope on a corn-ripening day in Iowa. "He's my daddy."

The word she'd vowed not to use again.

"Hon"—Geneva cleared her throat—"sometimes the bravest thing we can do is let the guilt go."

"Don't hold your breath."

"Don't hold yours."

"What?"

"Keep breathing."

"It's not automatic anymore." Jayne rested her forehead on the steering wheel. If it left a mark, so be it. She'd been branded by her father's "community service" projects. What was one more deformity?

"Jayne, let me come get you. Where are you now?"

"Parking Lot B at the university."

"What are you doing there? Oh."

"The appointment with my faculty advisor was a scene you'll find amusing. Imagine hearing the final verdict from the

TA who bops in with the good news, not knowing the convict's daughter is sitting in the room."

Geneva's pause communicated a paragraph of concern. "When do you start?"

"School? Never. Not here anyway. It would cause the administration 'discomfort' to deal with the press. What Dad did with his pharmacy degree isn't going to make it into the college recruitment brochure. Thanks to him, my name would apparently poison the student roster. Can you imagine roll call? 'Davis? Denmark? Dennagee?' Then gasps followed by silence."

"How can they have any complaint about you? This isn't your doing."

No. It's my undoing. "Have you ever walked through a barn and then noticed that your clothes and hair smelled like manure, even if you hadn't touched any?"

"I always said drama was your gift. Don't know why you chose nursing rather than the theater. But we can rehash that later. Let me pick you up. We'll go out to the lake. Give the press a chance to lose interest in you."

"The diner is expecting me for the four-to-midnight shift."

Geneva's sigh could have moved a Richter needle well beyond six point five. "Call. In. Sick. Good grief. Of all days, this would be the day to call in sick."

"Can't do that."

"Then call in 'done'."

"Geneva! Aren't you the one who always preached responsibility?"

"At this point, I don't think you can afford to stay at a place that shrivels your soul."

"I did for most of my childhood."

⸺◦◦◦⸺

"You aren't afraid the neighbors will ostracize you because of your association with me?" Jayne took the iced tea Geneva offered and settled back into the slope of the lime green Adirondack chair on the cottage's narrow deck.

Geneva's age showed when she lowered herself into a raspberry-colored chair with the same odd-to-get-into, comfortable-when-in, odd-to-exit slope. "Most are weekenders. We keep to ourselves."

"I haven't been out here for a while. I think I was fifteen the last time. The summer before Mom's illness had a name. After that, fun wiggled its way out of our family dictionary." She sipped her tea. The cold soothed her tense, raw throat.

"It shouldn't have happened that way."

"ALS is a consuming disease. All . . . consuming."

Geneva's tea glass landed on the arm of her chair with a pronounced thunk. "No disease justifies neglecting a child." She swatted at a sun-drunk fly. "It's as if they forgot you existed except as a caregiver."

Jayne could see the burning ember of the sun on the inside of her eyelids. Fading. Fading. "Sometimes parents give you away, but they make you stay."

She opened her eyes to find the source of the low, chugging rumble. A pontoon boat a few dozen feet offshore crossed their field of vision. An elderly couple and a golden retriever. No fishing poles. No hurry. No real destination, it appeared. They waved. Jayne waved back as if her life were no more complicated than theirs.

A phone buzzed. Geneva's. The woman glanced at the screen then held the phone facedown on her thigh. "Work can wait."

"Don't mind me. I'll rehearse my 'It's the first day of the rest of my life' self-talk. Go ahead. Take the call."

Geneva rose from the chair, phone in hand, then into action. "Hey, Jeff. What's up?" She retreated into the cottage. With the windows open, the building offered no privacy. Jayne heard every word. "Our counteroffer did not include the seller's help with closing costs. Where'd they get that idea?"

Jayne listened as the woman morphed from friend and confidante to savvy businesswoman. Real estate suited her. More a people-to-home matchmaker than salesperson, she played the part well. So much to admire about that woman.

A familiar guilt-like claw gripped Jayne's stomach and squeezed. She'd had no choice. Turning her father in had nothing to do with her resentment over his pathological obsession with her mom's illness, with the way they both emotionally checked out of her life and replaced their daughter with a disease. Nothing. It was her civic duty to report what she'd witnessed.

Her mom's desperate cries—*No, no, no!*—silenced by his knee on her chest while atrophied limbs flailed against the syringe needle. Her mother must have known it was a lethal dose. The look of terror on her face—

The screen door squeaked open, then bounced twice before settling into place.

"How about a snack? And it doesn't matter that you think you're not hungry." Geneva spoke as if the sentences were all one word.

Jayne caught a whiff of the ever-recognizable bacon. "Bacon is a snack now?"

"Don't tell my internist. And not merely bacon. I'm making BLATs. The *A* stands for avocado in our BLTs. Okay with you?"

What kind of hideous creature am I? The thought of a BLAT derails my guilt trip.

Her father had no doubt already heard the piercing clang of metal on metal when the cell door closed behind him. And she—noble woman that she was—pushed the scene aside at the mention of bacon.

2

There's a breeze here." Jayne put down her forkful of potato salad and extended her arms to catch the updraft.

With a toile-patterned paper napkin that matched the paper plates on the patio table in front of them, Geneva wiped a tomato seed from her chin. "Often is."

"No breeze in town. I noticed."

Jayne left her arms extended and leaned into the wind but remained rooted to her chair. No soaring today.

"Where are you?"

She lowered her arms and resumed eating. "You ask that a lot lately."

"This time, I mean. Where were you mentally just now, when you closed your eyes and let yourself enjoy the moment? Don't answer, 'Here.' That's too obvious."

Geneva always had made her think.

"Floating above all this, I guess."

"And in your mind's eye, where did you land?"

Jayne crunched a baby carrot and chewed it while she thought. She swallowed every tiny bit before responding. "I haven't been cleared for landing."

Geneva crossed her arms over her chest and tucked her fists under her chin. Head down. The posture of contemplation. Or was it a new prayer posture? She lifted her head and rested her hands on the surface of the patio table. "You can stay here for a while, if you'd like."

"I appreciate that. I can't go back to my apartment yet."

"I mean, longer-term. The cottage isn't winterized, but—"

"Long commute to work."

"Worth it?"

"Even if calling in 'done' hadn't been frowned upon by the diner establishment, I doubt I'll find a job of any consequence within a three-state radius. Who'd hire me? I betrayed my own father. I've only finished a third of nursing school and that took me four times as long as it should have because of taking care of Mom. And the Dennagee name isn't exactly a foot in the door, if you know what I mean."

"That will fade."

"Things like this don't fade. They ferment."

Geneva tugged a lettuce leaf from her sandwich and ate it. "Lots of great food depends on the fermentation process."

"Was that supposed to make me feel better?"

"You're welcome to stay here until the snow flies, or until you find a job elsewhere. How far are you willing to go?"

Jayne's ankle itched. A mosquito. She scratched at it, knowing full well it would only make it worse. "How far would *you* want to run from a reputation like my father's?"

Across the lake, a lawn mower roared to life. How well sound carried on water.

"I have brownies in the freezer," Geneva said.

"Good choice."

"Let's try to sneak into town tomorrow to gather your belongings."

Jayne could search every corner of her apartment—or her life for the last many years—and not find a crumb that matched the definition of *belongings*.

Longings trump belongings any day.

Living simply had been more from necessity than choice. She'd understood her parents' need to pour money into a litany of treatment options and pain reducers. She'd understood why they couldn't help her with college costs, or high school graduation costs, or the cost of shoes and jeans and jackets. They'd downsized how many times? It was the way they'd budgeted their affection for her—Scrooge-stingy with their love—that created the sense of living on the edge of emotional bankruptcy.

Except for the influence of a handful of people like Geneva. Then only a couple of people. When forced to quit college mid-semester after her mother's ALS took an even more prominent center-stage role, Jayne saw her world shrink to the dimensions of whatever part-time jobs she could slip between the hours she spent caregiving.

Her dad started staying later than the pharmacy was open, then rushed in and pushed Jayne aside as if no one could care for his wife like he could. How had Jayne become an annoyance when she'd started out as a product of their honeymoon?

Geneva tapped her on the shoulder, stirring Jayne from the dark hallways of memory. "Do you want to keep this?" She held a lamp with three graduated amber glass globes that reminded Jayne of a see-through snowman made from dirty snow.

"Belongs to the landlord. None of the furniture is mine. Not much of the décor."

"Good. I was beginning to worry about your lack of taste." Geneva smiled in the dim light.

So far, her "must save" items clattered against one another in the bottom of a box. What was the name of that movie with the office guy who fought the world to hold onto his red stapler? Even Jayne's stapler belonged to the landlord. The oceanview mouse pad was hers. And the verse-a-day flip calendar. And a bottle of Advil. She shook it like a maraca before dropping it into the box's cavernous mouth. Half a bottle left. Without a regular paycheck, she'd have to ration them.

Jayne picked up the box and used her hip to push the straight-backed chair tight against the flea market desk. The flip calendar lay open to a verse that read, "'There's a time for searching and a time for losing.' Ecclesiastes 3:6." Did that wisdom apply to the search for a place to belong? Lost. Time to admit it.

Had Bertram Dennagee's homespun Kevorkian actions made it impossible for her to know a true home?

She set the box on the bed beside an open suitcase she'd borrowed from Geneva. The dresser emptied in less than five minutes. Neatness counted little in the middle of the night. They'd managed to dodge the expected ambush of reporters. They'd be back at dawn, no doubt. Jayne and Geneva planned to be long gone before then.

The apartment hadn't been the refuge Jayne hoped when she moved out of her parents' latest downsize after her mother's death and her father's arrest. The one room seemed as cold as it had the day she became a renter. All the more so, shadowed as it now was, with a minimum of lights to illuminate their packing. It wasn't that she had no nesting instinct, Jayne assured herself. But *temporary* seemed stamped across everything she called her own.

Geneva grabbed a handful of hanging clothes from the closet and folded them over her arm. "We'll sort later, right?"

"Good plan."

"I got everything from the nightstand on the first trip to the car with those few kitchen things. Wish we'd thought to pick up more boxes."

Jayne glanced around the room. "We're almost done. How much is left in the closet?"

"Shoes." Geneva's whisper matched Jayne's, decibel for decibel. "You are not normal."

"What gave you your first clue?"

Her friend headed for the door with a tote bag over her shoulder and her arms laden with the hanging clothes. "Three pairs of shoes? That's all? Most young women your age count shoes by the dozens."

"Four," Jayne said. "I'm wearing the other pair."

Geneva halted her progress as if she'd neglected to measure the distance from the edge of the cliff until her toes dangled over it. "Jayne!"

"What?"

"We have company."

She raced to the window. A car slowed in front of the two-story building.

"Do you recognize the car? Neighbors?"

Jayne doused the light from the lamp and tugged the curtain tight around her face as she peered into the night. "No. Not unless the neighbors have taken to carrying fancy cameras with foot-long zoom lenses."

She felt her way back to the bed, closed the suitcase, and tucked the box under one arm. "Let's get out of here."

Not winterized? The cottage didn't seem *autumnized* either. With Willow Lake angry looking and raindrops pelting the windows, Jayne opted for thick socks and pulled a sweatshirt over her tee.

She checked her phone. No messages. Just as well. Her heart wasn't in any of the jobs for which she'd applied. It would take diligent saving to build enough reserve to resume her nurse's training somewhere else. She'd studied options online. Finding a reputable school of nursing in a town small enough not to have heard her father's name proved daunting.

Soup. Soup solves everything.

Leftover chicken. A good start.

Jayne played Rachel Ray, pulling together an armful of ingredients in short order. The healing aroma of garlic, chicken broth, and basil soon seeped into the chilled air of the cottage.

Before her illness, Jayne's mother's passion for soupmaking drew her daughter into the kitchen to watch the flurry of knives and herbs, vegetables, and wooden spoons stirred in a distinct figure-eight. The pattern made the product taste better, Mom insisted.

Jayne's heart muscle clenched. Soupmaking was one of the few times she thought her mother might change her mind about not wanting to have children.

"Honor thy father and mother." God had to know it would take more faith to obey that command than to believe seas part and God-followers walk on dry ground. Water into wine? Simple. Honoring Bertram Dennagee? The task required little spiritual stamina before he derailed.

When Mom's illness hit. When weakness made her mother little more than a puppet in Jayne's father's control. When husband and wife locked themselves in the tower of their consumption with ALS and refused to lower the drawbridge for their daughter. When her mother died.

By his decision. Against his wife's wishes. As Jayne walked through the door.

She stuffed the thought into the garbage along with the woody ends of the celery stalks she'd chopped.

Carrots? Only two left. One for soup, one for tomorrow's salad. This would be a great time to tap into a savings account. Jayne snorted. Her account stayed in a perpetual state of danger, dipping close to the minimum balance for reasons as innocuous as a new muffler for the Cavalier.

Job hunting—as pleasant a task as removing tar from the hem of her blue jeans. Now she dealt with the additional tar of the Dennagee name. She couldn't escape the name. Every job application started the same. *Name. Address.* And done. She was done. Before she could tackle *Education* or *Special Skills.*

Done.

Jayne set the soup to simmer and booted up the computer perched on one end of the pine table. Willow Lake wasn't known for its Internet speed. She picked up an emery board and smoothed the rough edges of four fingernails before the screen told her she could proceed. Connect. "Name Change Procedure." Search the Web.

And there it was. A reason worthy of a couple hundred dollars from her nursing degree savings account.

Sometimes to make money, you have to spend money.

Sometimes to get a life, you have to give up the old one.

"Jayne?"

"Hey, Geneva. I haven't heard from you for so long." Her heart warmed as if the morning sun sneaking into the cottage had a rival.

"I wish I could get out there more often. Is the fireplace enough for these chilly nights? A little early for a cold snap like this."

"I've only had to start a fire twice so far. Heard the temps are supposed to bounce back closer to normal next week. Geneva?" Jayne pulled the phone from her ear and checked the screen. Still connected. "Are you there?"

"I'm here."

She shifted the phone to her other ear. "What's up?" She swirled a wooden spoon through her oatmeal in a figure eight, disturbing the plump, slumbering raisins. She tapped the neck of the spoon on the edge of the pan. Three taps. "How's the real estate business?"

"I've seen better days. What's the opposite of a downswing?"

"Upswing?"

Geneva Larkin sighed into the phone. "From your mouth to God's ears. Amen and so be it."

Jayne smiled. The weight on her heart shifted. She could breathe a little easier, as she expected an asthma victim might after using an inhaler.

From the sipping sound coming through the phone, Jayne pictured her mentor nursing a cup of coffee or tea.

"I called with a job offer for you, if you're interested," Geneva said.

"Selling real estate?"

"No."

"Filing your paperwork while *you* sell real estate?"

"Jayne, your gifts would be sorely wasted on paperwork."

"Gifts?" She yanked open the diminutive refrigerator and pulled out a half gallon of milk.

"My sister is dying, Jayne. She needs you."

The milk jug slipped from her hands and hit the kitchen floor like a water balloon. Cold liquid exploded against the cupboard faces and Jayne's calves. The sting plunged deep into her soul and pushed out a moan.

"Oh, Jayne! Forgive me. I wasn't thinking how that would sound. My sister Aurelia needs you to help her *live* as long as she can. I didn't mean to imply—"

The cold white dripping into her socks would soon turn sticky. How many paper towels would it take to mop the pond on the floor at her feet?

Help someone live as long as possible? Now, that would be a switch for a Dennagee.

"She means a great deal to me." Geneva's voice faltered.

Jayne sidestepped the puddle and slipped into a waiting chair then leaned her elbows on the pine tabletop and rested her head and the phone in her hands. "I don't recall meeting your sister."

"No, you wouldn't have. She lives not far from Oceanside. I've probably mentioned her."

California, right? The distance between Willow Lake and California stretched forever before her. Perfect. But caregiving for a dying woman? Could she?

How ironic. She claimed her heart was in nursing. Driven by compassion to care for physical needs. She didn't have her degree yet but was already tempted to pick and choose whom she'd serve. "Doesn't she have family? I mean, other than you? Someone closer?"

"She has a son. Isaac. My nephew. Darling boy."

"Couldn't he go help her?"

"He lives there. In La Vida. He's struggling with all of this. Poor child."

Jayne pushed away from her slump and pressed her spine against the chair back. "How old is he?"

"He'll be thirty-four in January."

"Oh. Then . . . ?"

Sighs travel well over phone lines or fiber optics or whatever they're using these days. Geneva's sigh produced a level closer to a freight train than a simple expulsion of air. "Isaac is a busy young man. He's in real estate, too. Commercial. As much as he loves my sister, he's not handling this well. It's not his . . . his gift."

"Caring for someone in need isn't a gift. It's an obligation."

"It can be both. I hoped you'd feel that way, Jayne."

She dabbed at milk splash on the chair leg. "I didn't mean me."

"You didn't?"

Silence doubled itself like a healthy yeast dough. "Not me. I can't—"

"Can't what, dear? Can't make yourself care? I don't believe that for a minute. It's in your—"

"Mrs. Larkin, please don't say it's in my genes." That's what she'd do with the rest of her life—work on inventing a DNA eraser.

"Since when did you revert to calling me Mrs. Larkin? I shouldn't have sprung this on you over the phone. Could we meet? Can I treat you to lunch? Soon? I can't get away from the office long enough to drive out there. But we should talk about your salary requirements and transportation. I need to introduce you to Isaac. Phone call or video conference call. Something."

The room now beyond comfortably warm, Jayne juggled the phone while she removed her sweater. The oatmeal no longer looked comforting. After all Geneva Larkin had done for her, how could she refuse her request? Would her nephew micromanage every caregiving move Jayne made? Did he even know who she was? Once he found out, it was unlikely he'd go along with the plan.

"I'd recommend flying," Geneva said. Jayne must have missed a snatch of conversation. It sounded as if the woman was sure of the response. "But I can understand if you'd like to take the train or bus and see more scenery on the way. It's only another couple of days. But the situation's pretty desperate out there."

Geneva's words continued. Jayne's attention did not. It drifted on a sea of upheaval. Move across the country? Leave the wake of her father's crimes? Care for a dying woman?

Cold oatmeal waved its sticky fingers to remind her of the alternative. Stay. Find a new employer who didn't mind hiring a Dennagee, and a snitch at that. Bear the shame until the decades passed and the notoriety faded.

"Bus."

"Excuse me?"

"I'd like to take the bus."

3

Can't say I blame you for leaving," the landlord had said when Jayne gave her notice a week later. He waived the one-month rule.

"Course, you can't be hoping to get your security deposit back, what with no notice."

Ah, the rub. Mercy abounded at the Highview Court Apartments.

Jayne's molars played mortar and pestle. In the game of "Pick Your Battles" was that one worth the energy? Fighting for her rights meant lingering. Lingering meant languishing, the riptide of her father's choices pulling her deeper into her personal Bermuda Triangle.

She calculated the financial consequences of not having her security deposit to lean on should Geneva Larkin's nephew Ethan—no, Isaac—not approve of her as a caregiver for his mother. She'd need more than a pocket of change to start over somewhere else.

"Okay, fine." Mr. Heinrich's voice softened in the moments Jayne considered how to answer him. "Fine, you can have your deposit. It's against my better judgment. Rules is rules. But it's about time somebody gave you a break, I'd say."

Compassion? It seemed foreign on him. Jayne didn't argue. She waited long enough for him to cut her a check, thanked him, and headed for the bank. Her last transaction as Jayne Dennagee.

Now to meet with Geneva and explain what she'd done.

—❧—

"Changed your name?"

"Yes." Jayne shredded the paper napkin before her as if making kindling for a flea circus campfire.

"I won't ask why, but isn't that rather . . . ?" The older woman's eyes roamed the perimeter of the restaurant as if hoping the word she sought was stenciled where the walls and ceiling met. "Isn't that severe?"

"What Bertram Dennagee did was severe. What I did was a rational, carefully considered move to distance myself from him."

"He's still your father, Jayne."

"Jayne's father. Not mine. My name is Rosa Lorena Angelica Fortunatis O'Leary."

Geneva's eyebrows threatened to lift off the surface of her face.

"I'm not serious."

"Oh."

She reached out to lay her hand over the one that radiated kindness and concern. "I did change my name, Geneva. Legally. I have the papers and the ailing bank account to prove it. It's important to me that when I apply for this position with your nephew, I'm known by my new name only."

"He would understand."

Jayne withdrew her hand. "You haven't told him already, have you?"

"No, dear." Geneva toyed with the handle of her teacup. "I didn't see the need. He knows you're capable and willing and free to relocate. He also knows I think highly enough of you to trust my sister into your care."

"Good. I mean, thank you. Please honor this request. I want to start a life free of the leprosy of my old name and what my father did to it."

Geneva's heavy, artsy necklace clunked against the edge of the table as she leaned in. "Doesn't that border on deception?"

"I have a new name. By law."

"What is it?"

"Becca. Becca Morrow."

"Morrow?"

"Seemed like the opposite of Dennagee, somehow. Morrow. Like tomorrow. I picked a name like a novelist chooses one for a character."

"Becca." She fingered the necklace as she tested the name. "Oh, I get it. Clever twist."

"What?"

Geneva smiled and leaned back, her necklace thumping softly against her middle. "You don't see the connection?"

"What connection?"

"Isaac? Becca?"

"What about it?"

Across the room, a band of waiters and waitresses broke into a sappy reinvention of "Happy Birthday," to the chagrin of the intended target, a young woman whose husband or boyfriend hooted and clapped to the beat—such as it was—of the music.

The roomful of restaurant customers applauded in tribute to the stranger with a birthday. No one questioned their right to be there, to belong at the young woman's impromptu party.

The new *Becca's* heart fell out of rhythm for a moment, like the last measure of the song.

"We need to call Isaac," Geneva said, pulling her cell phone from her lime suede purse. She punched two buttons. Speed dial to her nephew. That said something.

Becca leaned closer, her facial muscles squeezing together as if being forced through the eye of a needle. "Please, Mrs. Larkin. Becca Morrow. That's who I am now."

The older woman gave a conciliatory nod before speaking into the phone. "Isaac. I think we have our answer."

4

The bus ride to the edge of Far Enough offered Becca time to think, if nothing else. Time to invent an answer to the fluttering, "What now? What are you going to do now?"

Of all her needs at the moment, conversation ranked lower than rhinestone snow boots. She needed silence and ideas and whatever medication would slow her heart rate. She did not need a chatty seatmate bent on drawing out her innermost feelings on everything from the joy of bus travel to microwave versus air-popped popcorn to pop stars' latest escapades.

She opted for an empty bus seat far from other riders. That lasted only until the first pause. A little town with a combination diner/bus stop. Ten minutes. Enough for the driver to pick up a fried egg sandwich and Chatty Cathy—a tabloid-reading, raven-haired, forty-something trying to look twenty.

"Is this seat taken?"

"I'm traveling alone."

"Me too!" the woman chirped.

The chirping wouldn't stop until close to dawn when the bus's air brakes burped and the driver called back, "All out for Remington and points north."

Tar-black hair swung like a horse's tail. "Sorry to cut our conversation short. But this is my stop."

The woman felt the need to apologize?

Chatty Cathy combed through unnaturally thick locks with well-manicured fingers as she stood to exit, adjusting her tote bag strap on her padded shoulder. "Enjoy the rest of your trip. Where'd you say you were headed?"

"West. Just . . . west."

"Hope you find what you're looking for. Nice talking to you."

Relief slid in when the woman waltzed down the aisle and out of Becca's life. She had to think. Had to formulate a plan of some kind.

By midday, the sun and time melted away three hundred more miles. The belly of the bus filled with daylight travelers. Happy people with clear destinations and something to smile about.

Was it unthinkable that she wasted so much of her planning time in prayer? Which served as the greater sin—that she failed to use the time efficiently or that after all these years, she dared to pray?

I don't know why You'd listen to me, God, but I need help. I hope it's true what Geneva says, that I don't have to deserve mercy in order to ask for it.

"Is this seat taken?"

By now, few choices remained in the crowded bus. She scooted closer to the window and forced herself to welcome a new traveling companion. "Be my guest."

Becca tried every conceivable sitting and sleeping position during the interminable trip that showed her the scenery on either side of four-lane highways across the country. If the bus driver's predictions proved correct—and why wouldn't they?—she had an hour left on the road. How could an hour be enough for her to fill the holes in her story? It takes time to create a persona from scratch. She'd purchased a believable, respectable name. Now she needed a credible and easily recalled history, one she could convince Geneva Larkin to help corroborate.

Invent a childhood. Troubled? No. Too real, complicated. Basically happy? Sure. An uncomfortable but short-lived season of rebellion. Four years of college, no two. Two. Enough to explain her better-than-average grammar, but not enough for people to expect more than she could deliver. Parents? Dead. Fire? Too melodramatic. Car accident? Better. Happens all the time.

Ten more miles ticked by, each conquered hash mark on the highway devouring precious milliseconds of preparation. She leaned her head against the bus window, feeling its air-conditioned coolness seep past hair and skin to the bones that cradled her overheated brain.

I can pull this off. I have to.

She shifted her trip-weary body one more time. A job half a country away. Working for someone who had no idea who she really was, if Geneva could be trusted to honor her request. How often did Geneva and her nephew talk? That could be problematic. The woman wouldn't intentionally let anything slip, but . . .

Becca's seatmate rambled on, as animated as a kindergartner high on Easter candy. With one confession, Becca could clear the seat. The bus. But her past wasn't a weapon, a tool she could pull out when convenient.

Thoughts of her father's other victims made her skin feel mismatched, as if created for someone else, as if the tag on the neckline had been removed and God had grabbed the wrong size from the rack. Their voicelessness cried inside her. A lava flow of pain circulated through her marrow and pressed against her spine.

Her dad made people past tense. Not dying, but *dead*. Not ailing. *Gone*.

And their families—those who labeled him sinner, those who labeled him saint—no doubt wrestled their own demons of relief and regret.

"Cool, huh?"

Becca coughed into her elbow, buying time to reenter the current conversation. Her fellow traveler's excitement could have been linked to a winning lottery ticket or a new flavor of gum, for all Becca knew. "Yeah. Cool." She feigned agreement a notch higher than neutral.

"I know. Right? So, here's my card." The woman thrust a hot-pink-and-black-polka-dotted business card toward Becca. *Dottie's Forever Yours Cupcakes*. Tagline? *Your dessert worries are over forever.*

Dessert worries.

Eternally resolved.

Becca suppressed a wholly inappropriate snort and an unspoken "What a relief!"

She'd been offered a choice—plane or bus. In the moment of decision, a drawn-out, slower bus ride held the promise of time for reflection, planning, thinking. It broke its promise with cramped muscles, frequent stops, and passengers intent on engaging her in conversation.

But the ride was over and she'd landed in a mid-sized town squeezed between larger ones in a scene where every street name demanded at least high school Spanish to pronounce correctly and few of the trees or flowers she saw as they pulled up to the bus station looked familiar.

Tiptoeing around the damp spots of unknown origin on the floor of the bus station ladies' room, Becca deftly changed clothes. Her jeans—accordion-pleated across the lap—recorded the length of the bus trip like rings on a tree measured years and floods and droughts. From her lone piece of luggage she pulled another pair of jeans and a fresh T-shirt to replace the one mangled by miles. She wouldn't need the jacket.

A jagged diagonal crack in the washroom mirror split her face into grotesque, mismatched halves. Ducking and tilting, she found a smooth-enough section of mirror to do a reasonable job taming her hair.

"Concealer would help," she thought, tracing her under-eye circles. "I'm going to assume my sallow complexion is this fluorescent light's fault. It has nothing to do with—"

The doorknob twisted and clanked. Twice.

"Just a minute." Becca zipped her suitcase, brushed a handful of stray hairs from her shoulders, and opened the door to the woman waiting on the other side. A grim-faced woman with a pint-sized version of herself in tow. The little girl—three or four perhaps—danced from foot to foot. Becca wasn't fully through the doorway before the two pushed their way past her, the mother jerking her daughter into the room as if a full bladder were an act of rebellion. Becca hoped it wasn't too late.

Would Becca ever lose the urge to rescue unappreciated children?

The encounter lasted mere seconds, but long enough for Becca to notice the pale trail—the path tears make when flowing down the face of a smudged child. Quickening her steps, she left the narrow, foul-smelling hall, breathing a brief, awkward prayer for the little one.

Outside the station, the air was no fairer. Bus fumes lingered like skunk perfume. But she thought she could detect, from somewhere beyond the fumes, a hint of sun-baked beaches and salted waves. According to the Google map, LaVida was only a few miles from the Pacific, with Oceanside to its north and San Diego to its south. She hoped it wasn't only her imagination suggesting the scent of the sea. Pictures and Mrs. Larkin's descriptions had been enough to convince Becca the ocean could play a role in washing away the detritus of the life she'd known until now.

Standing on the curb—and the edge of a carefully, though hastily, constructed new life—Becca debated her next move.

Hello, my name this week is Becca Morrow. You don't know me and have no reason in the world to trust me, but . . .

Without Geneva's employment matchmaking, she couldn't have hoped to get past the answering machine, or caller ID, or a diligent and discerning secretary. She thumbed the scrap of paper with the cell phone number and address of Hughes Realty.

5

Becca could smell the fingernail polish before she neared the receptionist's desk. The woman behind the desk, intent on covering each nail with two smooth strokes of liquid flame, made no acknowledgment of Becca's presence, as if the first move were Becca's responsibility. She hesitated a moment, taking in the picture the receptionist painted. "Excuse me, Miss." Becca bit her tongue. She almost called her Miss Cliché.

"Mrs." The woman's fingernails continued to hold her attention. But she did ask, "May I help you?"

"Is this the office of Isaac Hughes?"

The receptionist looked up, glanced behind her at the mahogany door clearly labeled *Isaac Hughes* and drew out the word "Yes" as if it had four syllables.

"My name's Becca Morrow. I'm here to see Mr. Hughes. Is he in?"

"No appointment?" The woman—Lila Gallum, if the nameplate on her desk spoke the truth and wasn't a joke—must have known the answer, but cast a cursory glance at what Becca assumed was a schedule book. "Doesn't appear so."

"He's expecting me. I'm here to fill the position as caregiver for Mr. Hughes' mother." Saying it aloud made the words taste like wet cement licked from an underdone sidewalk. All wrong. Bad idea. Bad idea with more than fifteen hundred miles pushing it.

"The man's crazy-desperate. You the one his Aunt Geneva sent? I told him my cousin would do it once she gets out of rehab. But no. He can't wait that long, he says."

Geneva Larkin, what have you gotten me into? "Could I please have a moment of Mr. Hughes' time?" Did that sound professional enough?

"He's not in."

Was it possible for motion sickness to strike after she'd stopped moving? "Do you know when he'll be back?"

"Oh, he's here. He's just not *in*, if you know what I mean." Mrs. Gallum pursed her lips and raised her eyebrows, her face a thumbs-down critique.

Becca counted considerably higher than ten before speaking. "I'm sorry. No, I don't know what you mean."

The receptionist used her thumbnail to carefully swipe away a stray blob of polish on her pinky. "He can't be disturbed. He's doing his God thing."

"God thing?"

"I don't know what all he does in there." She gestured with her head and a flame-tipped thumb toward the closed door behind her and to the left. "Suppose he prays or reads his Bible or something. I don't ask. Not my business. You're welcome to wait."

"Yes, thank you. I'll wait."

A week ago, could she have pictured herself in such a position? Her life resembled an episode in an improvisation class. Someone handed her a slip of paper with Isaac Hughes's name on it and directed, "Okay, here's your scene. Businessman is looking for a companion/caregiver for his elderly, ailing mother. You show up at his door as . . . better than nothing. Aaaaand . . . ACTION!"

Now what? Her first task—convince Mr. Hughes she could be trusted. She'd have to lie to persuade him. The paradox almost made her laugh aloud.

The door behind Mrs. Gallum opened abruptly. Both the receptionist and Becca drew to attention as if caught red-handed in the middle of their distracted thoughts.

"Lila," the man said without looking up from the smart-phone in his hand, "I'm heading over to the courthouse. Some problem's come up with the abstract on the Humbold property. Don't know when I'll be back. You can text me if you need to."

Becca stood, watching her opportunity aim for the exit.

Mrs. Gallum spoke up. "Mr. Hughes, there's someone to see you."

"Have to wait," he replied before glancing up and catching Becca's eye. The pace of his mission seemed to slow measur-ably when he saw her. "I'm sorry to be rude. Did we have an appointment? You are . . .?"

"Becca M-morrow. And no, I don't have an official appoint-ment, but—"

"She's here about your mother." Lila Gallum said the words as if they were juicy morsels of gossip, whispering them through overdone lips.

His dark eyebrows twitched. "You're Becca?"

"Yes." Like week-old shoes, the name fit better than it did when new and factory-stiff.

"I'm glad you're here. But I have to get to the courthouse before the noon hour break." Then suddenly, "Why don't you ride along with me? We'll talk on the way."

Split-second decisions had never been Becca's forte. That would have to change. Even minor deception, she was finding, demanded quick thinking and lightning responses. "Fine with me." Then, conscious of the bulk at her feet, she added, "Oh, my suitcase."

Mr. Hughes seemed to assess the entirety of the scene for the first time. "You came straight from the airport?"

"Bus station." The truth felt foreign.

His facial expression said he was thinking on his feet, juggling his previous dilemma with the new. "Why don't we haul it with us? When I'm done at the courthouse, we'll grab some lunch and talk about the caregiver position. Then I can drop you off wherever it is you're staying."

"I'll be staying with your mother." Where did the boldness come from? Becca smiled, both amused at her cocky answer and eager to convince Isaac Hughes it was enthusiasm not desperation forming her words.

Isaac shifted his briefcase from right hand to left and wordlessly reached for Becca's bag as if it were his responsibility to shoulder the burden. "Follow me," he said, turning toward the exit. He didn't look back until he reached the door, which he pushed open and held with his hip to allow Becca to pass. She turned sideways to slip through the doorway, avoiding his briefcase, her suitcase, and eye contact.

"Thank you," she said over the tension in her throat.

"You're welcome."

Manners. Nice.

Half a dozen vehicles waited in the lot in front of the office complex that housed Hughes Realty. From what little she knew of the man, Becca ventured that Isaac was not the minivan type. She couldn't picture him in a daffodil yellow VW. Nor did he seem the type to own a monster-wheeled pickup. That left two sedate sedans and a mercurial Corvette convertible.

She studied the man who led the way across the parking lot. Sharp dresser—olive slacks with a perfectly coordinated olive and black plaid shirt and black silk tie. He sported one of those casual, just-stepped-out-of-the-shower hairstyles that probably cost him a fortune. And his impeccably trimmed, jawline-tracing beard? The work of a stylist, no doubt. Even Isaac's stride seemed classy, polished. The man oozed confidence. Owned his own business. Had to be the Corvette.

"Your chariot awaits, Miss."

Becca caught herself before blurting, "You're kidding!" when Isaac held open the passenger door of a bronze Buick. Outwardly unflustered, she slipped into the seat while Isaac stowed her suitcase in the trunk and trotted around to the driver's side.

Isaac wiggled the key into the ignition, but did not start the car. He glanced Becca's way, then sighed and dropped his hands onto his lap. "Okay, we're not going anywhere until you tell me the truth." His eyes danced as he said it. What could that mean?

How could he have read through her mask so soon? She focused on smooth, adequate breaths. Mrs. Larkin's integrity must have forced her to spill the whole story.

"Tell me," he said, his words crawling across the space between them, "are you in the habit of riding without a seatbelt?"

"What? No."

"Then would you please buckle up?"

Her heart raced with explosive relief, and with some other emotion altogether. The concern in his eyes registered as genuine. It had been a long time since anyone other than Geneva had expressed concern for her safety. Years, if ever. Strange how she found his sincerity so attractive when Becca Morrow herself was a fabrication.

"There's a dichotomy for you."

"Where?" His question rang innocent enough.

"Did I say that out loud?" Her heart temporarily lost its rhythm.

"I'm not good at mindreading, Becca. Never met a man who was, to be honest with you." His smile breathed warmth and acceptance.

"Honest. Nice theory."

"Excuse me?"

Becca bit her lower lip as an addict might snap a rubber band on his wrist to remind him of his weakness. "Sorry. Long trip. I'm still a little road weary. Not firing on all cylinders."

Isaac's laughter filled the car's interior. "I can understand that. How about if we talk about simple things? Did you live near Aunt Geneva? Why did you decide to move to this area? Why are you interested in caregiving for an elderly woman in ill health? Do you like Asian?"

"The people or the food?" Could she avoid his not-at-all-simple questions with lame humor? "Yes to both."

"Great. Our plans for after the courthouse are secure."

Are they? Pulling the wool over this kind man's eyes, even if necessary, and even if it couldn't possibly hurt him—a harmless holding back of a few key facts—would stink.

"So, sell yourself."

Becca's eyes widened at his words. A stiff silence flooded the car. She could read in Isaac Hughes's face the moment he realized what he'd said.

"Oh, that couldn't have been worded more poorly. What I meant to say was that I'd like to hear you convince me I should hire you to take care of my mother. Sell me on the idea of Becca Morrow."

"She's a lovely young woman," Becca said, half-hoping to convince herself. "Compassionate and caring. Not afraid of a challenge. She took care of her . . . aging . . . father . . . when he was ill."

"He's gone now?" His voice quieted.

"Yes." Gone. Sentencing process complete.

"From . . . ?"

A question she should have anticipated. What did her father "die" from? Why is he gone? The bus ride would have been a good time to rehearse an answer. *Pinocchio, I'm glad you were fiction. I'd be tripping over my nostrils by now.*

A whisper of a Voice rattled deep in her ribcage. She couldn't afford to listen.

"Look, Becca, if it's too painful to talk about . . ."

She'd allowed herself so few meaningful conversations with guys, with anyone, for that matter, since her father's fall from grace. Awkward as it was with the truth, half-truths convulsed within her.

"It's . . . it's hard."

"Still too fresh?" Isaac's voice balanced expertly, socially gifted where she was inept. "I can understand. My dad's been gone two years. I still think about him every day."

Becca watched his Adam's apple move. He watched the traffic. When it settled into a workable rhythm, he turned toward her.

"And your mom? How is she handling your dad's death?"

His Aunt Geneva hadn't told him *anything*? As soon as she could afford it, she'd send the woman flowers.

I won't lie for you, Jayne, she'd said the night before they parted.

Becca.

Oh, yes. Becca. I won't lie. Believe me, I know what a tangled mess that can make. But I'll let you be the one to tell the story.

As if Becca ever intended to do that.

"Whoo. I'm batting a thousand on touchy subjects. Sorry about that." Isaac shook his head and changed lanes. "Let's talk about *my* mother instead."

The two-hour time zone change was to blame. Becca couldn't think fast enough to carry on a conversation. Great first impression. Who wouldn't have total confidence in hiring a woman who couldn't spit out a one-sentence answer? She watched palm trees whip by as the car dodged mid-day traffic.

"Okay." *Brilliant, Becca. Good work. Two whole syllables. Way to win him over.*

"I have to warn you that Mother is not . . . how can I say this? She's not the sweet-tempered woman she once was. She's demanding, feisty, bordering on ornery, and her care is enormously time-consuming."

"Nothing new for me."

"I love her so much, but I can't do this myself."

"Your job must require a lot of your time and energy."

Isaac rested his left elbow on the door. He leaned his head into his waiting hand and confessed, "Even if it didn't. Even if I didn't have the job responsibilities I do, I don't know that I could care for her 24/7. We grate on each other these days."

Becca tried to imagine how a man with Isaac's much-more-refined-than-his-years gentility could grate on anyone, much less his beloved mother.

"Sometimes . . ." She drew a breath and fought for courage. "Sometimes it's the disease. I don't know all that your mom is battling, but I've found that an ailment can profoundly alter a loved one's personality." *Too close to the edge again!*

Sitting upright while negotiating another lane change, Isaac said, "I'll take you to meet her after lunch, if you have the time."

"Do *you* have the time?"

"My job is demanding. Almost as demanding as Mother. But at least at work, I'm the boss. If I take the rest of the afternoon off, who'll complain?" He affected the ultraproper facial expression and posture of a British butler. "I'm disinclined to fire myself. Bad for business." His glance held a faint twinkle of humor.

"Mr. Hughes?"

"Call me Isaac."

"Isaac, I may not be the most qualified person for this position, but I would appreciate a chance to prove I can do a good job caring for your mother. Would you consider a trial period? Six months?" By then she would know if her plan had successfully removed her from her father's reputation.

"Six months? She may not have that long."

"Oh. I'm sorry."

"Then again, she's stubbornly outlived every projection the doctors have offered. So, who's to say? Well, that was dumb."

"Dumb?"

"God is the one who will say when her time is up."

Not necessarily. She flashed back to the bone-crushing weight of the people who died because her father decided they should.

6

The floor where Becca waited outside the offices of the County Clerk and Registrar of Deeds was free of police officers and black-robed judges. Still, she shivered. She shifted her weight, crossed then uncrossed her arms and legs. She counted the holes in the perforated ceiling tiles. A hundred and forty-seven per square. Arching her back, she rehearsed the script of the lunch conversation soon required of her.

"Ready to go, Becca?" Isaac's voice rescued her from whirling thoughts.

"Done already?"

"The clerk had all the information waiting when I walked into her office. Answer to prayer. She'd ignored what the computer told her and pawed through the old-fashioned file folders. Problem solved." He brushed his hands in a glad-that's-done motion and invited Becca to follow as he led the way to the car.

His pace was quick, his strides long and confident. Although he wasn't more than six or eight inches taller than Becca, she took three steps to two of his in order to stay even. At the car, he again held the door for her. She eased into the passenger seat and noticed for the first time that his car smelled of day-old French fries and vanilla. The crumpled In-and-Out fast food bag in the console explained the first. The leaf-shaped air freshener hanging from the rearview mirror explained the second.

Becca made a show of buckling her seatbelt. Isaac smiled, slipped almond-eyed sunglasses on his face, and eased the Buick out of the courthouse lot.

When the questions started, Becca grabbed the chest strap of her seatbelt and lifted it from its lung-crushing position.

What kind of son would not ask questions like the ones Becca skirted as if skipping through a minefield? Light on her feet, but adrenaline-charged, she dodged a bullet here, a missile there, felt the tension of a trip wire in time to sidestep disaster.

"So," Isaac asked again, "your family?"

"Gone." She'd already told him she'd cared for her father until he died, so she revised her earlier, bus-born idea. "My mother died when I was a teenager. Car accident. I was an only child." *One more than my parents ever wanted.*

Isaac lifted his chin slightly. Was he considering the veracity of her story or his own response? "Must have been difficult not having your mother around when your dad was so sick."

The thought fed her another diversionary idea. "Isaac, you said your father isn't in the picture?"

"Aneurysm. On the golf course."

"I'm so sorry."

"He wasn't." Isaac deftly laced the car through traffic as he spoke. "I mean, he didn't relish the idea of dying, I'm sure, but he always said he'd like to go with his spikes on."

"Excuse me?"

"His golf shoes. Like the cowboys who wanted to die with their boots on. It was an honor thing, I guess. Dad said since he had to go sometime, he wanted to step from one fairway to the ultimate *fair*way. Knowing he was doing what he most enjoyed right up until the end has been a comfort to my mom and me."

"I can see it would be. How long did you say he's been gone?"

"Two years."

"And you took over the family business?"

"Hughes Realty? No, that's my own folly. Dad was a banker. Chief loan officer, actually. He rode the wave of success, stepping into the waters when the climate was good and stepping out before the economy took all the fun out of it."

Becca leaned forward against the restraining arm of the seatbelt, grateful she could observe him more freely than he could observe her. "And you're an only child, too?"

"Yes. Did I give that away? Is it obvious I was spoiled rotten? When I was younger, mind you." The corners of his eyes creased, signaling complete comfort with self-deprecating humor.

"No, I just assumed. The responsibility of caring for your mother is on your shoulders alone. You're either the oldest of your siblings, the youngest, the most devoted, or an only child."

"I wish I could say I was the most devoted. I'm adopted. Didn't Aunt Geneva mention that? I was adopted as a newborn, from what little I know. Aurelia Hughes is all I've known as a mother, though. And she's been"—his voice caught— "wonderful. It's hard for me to watch Mom slipping away. And sometimes my discomfort shows itself as irritation and impatience with her. I'm not proud of that. My Aunt Geneva must have told you that much. Still working on it. That's why it's important for me to find someone to help with the caregiving. Which brings this interview back to where it should be, my asking questions of *you*. Your work experience?"

Becca pressed her back against the seat, eyes riveted to the view through the windshield. "How much farther to the Chinese restaurant you told me about?"

"Becca?"

"How far?"

"You can see the sign from here. We'll be digging our chopsticks into Moo Goo Gai Pan or Yi Shang Pork within minutes."

"Then, I think I'll save my story until we've ordered, if you don't mind."

"Fair enough. I'll be able to focus better without having to maneuver between insane drivers."

And I'll be able to figure out how much I can tell you about who I am.

<hr />

Garlic and ginger, sesame oil, hot chilies, hibachi something . . . Good choice for lunch. The smells hung so heavy in the air she thought she could taste them. How long since she'd eaten? She'd squirreled her money, eating sparingly on the trip, and tucking the rest of her meager funds in a concealed—and now inaccessible—leather pouch under her shirt.

It hadn't occurred to Becca that conversation would not form the only awkward moments at the restaurant. Isaac hadn't specifically said he intended to pick up the tab. What was protocol for an impromptu job interview?

Behind a party of six at the "Please wait here to be seated" sign, Isaac and Becca stood shoulder to shoulder in the tight quarters of the small foyer, temporarily disengaged from communicating with each other.

The heavyset man paying his bill at the cashier's stand searched his wallet for a credit card. Something fluttered from his pocket. Becca could clearly see he'd dropped a folded twenty. *My provision? Is this for me, God?*

Becca edged closer and planted her foot over the bill. No one else seemed to have noticed the man's loss. Another divine intervention? The tight press of a noon-hour crowd of patrons coming and going. The man's own shadow-casting presence. The clang of the cash register and the high-pitched, fast-paced chatter from hostess to waiter to busboy to kitchen.

She could feel the bulk of the bill, thin as it was, under her foot. *How many commandments will I have broken if I stoop to stealing, too? Honor thy father and mother. Honesty is the best policy. Thou shalt not steal. Is that how they went?*

Becca bent down, picked up the twenty destined to solve her immediate financial dilemma, and tapped the man on his Pillsbury Doughboy shoulder. "Excuse me, sir? I believe you dropped this."

"What? Oh, thank you. I 'preciate it." The man slipped the bill back into the protection of his wallet. The incident was over. Her answer rested in someone else's pocket. She'd have to excuse herself to the restroom and fish out enough to pay for her lunch, just in case.

"Good deed for the day, Miss Morrow?" Isaac's voice whispered close behind her. If only he knew how tightly her good deed had walked to the cliff edge of sin.

"I guess no one else saw it fall out of his pocket."

"Just for that, lunch is on me. Let's go. Our table's ready." Isaac steered her forward with a warm, comforting hand in the small of her back. As they walked, he bent to say, "Not that I wouldn't have picked up the tab, anyway. But it makes me sound philanthropic, doesn't it?"

Isaac treated her as if she were an ordinary, authentic person. His heart seemed light. Hers was an anvil of guilt and regret. But somehow the helium in his spirit buoyed hers, pulling it up off the bottom.

As agreed, Isaac reserved his questions until they'd ordered. His "Where are you from?" competed with the lure of Sizzling Sensation floating past their table on the way to satisfy someone's appetite. Becca fought to focus on her interrogator, ignoring her snarling, insistent hunger.

"From? Have you ever been to northern Minnesota?"

"No."

Good. "I'm from a little town a few dozen miles west of Duluth." She watched his face for signs that she needed to feed out more line.

"A sight warmer climate here," Isaac said, pouring oolong tea into two white, handle-less cups. "They say we have four seasons, too. Summer. Not Quite Summer. Almost Summer. And Oh Hey Look It's Summer Again. Is that the reason for your move?"

"That's part of it. Sure. The climate."

"You seem hesitant. Look, Becca," Isaac Hughes reached across the table. His touch on her hand startled and calmed her at the same time. "You don't owe me any more information than you'd like to share. But I don't think it's out of line for me to get to know you a little better before recommending you to my mother."

"Recommending me?"

"Yes. She'll make the final decision. Officially. But I've no doubt she'll lean heavily on my counsel. What would you like me to tell her about you?"

"Would I have to have a nursing degree?"

"No, not necessary. Her medical needs are taken care of by her physician and sometimes a visiting nurse. What she needs is a companion. Someone to do light housekeeping. Someone to see she doesn't neglect her medications, that she's eating when able, that she doesn't try to get out of bed without help. There would be some not-so-pleasant personal-care responsibilities." Isaac wrinkled his forehead and nose as he waited for her response.

The corners of Becca's mouth lifted slightly. "I understand. As I mentioned in the car earlier, I'm sure there are others more qualified. But I think I could give your mom the care she needs."

His grin revealed teeth bright white in contrast with his sun-bronzed skin. Obviously, he wasn't stuck in his office on weekends. A surfer? Dude.

"I'll devote myself wholeheartedly to your mother's care, if you trust me to do so." It sounded stiff, even to her.

"I'm not going to discover much about Becca Morrow by asking, am I?" Isaac conceded.

"You're welcome to anything I know about her," Becca dodged, momentarily amused by the irony.

"My Aunt Geneva speaks so highly of you." He smiled as if thoughts of Geneva Larkin tugged at the corners of his mouth. He appreciated her. They had that in common.

The waitress brought a welcome diversion. A bowl of fragrant Jasmine rice and an overflowing platter of Moo Goo Gai Pan.

In some households, when food arrives at the table, talking stops. Apparently not the kind of household in which Isaac grew up.

"So what did you do?" he asked while dishing up his foundation layer of rice after allowing her to build her own.

"What did I do?" *I'm not ready to tell you that yet, Mr. Hughes. I may never be ready. I came home too late to stop my mom from dying. And I called the cops on my dad. There's a "character" reference for you.*

"Before you decided to move out here. For your former employer."

Becca arranged the pieces of tender chicken with her fork, evenly distributing them among the onions and mushrooms and bamboo shoots and water chestnuts. The green of the broccoli and bright orange of the carrot slivers helped make the plate as delicious in appearance as it must have been in taste. Becca's rumbling stomach begged her to figure out how to gracefully put a forkful in her mouth between questions.

Isaac postponed her agony a little longer when he said, "Before you answer, would you mind if I asked the Lord's blessing on our food?"

"Not at all. Please do."

"Great God and Father, Creator, Redeemer, Friend, Provider, we thank You for the meal before us. Thank You for the opportunity to meet Becca. If it's in Your wise plan that she become Mom's caregiver, I ask You to make it clear and help us work through the details. For Your glory. And it's in Your Name that we pray, Jesus. Amen."

What was this wave of peace? The first she'd felt in longer than she could remember. And who was this guy who could pray like that but couldn't cope with his mom's disease?

"Tell me about your mother's illness." It was time to get back on the offensive again. If she were asking the questions, her likelihood of getting tripped up decreased significantly.

"A lethal combination. She has a weak heart and is battling mid-stage Alzheimer's. Some days she's as lucid as you or I. Other days she's living in some other era on some other planet."

"The doctors can't do anything about her heart? Bypass surgery? Pacemaker?"

Isaac put down his chopsticks and dabbed at his mouth with his napkin. "The heart muscle is growing weaker. It's genetic, I guess. Her mother and grandmother both died from this. If Mom were twenty years younger, the medical community would probably insist on a transplant. But especially now with the addition of the Alzheimer's . . ."

"Too much room for dangerous complications?"

"Yes."

"Isaac, I'm sorry."

Isaac held her gaze for longer than Becca felt comfortable. How could she look away without appearing insincere? He seemed to study her face. This man was in serious pain. How selfish could she get? When she first read Isaac's name on the door of his office—*was that only an hour ago?*—she saw it as flat letters. But the name belonged to a person. Someone she intended to use to help mop up her mess like a waitress cleaning tables. Someone she needed to legitimize her identity and presence in that town so far removed from "before." Someone to hide behind while she detoxed from her previous life. Isaac Hughes and his needy mother—her only current options.

7

Isaac hadn't expected his aunt's recommendation to come so beautifully packaged. Younger than he'd expected, too. Aunt Geneva described her as a friend. Interesting. He'd pictured someone closer to his aunt's age.

This was better.

He stabbed a piece of chicken and reined in his thoughts.

Aurelia Hughes' home was familiar to Becca. She'd seen it many times in her dreams. Not this exact home, but one much like it. Deep front yard with mature trees and flower beds, although the species of trees and flowers weren't all familiar to her. Georgian two-story house—white. Not typical of others in the neighborhood that boasted Mediterranean influences and clay tile roofs. This one had wide window boxes under the twin bay windows on either side of the double-wide front entrance door. A *home* home. She'd seen it. Aha. The *Father of the Bride* movie.

A chorale of birds seemed at ease and safe in this yard. Would she?

"We'll go through the garage," Isaac called over his shoulder as he bent to hoist the heavy wooden garage door. "Why Mother refuses to let me put in an automatic garage door opener for her, I'll never know. This way."

Isaac beckoned to her from where Becca stood near the passenger door of his car, drinking in the thirst-quenching scene. *Please, another moment?* Some heavenly fragrance—mock orange?—called to her from somewhere in the yard. And a sea of roses cried out to be appreciated.

"Becca?"

"Coming. Should I bring my suitcase?"

Isaac's throaty laugh again. "My, you are the confident one, aren't you?"

Far from it.

"Why don't I introduce you to my mother first. I'll be more than happy to make a trip out to the car to retrieve your suitcase, if need be. Frankly, I'll probably need the escape from her ramblings. You'll be doing me a favor if you just let it sit where it is for now."

As she followed Isaac through the garage, skirting Aurelia's collector-quality ancient automobile, Becca thought to ask, "Who takes care of your mother while you're at work?"

"A constantly changing flow of temporaries. That has to be resolved. There's no consistency. Because today's caregiver doesn't have a clue what she pulled yesterday, Mother is getting away with murder."

Becca flinched at the word. *Murder?*

The door from the garage led into Aurelia's kitchen. Classic white cabinetry and intriguing granite countertops with iridescent flakes kept it from looking dated, although the wallpaper and curtains revealed it had been some time since anyone had had the energy to update them.

"Grab yourself a cup of coffee, if you'd like, Becca. I'll prepare Mom to meet you. I might just send the temp home for the day. Remind me to call Mrs. Gollum later and tell her I won't be in until tomorrow." His secretary's name came out slightly growled, not spoken.

"What did you call her?"

"Pardon? Oh, did I let that slip?" Isaac rubbed his forehead. "Sorry. I'm not proud of that. Have you seen *Lord of the Rings*?"

"Seven times."

"Me? Eight."

"Would have watched all three an eighth time, but I—."

"Gallum. Gollum. It's just too . . . too . . ."

"Prrrrecious?" Becca twisted her hands as she'd seen the ex-Hobbit victim/villain Gollum do in the classic trilogy.

Isaac's eyes shifted from left to right. "She must never know!"

"Our secret," Becca assured.

Isaac cocked his head as he looked Becca's way. "You know, if for some reason my mother doesn't approve of hiring you—and I can't imagine why she wouldn't—there may be an opening down at my office."

Her heart hadn't lost track of its rhythm for any reason other than fear . . . until that moment.

Footsteps overhead told Becca that Aurelia's room was probably directly over the kitchen. Considering the report of the older woman's condition, Becca doubted she ever saw the downstairs of her own home anymore. As Becca waited for Isaac to pave the way for her entrance, she ventured from the kitchen to explore the rest of the first floor.

Formal dining room. How long since it had been used? Serene, ultraformal living room with carefully arranged conversation groups of chairs and couches, elegant lamps, what must have been important artwork, polished cherry side tables, and no one to use them to entertain company.

Curious as she was, Becca resisted the temptation to open the two closed doors off the main entrance hall at the front of the house. One was no doubt a closet. The other would have to remain a mystery for now.

A scented candle would go a long way toward evicting the staleness in here. Or someone should open a few windows. Her mind played with what chores she would tackle first if given the chance.

A deep sunroom ran almost the full length of the back of the house. It was the one bright, unexpected room in an otherwise museum-like home. Windows on three sides of the sunroom offered unencumbered views of the lush backyard and garden. Becca couldn't tell if neighbors were close in back. A heavy growth of suburban forest—palms and vines and shrubs Becca had no Midwestern reference with which to identify—kept her from knowing.

She could picture white wicker in this room. Lots of it. Right now it served as a storage area, it seemed. Empty cardboard boxes. Rusty folding chairs. A wooden-legged ironing board that had seen better decades.

"There you are."

"Isaac!"

"Sorry if I startled you."

"Day-dreaming."

Isaac drew a deep breath. "This is a good place for it. I used to love this room."

"It's not used anymore? That's a shame." She traced her finger along the top of an on-the-edge-of-shabby lamp table.

"It hasn't seen any life since Mom's health began to fade. She's confined to her room." His gaze drifted to the painted floor. "You haven't asked why she isn't in a nursing home."

"I think I know the answer. If there were a facility close by that met your expectations for her care and her expectations for comfort, that's where she'd be."

Isaac crossed his arms and leaned against the archway connecting the sunroom to the rest of the house. "Very perceptive, Miss Morrow."

"Thank you, Mr. Hughes. May I have the honor of meeting your mother now?" *Becca, you're not auditioning for the part of a governess in Victorian England. Lighten up.*

As if he'd heard her self-chiding, Isaac smiled broadly and answered, "It will be her honor to meet you."

⸺

Isaac paused in the upstairs hall. This could go either way. *Mom, please be on your best behavior.* "I have to warn you, she was clear-headed a minute ago, but she may be broadcasting from Neptune now."

"Then I'll talk Neptunese, if necessary," Becca countered. "Let the games begin!"

Isaac pressed his lips together and opened the bedroom door for her.

⸺

The room lay on the north side of the building, which even in California meant less light reached its pale resident. Aurelia Hughes's fragile form barely registered under the bedcovers. A slight ridge of frail bones and thin skin arrowed the eye upward to a gray-haloed head resting on the bed pillow.

"Mrs. Hughes, I'm Becca Morrow."

"No, you're not." The woman's voice was twice as big as her body.

"Mother!" Isaac stepped forward as if to referee the exchange.

The raspy voice continued. "My son said a beautiful young woman named Becca Morrow is here to apply to be my baby-sitter. Until you march on over here and let me see your face, how do I know it's you?"

Becca and Isaac traded eye-sighs. *Wait a minute! Beautiful? He used the word* beautiful?

"Sorry, Mrs. Hughes," Becca said as she neared the bed. "I'm the ugly stepsister. But they call me Becca, too." She twirled with arms extended, giving the old woman a full view.

"Isaac," Aurelia motioned with a weak, parchment-skinned hand, "make a note to call my lawyer. If this is ugly, then I'm changing my name to Becca."

If only the woman knew how direct a hit her sentence had made. But, one hurdle conquered. The temp nurse whispered something to Isaac, then left the room.

Becca sat lightly on the edge of the bed. "So, what have you learned today, Mrs. Hughes?"

"Pardon me?"

"Most people start with, 'How are you feeling?' Seems obvious if you were feeling spunky, you'd be out of this bed dancing in your garden on a day like today, working on your tan, hiking around the block. I think it's a smarter question to ask what you've learned with the extra time you've been given to think."

Aurelia cocked one ghostly white eyebrow. "How did you know I was a dancer?"

Isaac shook his head no. Becca caught the movement and hoped Aurelia hadn't.

"Isaac, I like this one."

"Me, too, Mom." He didn't look at Becca when he spoke. A blessing.

"Mrs. Hughes, I would very much like to work for you. As I proposed to your son . . ."

"You proposed already?"

"An idea. I proposed an idea."

"Oh." The twinkle in Aurelia's eye told Becca she knew very well what the younger woman meant.

"I suggested a trial period of six months. But now my thought is to work for you, at no charge, for the first six weeks. All I ask is room and board. If at the end of that time you're dissatisfied with my performance, you can send me packing." *Performance. Watch your word choices, Becca.*

Isaac stepped closer to the side of the bed. "We can't have you work without pay. How would that be fair?"

"Remember the fair of 1920, I believe it was?" The gray halo trembled with the effort of thinking.

Isaac shot Becca a look that warned her his mother was wandering off.

"Or it might have been '21. My sheep won a blue ribbon."

"Mother, you never raised sheep."

"That's right. It was a pie. Is that what you call it? Cherries in the middle and a cross on top?"

Becca sat on the edge of the bed and took Aurelia's hand in hers. "Was it a cross on top, Mrs. Hughes, or criss-crossed pastry? A lattice-topped pie?"

"I believe it was. Yes. A cherry pie. Blue ribbon. Well, we can talk about that tomorrow when you bring me my breakfast, Becca."

Isaac reached to put a hand on Becca's shoulder. "Looks as if the job is yours, if you want it. I'll go get your suitcase."

A foot in the door. She had a foot in the door. Becca glanced down at her worn ballerina flats. Better a foot in the door than in cheap foam institutional flip-flops. Classic black to contrast with prison orange.

Dad, get out of my head.

8

As he pointed his remote fob toward the trunk and popped its lock, Isaac rewound the brain-tape of the last few hours. *What just happened?*

Someone had thrown the switch for the tracks on which the locomotive of his life clack-clack-clacked. He veered to the left now. The well-worn track of familiarity and routine grew farther and farther distant. With ocean-deep eyes and a disarmingly shy smile, Becca Morrow changed everything.

He'd opened the office door and practically stumbled over her. Stumbled over the answer to his mother's needs. When had Aurelia Grace Hughes last sparkled as she did in Becca's presence? Which of the temps handled his mother's wanderings as well as she did? Five minutes. In five minutes' time Becca wormed her way into his mother's heart.

And his.

Where did that thought come from?

Isaac hoisted Becca's suitcase from the trunk of the Buick. Halfway across the country with only this little bag? No ordinary woman. Anything but ordinary.

Isaac, get a grip! You've known her part of an afternoon. Not even long enough to form an opinion. And what did he really know about her? Becca used SuperGlue for lip gloss. He'd pried all through lunch and wrangled only the briefest sketch of her personal history. Mega-shy? Hiding something? No. That sweet face? Impossible. Protective of her personal information, that's all.

"Some of it lives in this suitcase. I could play Airport Baggage Handler and see what falls out. I can't believe I just said that. Have you lost your mind, man? Must be the stress of the Humbold deal. And . . . I'm talking to myself. Great."

He tugged on the telescoping handle of the suitcase and commanded it to "heel" as he headed toward the house. Curiosity reined in if not abated, Isaac attempted to shake off thoughts of the twenty-something woman who won over the heart of his mother without breaking a sweat. How did she do that? Another mystery.

Isaac paused at the doorway of his mother's bedroom and drank in the scene like a dehydrated marathon runner. The race of concern for his mom stretched on beyond the horizon. Muscles he needed for the challenge sagged and rebelled against the strain. He hadn't trained for it. This early into the race and he could already feel the tension in unused, flabby caregiving limbs.

But Becca stepped onto the course with winged running shoes, flying over obstacles that smacked him in the face and shins. A few brief moments and he already noted the differences between them. His bedside manner could best be described as klutzy. Hers was grace.

His mother was laughing. Laughing! He'd missed the joke, but didn't mind. Hearing her laughter meant more than any punch line.

"Sorry to break up the party, ladies, but I need to know where to put this." Becca would know full well how light the suitcase was, so there was no point in his feigning muscle strain.

"What's right across the hall?" Becca stepped around the end of the bed toward him.

"That's a little sewing room. Nothing more than a daybed in there. Should we put her in the room at the end of the hall, Mom?"

"What's that, dear?"

"Shall we—? Never mind. Let me show you the larger room, Becca."

But she stripped the case from his hands and headed across the hall. "I'd rather have this room, if you don't mind. It's closer. I'll be able to hear if Aurelia needs me in the night."

"You'd be a lot more comfortable in the end room."

Tears? Why did tears pool in her eyes?

"This is all I need. Thank you, Isaac."

So it was settled. The arrangement, that is. Not his heart rate.

<hr />

Sea glass.

Blue-green sea glass with tears. What must the world look like viewed through pale blue sea glass every day? Isaac backed the Buick out of his mother's driveway. Twenty minutes and he'd be unlocking the door of his condo. Becca would be making a nest for herself in a cramped sewing room.

She'd been quick to pick up on the instructions for his mother's care that afternoon. With so many temporary caregivers in and out, the procedure manual came in handy. More than once, Isaac flinched at the revelation that the manual knew more about her needs than he did.

Isaac had walked Becca through the rest of the house while his mother took her prescribed nap after their canned soup supper. He smiled now thinking about her almost childlike delight over the home's architectural features. He remembered asking about her childhood home. Why couldn't he remember her answer? Had she changed the subject? Happened a lot.

Usually the drive home passed like the pull of a magnet toward a long-awaited destination. Tonight it felt like the other pole of the magnet. A palpable repulsion.

He debated a half second too long on a yellow light, then jammed his brakes after checking his rearview mirror for tailers. The abrupt stop threw his briefcase forward off the backseat and onto the floor.

My briefcase. The Humbold property! I haven't given it a minute's worry since . . . since I met her.

Isaac, you need to bolt your head on tighter. You're leaking brain cells, dude.

With Aurelia settled for the night, Becca walked across the hall to the sewing room. A dressmaker's form in the corner and a professional quality sewing machine told her Aurelia's seamstress abilities outshone the typical mended hem or loose button. The headless figure held nightmare potential, so Becca relegated it to the small closet.

She opened the casement window on the south wall. A light breeze—perfumed with some overachieving night-blooming garden flower—floated into the room and chased out the stale air of disuse. She pulled back the coverlet on the daybed. Not that it would have made any difference, but she gave the sheets the sniff test. Clean. She couldn't imagine how long it had been since the bed had been used, but it was put away clean at least. The joy of not having to sleep upright on the seat of a bus ought to have been luxury enough for her. Clean sheets were a bonus.

Unpacking her suitcase took all of four minutes. If this worked out, she'd ask Geneva to ship more of her things. Not that it would be much of a chore. She padded down the hall in her bare feet to the white-tiled bathroom, toothbrush in hand. Frowning at her reflection in the mirror, she brushed her teeth and washed a few days of history off her face.

A day at a time. She'd be grateful for a day at a time.

Deep in the bowels of the house, an ancient clock marched off the seconds. Tup, tup, tup, tup. She'd have to see about silencing the thing. The mocking tups seemed a countdown that drew her closer to the moment her veil would unravel, when her father's reputation would disturb the fragile peace. It always did.

She'd attend to that clock in the morning. Right now the little daybed called to her, and an old woman's purring snore offered to sing her to sleep.

9

Not in the habit of swinging past his mother's house on his way to work, today Isaac thought it wise to check in on the women. Eight o'clock. If no one was awake, he could at least start a pot of coffee or something.

No need for that. Becca stood at the table, putting the finishing touches on a breakfast tray when he entered the kitchen.

"Sorry," he offered. "Should I have knocked? I'm used to just walking in."

"I was ready for you. Fresh coffee's on the counter."

"What smells so good?" And how did she know he'd come by this morning?

"I sprinkled a little cinnamon and brown sugar on the coffee grounds."

"Nice."

"Have you eaten? Not much for groceries in the house right now, but I managed to find the fixings for French toast. Help yourself. I'm on my way to your mother's room."

"Can I carry that up the stairs for you?"

Becca stopped in her tracks. "I'll take you up on that. If my plan works out, it won't be necessary much longer. But if you grab the tray, I can get a caráfe of ice water for your mom."

"Your plan?"

"We'll talk about that after a bit. Your mother is going through an impatient phase this morning. I'd rather not rattle her any more than needed."

Isaac suppressed the smile tugging at the corners of his mouth. "A phase, huh?"

Three steps up the stairs to the second floor, Isaac noted that the grandfather clock in the foyer wasn't ticking. *Have to take a look at it later.*

Breakfast sailed on rough waters that morning, according to Becca. Nothing suited Aurelia. Not even the rosebud Becca had clipped from the garden and stuck in a tiny crystal vase for the tray.

"I'm sorry about that." His words bounced off the kitchen ceiling as the two ambulatory humans in the house unloaded the tray of half-eaten, rejected food.

"You act embarrassed by her behavior, Isaac. Don't. Please." Becca squirted dish soap into the sink and turned on the faucet full force.

"How can I help it? This is not the mother who raised me. I wish you'd known her then."

"I see glimpses of that woman. Enough for me to know she was once easy to love."

"The easiest. You still want the job?"

Becca shut off the faucet and leaned on the sink edge. "Yes. Very much." She didn't look his way. Her breathing changed, though. He saw her thin shoulders lift with each breath, as if she waited for an ax to fall.

He checked the time on his cell phone. "You wanted to tell me about your plan?"

Now she turned. She seemed to notice the phone still in his hand. The skin between her eyebrows wrinkled. A smile fought to break through whatever emotion churned within her.

"I'd like to move your mother to the sunroom. I think half her battle is loneliness. If we relocate her to the sunroom, she can see outdoors, even from the bed. She'll feel more a part of the life of this house. And it will be more convenient for the wheelchair."

"The wheelchair?" He hadn't considered his mom could tolerate sitting in one, much less be wheeled around. Something in his chest caught, as if he were afraid of his falling, not hers.

"We can rent one if you'd rather not purchase. Most home-health-care agencies have them."

Becca oozed hope out of every perfect pore.

"You think she's up to sitting in a wheelchair?"

"We won't know unless we try, will we?" She gestured with raised hands. "I didn't note any doctor's orders against it in the instructions for her care."

"I'll see what I can do."

"Do talk to her doctor first. Unless you'd rather I called the number in the manual."

Isaac took the smartphone out of his sport coat pocket again. "Noted. I'll take care of it as soon as I get time." He noted she flinched at the word, in harmony with his own twitch.

"And we need music."

"Pardon me?"

Becca slipped into a chair at the kitchen table and leaned Isaac's way. "The woman needs music in her life, Isaac."

"She used to play the piano."

"Yes, she told me. A woman with a love for music will dry up and shrivel in her spirit if she's denied it. Can we get a radio or a music system in that sunroom, too?"

The phone flew into use again, his thumbs taking notes. "Anything else?"

"A baby monitor."

"A baby monitor." Isaac knew his voice dripped with sarcasm, but let it.

"Yes. That will free me to clean or cook or go out to the garden without wondering if she's okay. I'll be able to hear if she's having a coughing spell or calling out to me or trying to get herself out of bed."

"She's up to that trick again?"

"Twice this morning already."

"One baby monitor. Check. Is that it?"

Becca folded her hands before her on the table. "How would I go about getting free for a couple of hours for grocery shopping and to . . . to pick up some personal items?"

"If you make a list, I can stop at the store on my way home from work today. It's likely to be late."

She lowered her head without lowering her eyes and pursed her lips. "Isaac, I need some . . . *personal* . . . items."

So that's what a blush feels like. His cheeks grew warmer than flat rocks on a beach. "How about if I send one of my friends to watch Mom this afternoon so you can do the grocery shopping yourself? *Call . . . someone.* Oh, hey, since you are apparently hired, I need to reimburse you for your trip." He finished keying a note into his phone and looked up.

"Thank you."

"Are you sure that's all?"

The smile seemed genuine this time. "All for now. I've only been here one night."

"How'd you sleep, by the way?"

The sea glass sparkled. "Better than I have in a long, long time."

Would he ever hear the story behind that admission?

10

If Isaac followed through and found someone to give her a couple of hours away from the house, she could supplement her leave-it-all-behind wardrobe. She'd shop frugally, as always. A nightgown, two or three summer-weather tank tops, and "personal items." Oh, and sunglasses, she thought, squinting. She could go most of the year at home without sunglasses.

He intended to reimburse her for the bus fare. That would help her establish the beginnings of a new "finish college" fund. The more she thought about asking Geneva to send anything from her old life, the less appealing that seemed. Clothing limitations would force frequent laundering and creativity until at least six months from now, when her new job brought a legitimate income.

Legitimate. She needed a new attitude. Why couldn't she think of herself as something more honorable—perhaps redefining herself because she was in the Witness Protection Program? In a way, she was. What she'd witnessed . . .

Maybe she wasn't as despicable as her conscience tried to tell her. Her dad was the guilty one. Maybe the fact that it troubled her to layer one half-truth on top of another like a stack of pancakes was a good sign. She had a conscience.

This isn't what You expected of me, is it, God? Did You lie awake and dream of what I'd be when I grew up? I'll bet this wasn't it.

———

She shouldn't have had to remind him. Isaac rubbed the kinks out of the back of his neck. With all she'd given up to move out here, with all she'd done already, he should have remembered to call in help so Becca could have time to shop and get a little more settled. She'd gone to work within minutes of arriving. The fickle economy meant if he were going to be successful, he'd have to be okay with putting in outrageous hours, working through lunch, cutting to the chase.

But she shouldn't have had to remind him to give her a break to go get groceries.

Peter's wife, Ginger, would have done it if he'd called soon enough. Did he expect the temp he'd fired yesterday to jump at the opportunity to come back for an afternoon? Maybe not. But he hadn't been called a name like that for almost twenty years—to his face.

He'd cleaned out a hundred e-mails before he thought about it again. Becca had been waiting most of the day to hear from him by the time he found someone to sit with his mom. She hadn't sounded irritated. *Disappointed* was a better word.

———

Committed to his work or addicted to it? Becca shouldn't have called his office. He was a busy man. He hadn't forgotten about her need. Not like her father. Isaac had gotten tied up in a project, that's all.

Her shoes tapped a sidewalk rhythm—*Why . . . does life . . . have to be . . . so complicated?*—as she walked the eight blocks to the shopping center. Nothing else occupied her brain. The reality that distance in miles doesn't equal distance from pain used up all the elbowroom.

A hot, penetrating late afternoon sun made her skin prickle and dew. *The sun shines on the innocent and the guilty.* Was that from the Bible? Truth is truth. She crossed the wide expanse of asphalt in the parking lot of the supercenter. Becca Morrow—one of many people on whom the sun shone that day. Most of them innocent, no doubt. If her father were here, the sun would shine on him, too. Nothing visible would mark him the guilty one, or mark her the ashamed one.

She slipped through the entrance doors as if it were the most natural thing in the world to have a murderer for a father, invent an identity to cover the fact, and want so desperately to belong where she'd landed.

Next time, oh wise one, as you fill the shopping cart with abandon, give at least a moment's consideration to the concept of hauling the items home. Home. The word rested on her mind's tongue like rich caramel. Soothing as it melted. Nice, lingering aftertaste.

She shifted one of the three plastic bags from left hand to right. Balance was impossible with an odd number of bags. She'd list to the right for another block or two before switching back again.

Grocery bag plastic makes a decent tourniquet. Good to know, should I sever a limb.

A soft, scented breeze dried the perspiration on her brow. Somewhere just a few miles west of where she stood was an ocean she'd seen only in images and imagination. She pinched her eyes shut for a moment. No wave sound, only people-noise.

But the breeze made its presence clear. *What was in Your mind, God, when you invented breezes? Great idea, in my opinion. My compliments.*

Since when did she high-five the Creator of the universe?

Her mood had shifted when she'd walked past the impulse racks at the checkout and not seen a grainy, morbid tabloid image of her dad with his ankles and wrists shackled. Old news now. No reason to do a side story about the effects of his choices on his tormented daughter. Insert photo here.

She should have colored her hair in case a slow news day resurrected interest in Bertram Dennagee and the daughter who made sure he went to prison. Hair color? New hair style?

Pointless at this stage. Isaac and his mother and Mrs. Gallum and the wait staff at the Asian restaurant had seen her in her traditional peanut-butter-colored stuff. Hardly seemed worth it to change to mahogany or chestnut or platinum now.

It won't be a clever disguise that gives me a new life. It'll take a miracle.

Her thoughts weighted her legs. Two tons of lead poured into size-eight jeans. Molten lead plopping like muddy footprints on the sidewalk that led to Aurelia's.

Becca focused on the pale gray sidewalk stretching out before her. Smooth. An upper-middle-class sidewalk—absent of pockmarks and uneven, toe-stubbing breaks, trimmed in lush, irrigated green or stylish rock landscaping materials to support the desert succulents and wispy tufts of exotic grasses. Yet another study in contrasts between her present and her past.

Somewhere in America, trailer parks sport sidewalks and neat lawns with wide spaces between trim mobile homes. Somewhere she'd never seen. The lawns in her father's neighborhood—the last of five moves in five years, until the court system moved him—grew grass like mid-chemotherapy hair.

The closest they came to ornamentation or landscaping—aluminum lawn chair skeletons without webbing, rust-encrusted one-wheeled bicycles, and someone else's beer cans.

Sidewalks? What a waste they would have been.

The one on which her feet now fell held purpose. The purpose-driven walk. Pathetic as it sounded, it would take her to the closest thing she knew to home.

The door opened to her before her foot hit the bottom step.

"Here. Let me get those for you."

"Thanks, Isaac." Her cramped hands and arms screamed their gratitude.

"You walked the whole way?"

Becca warmed at his concern. "It was good for me."

"Still working out the kinks from the bus ride?"

Working out kinks. Definitely. How many walks would that take?

"Becca?"

"My mind wandered off again. Going to have to consider sending it to obedience school." A nerve in her neck shivered. Normal. The fake "her" was supposed to be normal. "That small bag is mine."

Isaac slid it toward her on the kitchen counter and began unloading the others. "Nectarines. Mom loves those."

"I thought she might."

"Apricot jam?"

"I have a recipe for pork roast glazed with apricot jam."

"You brought a cookbook in that little suitcase?"

"In my head. The recipe's in my head. Explains why there's not much room for anything else at times."

"Personally, I claim computer overload. I don't need a transplant. Just a new hard drive." He tapped his head as one might to dislodge dust. He succeeded in dislodging one perfect forehead curl. Good enough.

"Are you staying for supper? Somewhere in one of those bags is low-sodium, low-fat bacon for a BLT salad."

"Low-fat bacon. Kind of defeats the purpose, doesn't it?"

Becca took in his anything-but-lumpy physique. What was her heart doing in her esophagus?

Isaac didn't wait for her response. "I'd love to stay, but I'm years away from my goal of the business running itself. Two critical appointments yet this evening."

"I hope I didn't make you late." Becca moved closer to finish putting away the groceries herself.

"No. Mrs. Gallum rearranged a few things for me."

"Bless her."

Isaac raised his hand as if to tweak her nose. Less than gracefully, he pulled back and rubbed his own. "I've got to go. Have fun with Mom. Thought I stole her Barbie doll this morning. She's sleeping, last I checked. I'll stop by after work. Oh, I made a few phone calls while I waited. A crew will be here Saturday morning to help move her bed to the sunroom. I have an air-conditioning/heating guy coming tomorrow to check out the vents in there. Start a list if you think of anything else."

Impressive. "I think this will be good for your mother, Isaac."

Isaac's lingering gaze heated the air between them. "I think *you'll* be good for her."

"Mrs. Hughes?"

"Come on in. No need to whisper. I'm more in need of company than I am a nap."

"It sounded as if you were having trouble breathing."

"Par for the course. Isaac turned off the ceiling fan before he left. Thought I'd catch a draft. But it helps to have the air moving, for some reason."

Becca caught the childish longing in the dove-gray eyes. "I'll turn it on low. How's that?"

"It'll be better soon. Some things, I can't explain." Her eyes glistened. "May or may not be a medical reason for all I feel. Like needing moving air."

"I hope you'll be patient with me while I learn what you require, Mrs. Hughes."

"I was going to ask you to stop calling me that. But it does add a little dignity back into my sorry existence."

Becca sat on the edge of Aurelia's bed and brushed a stray feather of silver off her forehead. "You're going to have to clean up your mouth around me, Mrs. Hughes. It hurts my ears to hear talk like that."

"Yes, Admiral." The effort to salute took the starch out of Aurelia Hughes's sails.

"Bad day?"

Aurelia's eyes widened. "Becca, will you look at that?" The conversation derailed.

"What is it?"

"See here in my palm?" The older woman held one shaky hand toward her. The skin was so white-pink it looked bleached, and so thin Becca wondered how protective it could be anymore.

"I don't see anything. I'm sorry."

"No. You wouldn't." Her expression darkened. "Nothing's written there." Pale as they were, her eyes lit. "But my name is written on God's palm."

Becca envisioned *Aurelia Hughes* inscribed in beautiful penmanship on an enormous, calloused Hand.

Aurelia closed both her frail fist and her eyes. "Some days, that's the only thing that keeps me going."

Her breathing deep and unhurried now, she seemed not to sleep as much as rest in that thought.

———

The room stilled except for the mildly annoying click in the ceiling fan's cycle. Becca sat in a cabbage-rose chintz chair in the corner, her feet tucked under her. The pages of the book in her lap were thin as onionskin and rustled like dry leaves when she turned them. So she crept through her reading, her search.

"What are you looking for? Money?"

"I didn't mean to wake you, Mrs. Hughes."

"I don't keep my money in my Bible, if that's what you were thinking."

Becca waited for clearer signals about Aurelia's mood, mind-set, and motivation for asking. When none emerged, she answered, "I hoped to find that verse."

"What verse?"

"The one about your name being written in the palm of God's Hand. Your sister Geneva quoted that to me once."

"Come here, girl."

Becca unfolded her legs, slipped back into her worn flats, and crossed the room to Aurelia's bedside.

The older woman winced. "What did it say?"

"What did *what* say, Mrs. Hughes?"

"My hearing's not what it should be. I know it was whispering something, something not too kind, either."

"What was whispering?"

"That!"

Becca followed the path Aurelia's arthritic finger indicated. "Your African violet?"

"Yes. Beady little yellow eyes. Jaundice, I suspect. Probably liver trouble."

"Your plant?"

"Oh, never mind. He shut up now. You're no help at all."

Becca grieved Aurelia's first unkind words to her. The first of many, no doubt.

As if jumping an invisible boundary, the woman's voice skipped now. "Don't you think we should get started?"

"With what, Mrs. Hughes?"

"Our lessons."

Becca closed the Bible and replaced it on the lower shelf of the bed stand where she'd found it. "What lessons did you have in mind?"

"Ballet, silly girl. Where is your mind today?"

If she suggests I help her into her tutu, I will have to put a stop to this train of thought. "I wasn't sure you'd feel up to ballet today."

"Why not?" The innocence on the deeply wrinkled face twisted something in Becca's heart. Aurelia's lower lip slipped into a perfect preteen pout. "I've been practicing."

"I know, honey. But with . . . with the recital right around the corner, I thought you might want to take it easy. Rest up for it."

"Rest up?" The rheumy eyes, faded as mourning dove feathers, bore into Becca's as though searching for a connection to the reality that scooted and broke apart like beads of mercury when she touched it. "Yes. I should probably rest. Save my strength for the recital."

Becca's relief mirrored the relaxing of thin shoulders that rested against the pillows. A sound bite from an almost forgotten television talk show flashed through her mind. "When dealing with Alzheimer's patients," the expert guest counseled, "don't worry about being right or proving the patients wrong.

They don't need to know the truth. They need to know they're loved."

For the sake of Aurelia's happiness, Becca chose to walk through the looking glass into a make-believe world with elderly ballet stars and gossipy houseplants.

If she had wanted adventure, she had found it.

Adventure. That had never been the point. She wanted to belong.

11

His mom wasn't proud of him anymore. She couldn't be. Some days she didn't realize her name was Mom.

Isaac glanced at his planner. More black ink than white page. Notes and phone numbers and tri-color highlighted events or appointments—Red for Vital. Yellow for Close to Vital. Green for Now! A full day. Important client contacts. They wouldn't all turn out as he'd hoped, but some would. He'd see to it.

Most of the time, she was beyond caring whether he landed a sweet deal or not.

No. Not beyond it. She didn't know she was supposed to.

His dad? Definitely beyond caring.

His birth dad—whoever he was—had probably never cared. Was that unfair? Isaac didn't know the story. Didn't know if his birth mom was a fifteen-year-old abuse victim or a thirty-year-old on her way to rehab.

Shouldn't matter.

But it did. Loose ends.

Speaking of which . . . He closed his Bible at Proverbs 29:23 with its embedded thought-detour—"Pride lays people low, but those of humble spirit gain honor."

Enough thinking. Time to get to work.

"How was your day, Becca?"

Isaac's question hung in the air while Becca pondered how odd an ordinary question sounded, given the abnormal circumstances.

"Good. It was good. Yours?" She busied herself chopping tomatoes. The less eye contact, the better.

"I survived. Enough said. Oh, I got this. Hope it's what you had in mind." He pulled a colorful box out of the shopping bag he carried under his arm. "Two remote units plus the base. Noise filter. Battery backup. What do you think?"

"The baby monitor. Thanks for attending to that so quickly."

"I wondered at first if you wouldn't prefer an intercom system or walkie-talkies. You know, she could buzz you to say, 'Becca, bring me a glass of water,' and you could buzz back and ask if she could wait until you brought her lunch tray. Save you a few trips up and down the stairs. Well, I guess that'll be a moot point once she's in the sunroom."

"I thought the baby monitor idea would save pennies, if not steps. Should work fine for our purposes. Can we give it a try for a while, then decide if we need to go high-tech?"

"Sounds like a plan." Isaac stripped off his suit jacket—must have had an important meeting—and hung it over a ladder-back kitchen chair.

Robin's-egg-blue shirt. Robin's-egg, chocolate, and silver striped tie. Nice.

"How can I help? I'll trade some manual labor for a chance to share that pork roast."

So, he'd noticed the heady aroma curling through the kitchen. "Did you want to say hi to your mom first?"

"Right. Sure. I'll pop in, set up the base unit of the monitor next to her bed, then come down for kitchen patrol."

"Take your time, Isaac. These potatoes need to boil for a bit."

As he headed for the stairs, he called back, "Hey, turn on the monitor receiver. After I get the base plugged in, I'll talk quietly so you can see if it picks up low-level sound from up there."

"Give a guy a new toy . . ."

"What?"

"Over and out!"

Becca heard his footsteps pause in the entry, then pound up the stairs, two at a time, it sounded. Then the creak of old floorboards giving a little under his weight as he entered his mother's bedroom. Within minutes, a low background hum in the receiver told her Isaac had found an outlet for the monitor's base unit.

"Testing, testing."

Becca smiled. His affective voice wasn't ready for radio.

Now softer. "Testing, testing."

"Son, what are you doing?" Hearing the shaky voice coming through the receiver, Becca could picture Aurelia rising up on one elbow to watch Isaac. "What's that thing?" Becca heard her ask.

"It's a . . . a health-care monitor, Mom. When Becca's in other parts of the house, she'll still be able to hear if you need her."

"I've got a scream could peel paint off the *Titanic*, you know."

Becca's discomfort over intentionally eavesdropping on their conversation lessened as the comedy routine progressed.

"Yes, but wouldn't you rather just say, 'Becca dear, would you be so kind as to bring me a cup o' tea?'"

Isaac's falsetto made Becca laugh out loud. Could they hear her through the floorboards and ceiling plaster?

"So I just talk into it?"

"You don't even have to get close to the base, Mom. Just talk naturally. If this works as it should, she'll hear you."

"Becca?"

"Don't wait for her to answer you. She only has a receiver on her end. She can't respond."

"Becca, if you're there, pick up."

"It's not like an answering machine. Oh, here." His impatience translated well through the sound waves. "Let me show you." Isaac's voice dropped to a whisper. "Becca, it would be ever so lovely if you would join us upstairs when you have a moment."

"She'll hear that?"

"I hope so."

"My."

"What?"

"There goes my privacy."

Becca cackled, then slapped her hand over her mouth.

"Are you worried about privacy, Mother?"

"No, I guess not. Actually, this will be good. I'll have proof, a witness."

A fear with barbed feet crawled up the back of her neck.

"A witness for what, Mom?"

"For when that fool African violet starts up with its slander against me."

Becca missed the next minute or two of their conversation. With the potatoes simmering she could leave the kitchen and respond to the hushed request.

She tapped lightly on the open door as she entered. "Here I am. Did you need something?"

"No, just testing," Isaac answered, patting the top of the monitor base as if it had earned an atta-boy.

"Yes, as a matter of fact, I do." Aurelia lay back against her pillow nest and touched her pointer finger to her lips as if pressing the button on a machine that held answers to her imponderables. "You need to find the bleeding heart, Becca."

Becca and Isaac exchanged questioning glances. Isaac's sigh told her his tolerance of rabbit trails wore thin.

"Your heart isn't bleeding, Mrs. Hughes. From what I hear, it doesn't get *enough* blood. But it's not leaking or anything, if that's what you're worried about."

The frown on Aurelia's face created bottomless caverns of skin. "Not mine. Yours. For you."

"I'm not sure what you mean. Can you tell me another way?"

"Find it. You'll see."

Aurelia's strength dissipated like the sun drained of its potency by a passing cloud.

"Just forget it," Isaac bent to speak low in Becca's ear. "Half the stuff she says wouldn't make sense if you had a month to think about it."

"I can hear you, Son."

"Sorry. I thought you were asleep."

Retreating to the kitchen afforded a respite from one awkward moment, but plunged them into another.

"That's part of the problem," Isaac said, slicing cucumbers for the salad. "I never know when she's 'on' and when she's 'off.' When she's in her right mind, she's so easily offended if I talk about the Alzheimer's. When she's wandering, it doesn't matter so much."

"I guess the safest path is never to say anything you wouldn't feel comfortable saying to her in her brightest moment." Becca longed to grab the tail of that sentence and pull it back in. Too late.

"I don't recall your résumé indicating graduate-level work with dementia patients, Becca."

He was riled. But an apology that started with his eyes followed closely on the heels of his sarcasm. "Forgive me. You're doing a wonderful job with her. I'm the one with a problem."

He stopped slicing and wiped his hands on the dishtowel tucked into the waistband of his Dockers. "It wasn't the diagnosis that cut so deep, but watching the slow descent. For years we didn't know anything was wrong. She was just . . . Mom. A little forgetful, but in a comic way. Entertaining. Then it became worrisome."

If Isaac knew how blessed he was to have a *worrisome* mother rather than a dad with a nefarious last name . . .

"She'd call home from the mall without a clue where she'd left the car in the parking lot. Or she'd be frantic at church, pacing the sanctuary, thinking Dad left for home without her when he was off talking with friends in the foyer. The clincher was Christmas three years ago."

He paused. Was the pain of remembering too scalding to discuss with her, a relative stranger without the relative connection? Or was he waiting for her to reveal she cared to know the details?

"What happened, Isaac?"

"What made it so bizarre is that Mom always prided herself in a well-dressed table, a meal to rival the best the gourmet magazines have to offer. She never was and isn't now pretentious. But she didn't save her best efforts for company. Family was reason enough to pull out all the stops."

"Not that year?"

Isaac's chin tilted and he drew in two quick breaths. "I got to the house by nine Christmas morning. As always, Mom planned on brunch first, then presents, then a traditional Hughes feast. Maple-glazed turkey, mashed potatoes, brussels sprouts in bacon, homemade cranberry salsa . . ."

"Back home, we called it cranberry sauce."

"And I'll bet the oranges for the recipe didn't come from the backyard, did they?"

"No." Becca cringed. Back home?

"Anyway, when I walked in, Dad was sitting in the entry at the bottom of the steps, waiting for me. I asked him where Mom was, fully expecting he'd tell me she was in the kitchen. He pointed toward the living room where Mom sat cross-legged on the floor in a cloud of spent wrapping paper. She'd opened all the presents. Hers, mine, Dad's, Aunt Geneva's, Sissy's and Bud's, and their children's . . ."

"Sissy and Bud?"

"My cousin and her husband. Dad's brother's daughter. Their two kids are the closest thing my Mom has to grand-children, so Mom always goes a little crazy with gifts for them. Mom sat there struggling to pull a hot pink bikini over Malibu Barbie's head. 'I don't know how she manages such an even tan,' Mom said. I mean, how do you answer a statement like that? Dad and I left her there and came here to the kitchen so we could talk privately. But—"

"But what?"

"She'd been there already. Couldn't have slept much the night before. The counters were full of food."

"So she'd managed to make the meal."

"Of sorts. Platters and bowls and cake plates and a punch bowl and fancy glasses full of mashed potatoes. Mashed potatoes. That's all. It was as if all she could recall about a holiday meal was mashed potatoes, so she made lots and lots of them."

Becca grew uncomfortably aware of the pan full of boiled potatoes on the stove waiting to be mashed. *Buttered parsley potatoes go nicely with pork roast.* She moved to the stove, turned off the burner, and slid the pan from the heat.

Her back to him, she asked, "What did your dad do?"

His answer was so long coming, she turned to see if he'd left the room. Isaac gripped the edges of the counter. Head bowed, he drew in air like a winded jogger. "He didn't have to decide. Mom stood in the doorway with a half-clad doll in her hands. She looked from Dad to me to the banquet of potatoes on the counters and asked my father if he thought Dr. Lambert had office hours on Christmas Day."

"Your family doctor?"

"Right. Dad told her he was sure the good doctor would be stopping by later with a batch of his wife's fudge, as always. She told him she was glad. Fudge would help balance out the meal. Then she went upstairs for a nap."

"I can't imagine how he kept his own sanity."

"He died less than a year later."

"Oh, Isaac!"

"Not sure what the Lord was thinking. Dad would have handled all this with much more finesse than I have. I don't have his genes. Or his grace."

A month of thinking and a desk full of dictionaries. A crash course in grief counseling. Live feed from an eminent psychologist. Nothing was equal to the task of responding to Isaac's story. Becca wept—quiet tears falling single file.

A twenty-first century segue launched them out of the quicksand onto more stable soil. Isaac's cell phone jangled.

"Isaac Hughes. Hi. What's up? No, not until tomorrow. Double-checked. Seriously? Why now?" Isaac looked across the room and caught Becca's eye seconds after she'd dried her tears. "It's not the best time. Okay, okay. I'll be there. Give me twenty minutes to get across town. No, it'll be fine. Don't worry about it. See you in twenty."

He tapped his phone to end the call. Pointing to it as the source of his begging off supper, Isaac snatched his jacket from the chair and backed out of the room toward the garage entrance. "Give Mom a kiss goodnight for me?"

"Sure, Isaac." *And I'll give her one for me, too.*

The evening routine of serving Aurelia's supper, tending to her personal-care needs, juggling her medication requirements, and dodging questions about her own past exhausted Becca. Or did the emotional scene in the kitchen drain her more than she realized? She'd heard sob stories before. She'd lived them. One would think a person like her would have tougher skin.

"This is from Isaac," she said as she bent to kiss the soft-as-cashmere cheek. Aurelia slept through it. Her purring told Becca she was out for the night.

Becca's bed across the hall called its invitation, but she turned back and lifted the Bible from its resting place on the bed table. A sliver of moonlight from the edge of the window shade lit her way around the bed and out the door to her room.

The overhead light seemed a harsh idea on a night like this, so she padded her way to the small dressing-table lamp. She laid Aurelia's Bible on the comforter on her bed. *The Comfort on the comforter. Someone should paint a picture of that.*

She reached under her pillow for her nightgown but stopped mid-action. A fragile string of graduated flowers stuck its head out of the pages of Aurelia's Bible. Becca opened to the bookmarked page. There it was. Isaiah 49:16—"Behold, I have graven thee upon the palms of my hands." *Belonging.*

Bookmarked with bleeding hearts.

12

As much as she looked forward to it, Saturday morning dawned a few hours early for her taste. The doorbell woke her at six. An insistent sound, impolite and relentless.

For lack of a robe, she wrenched the comforter off the bed and wrapped it around herself, kicking its dragging ends out of her way as she flew down the stairs. Her hand on the knob, she peeked through the curtained, narrow windowpanes flanking the front door. A sober-faced cop! With more than plenty of plainclothes backup behind him.

She jumped away from the door as if it had burned her. How had they tracked her here? What did they want? What had her dad done now? She peeked through the curtain again. The men laughed about something. The lead officer raised his fist to knock again.

Her respect for their detective skills soared with her pulse rate. *I have nothing more to give to my father's case. It's done. And still, the world he thrust me into clings to me like stale cigarette smoke. Changing my name wasn't enough. How naive could I be?*

Her stomach churned as she opened the door. "Yes?"

"You're Becca Morrow?"

Was it that obvious her name was stiff and new? Was it a trick question? Not that it mattered anymore. "Yes. I'm Becca."

The man seemed embarrassed by her comforter outfit, although it more than covered her trembling form. He stared at the threshold between them. "I'm sorry. I thought Isaac told you we'd be here by six."

Isaac knew her background? How long had he known? And what gave her away?

Her Social Security number. People could trace her old identity through her Social Security information, apparently. She should have thought of that. All that money to do things legally, for nothing.

"Be here by six?" She knew the confusion on her face must have added to the ridiculousness of her ensemble.

The guy in charge looked over Becca's shoulder to the interior of the house. "Can I use the bathroom to change? Just got off duty."

Change? The plainclothes "officers" were in work duds. Carrying tool belts and power tools.

Standing on the porch was her work crew, not an investigative team.

"Please, come in. I'll make coffee." Her static laughter read transparent and strained, even to her.

She directed the off-duty cop to the first-floor powder room and led the rest into the kitchen. Before she could fill the coffeemaker reservoir, one of the workmen took over that task and encouraged her to find something a little less cumbersome to work in than a quilt.

She took the stairs Isaac's way—two at a time—and winked at deodorant, toothbrush, and hairbrush before dressing and turning to head downstairs. Aurelia still purred behind her bedroom door. Becca told herself to turn on the monitor receiver the minute she got to the kitchen.

"Got any syrup?" a burly, red-bearded Viking knock-off asked when she entered. "Lyle's makin' waffles."

Under a cloud of flour and a gaggle of eggs, Lyle was indeed making waffles. The hot, buttery smell of the heating waffle iron made Becca's stomach growl. Or was it the incongruity of a police confrontation turning into a breakfast buffet? No wonder her limbs shook. She'd dodged a bullet. Or a shower of them.

Laughing and jostling each other, two workers entered through the back door with their T-shirt hems scooped up like aprons, bulging with oranges. "Fresh-squeezed juice. Nothing like it," the taller of the two proposed to the others. "This much muscle in one room, won't take long."

The frat party mood turned Becca's jitters into Jell-O. She darted between the men, directing them to utensils and ingredients, grinning as if she were an ordinary housekeeper/caregiver with a pristine genealogy.

Joy is noisy, Becca discovered. She almost missed Aurelia's call through the monitor. Almost. Her ears were tuned to her responsibility like a mother noting her baby's cough from the depths of hard-earned sleep.

Mrs. Hughes's morning care routine occupied Becca so long, the men were cleaning up the kitchen before she returned. They'd saved her two waffles and a dribble of syrup. But they were eager to get to work. She left the plate on the counter and led the conga line of testosterone to the sunroom.

The 1980's era indoor-outdoor carpeting met an untimely end, its grassy roughness a mere memory by the time Isaac arrived loaded down with paint cans.

"Sage green, you said." He frowned playfully in Becca's direction. "Do you realize how many shades of sage green the paint store carries?"

"So, what did you choose?" Considering the depressing blandness of her parents' last several homes and the cold white of her short-lived apartment, almost any shade of any color other than beige would work, in her opinion. But she couldn't resist the question.

He cringed as he confessed, "One of each?"

From their various workstations in the room, the men hooted, chuckled, or chortled.

"Isaac, one quart of anything won't do the whole room."

"I know," he said. "I plan to go back to the store for more once I know which one is *the* one."

The monitor receiver clipped to the belt loop of Becca's jeans sputtered a message Becca couldn't decipher. "Sorry, I have to get upstairs. I trust you guys to make a wise choice. Be back in a minute."

It took more than a minute to reassure Aurelia the noises she heard were workmen, not alien invaders. When Becca returned to the scene, she collapsed in laughter. Each narrow strip of wall between the far windows bore a different shade of sage. The men stood in a line facing the windows, arms folded or hands on hips, extolling the virtues or critiquing the vices of each one in turn.

"I like the subtle undertones of earthiness in this choice," one said.

"That looks too much like what I found in my toddler's diaper last night," said another.

"What's this one called again? It reminds me of the walls in the barracks at boot camp. Puleeze!"

"We're deadlocked, Becca." It was the voice of the policeman. "Hung jury. Your call."

If he only knew how those words rattled her.

Shaking the thought from her mind, she walked to the wall of samples and pointed. "How about this one?"

"Of course! Perfect! Genius!" they chorused, visibly relieved to return to their hammers, window squeegees, and debris patrol.

Within hours the room boasted a fresh coat of paint, clean windows, and new, prefinished hardwood floors. The amateur electrician in the group had rewired the room to provide more convenient outlets. At Isaac's urging, the door leading from the sunroom to the backyard and garden gained a new dead-bolt and security chain. Between trips upstairs, Becca chose a cheery drapery fabric that Isaac ordered over the Internet. The newly installed plantation shutters promised privacy and light diffusion until the drapes arrived for ambiance, a word the men seemed to delight in tossing around as they worked.

Where did Isaac find these people? Becca couldn't remember a gathering of more than two men where alcohol or tawdry jokes didn't take center stage. These guys begged for ice water and lemonade, but didn't lack for camaraderie and fun. As noon neared, Becca stole away to the kitchen. Somehow, she had to find a truckload of Hungry Man dinners in the pantry supplies designed for herself and an ailing widow. Or so she thought.

Startled by the wild thumping at the kitchen door, Becca opened it to discover a two-foot stack of pizza boxes with tall, tan legs. "A little help, please?"

Becca removed the top four boxes.

"Hi!" the voice belonging to the legs chirped. "Ginger. Ginger Jarr. Yeah, I know. What was I thinking marrying a guy named Jarr? My husband has it worse, though. You've met him, right? Pete? They call him Pickle?"

Pickle. The surfer guy with the shoulder-length blond hair. Amateur electrician. Pickle Jarr. "He's your husband?"

"He's the only one of the bunch I'll claim. Are they giving you a hard time? When that group gets together, you never know what will happen."

Becca slipped her pizza boxes onto the counter and relieved Ginger Jarr of the remainder. "They've been wonderful. It's amazing how much they've accomplished."

"Pete called on the cell an hour ago and suggested I drum up some lunch for everybody. Wish I'd thought of it myself. Sometimes he just puts me to shame with his thoughtfulness. Such a problem, huh?" Ginger's face seemed locked in a perpetual smile. "Pizza's okay, I hope."

"Oh, that's great. I was about to go exploring for possibilities. This is a huge answer. Thanks."

"I have paper plates and cups in the car and a case of soft drinks. Do you have ice?"

How had Becca so quickly gone from being strapped for an idea to needing only to supply ice? "Yes, plenty."

Ginger bounded on athletic legs toward the back door. "Can you round up the troops? I'll be back in a jif."

Small talk. Becca's nemesis. Even in the rarified air of the garden patio, the friendliness factor threatened to undo her.

"Where ya from?"

"Why'd you decide to move here?"

"What was life like in northern Minnesota?"

"Isaac said you know his Aunt Geneva? She's in Iowa, isn't she? She doesn't live far from the town where that Kervorkian-like guy lived. Denagree?"

"Dennagee. Bertram Dennagee. What did you say was your hometown?"

"Family?"

Simple questions. If Becca weren't making up the answers as she went along, the responses would cost her nothing. As it was, the crew's desire to get to know her better exhausted her. Juggling the plot points of her new life's script required enormous gulps of energy.

"A few miles east of Duluth, you said?" Tony, the off-duty cop, asked.

"Yeah."

"There's nothing east of Duluth except Lake Superior. A tiny corner of Wisconsin is east of a tiny corner of Duluth, if I remember right."

"And if you're a Minnesota Vikings fan," Pickle said, "that means there's nothing east of Duluth . . . period!" He elbowed Tony with his non-pizza-hoisting arm.

Becca couldn't show anxiety at their questions. Commanding her heart rate to slow, she answered, "Did I say east? Where is my brain today? I meant west. I'm directionally challenged. My friends back home can attest to that."

How far should she go? "One time, it was my responsibility to serve as navigator when a bunch of us drove down to St. Paul for a concert. When we saw the sign that said, 'Welcome to Canada,' I knew my role as navigator was over. They still talk about how much time we wasted on that trip because I couldn't tell north from south."

Did a wave of doubt flash across Tony's face?

"You must miss them," Ginger said.

Becca answered her, but couldn't take her eyes from Tony's tented brows. "Who?"

"Your friends."

"Oh, yeah. Of course. They'll . . . they'll probably fly out to see me sometime. I've been so busy settling in, I haven't taken time to call them or anything."

Isaac joined the discussion. "Well, Becca, by all means, call! Why didn't I think of that? You need to let your people know where you are, give them your new address and phone number, tell them you arrived safely. I apologize for not being sensitive to that. We have unlimited long distance."

Tony's broad hand rested on Isaac's shoulder. "Brother, maybe she should just . . . wait a while, make sure this is where she wants to stay."

Isaac's expression spoke of confusion and shock. "Why wouldn't she want to stay?"

"Well, there's you, for one thing," a smirking hammer-wielder quipped.

Another added, "And then there's us."

"I'm just saying," Tony said, "we don't know an awful lot about her. She might have . . . other goals."

"Becca?"

Ginger's voice broke the awkward silence that followed with an insistent, "Becca."

When the lap guard on the tilt-a-whirl shakes loose, body parts go flying. Her stomach in her neck, her mind leaking out her ears, Becca tried to gather the pieces and direct her thoughts toward the person calling her assumed name. "What is it?"

Ginger lifted the battery-operated monitor receiver and held it out to her. "Sorry, hon. Duty calls."

Like a carnival ride picking up speed for another go-round, the end of lunch conversation escalated to its previous frat party pitch before Becca's feet reached the threshold into the house.

"Come on, guys, give her a break," she heard Ginger admonish. "She's shy. A batch of rabble-rousers like you would make anyone nervous. Cut her some slack, will ya?"

Becca left the scene and headed to the stairs. She stopped the pendulum on the hall clock. Clinging to the banister with both hands, she pulled herself up one step at a time. Tony's observations had struck too close for comfort.

"I missed you, Becca." Aurelia's cocker spaniel expression melted the iceberg forming in the caregiver's heart.

"I'm sorry. I missed you, too. It's been crazy downstairs." *Crazy. Good word for it.* "I hate to leave you alone so much today, but the guys have questions and for some reason, they think I have the answers."

"Will they have my bed set up down there today?"

"I hope so."

"I haven't been downstairs in my own home for so long." Her sigh hovered in the air.

"Mrs. Hughes, if you don't like what we've done with the sunroom, please say something. We'll move everything right back up here, if needed." Becca couldn't imagine the courage required to ask the crew to return and undo all they'd accomplished. But Aurelia's comfort took precedence over other concerns at this point.

"Where will I go when they have to take this bed apart?"

The moment had arrived. "Your son ordered an electric bed for you."

"A hospital bed?"

"Yes, but I helped him choose the model. I think you'll be pleased with how classy it is."

"A bed for the dying."

"Or for those who want to live—however long they can—in greater comfort. Think of it as a luxury item you've earned, rather than a medical necessity. All the latest rage."

Aurelia smiled. "You're a gifted liar, Becca."

"But I—"

"Charming, too. I'll reserve judgment until I've adequately road tested this luxury item."

Becca stayed at Aurelia's side, finding safety in the woman's tenuous hold on reality. "When the men have gone back to work"—*and there's no danger I'll run into them in the kitchen*—"I'll fix a little lunch for you."

"I'm rarely hungry anymore."

"I know. That's part of my reason for being here, creating delectable dishes you can't resist." Becca smirked and tickled Aurelia's ribs as if the woman were seven rather than a prematurely aged seventy. The rib-tickling brought a frown. *Wrong move, Becca. She wasn't in the mood.*

Aurelia's gaze drifted to the window. "Not getting much snow this year."

Becca wondered when Southern California last saw snow. "No, that's true. It's early yet, though."

"Early?"

"September."

"I'll have to show you where I keep the Easter baskets, then. I don't have the energy for blowing eggs today, though."

"I don't blame you, Mrs. Hughes. That can wait."

A coughing spell brought an end to their tetherless discussion. Becca helped her sit more upright until the fit passed, as she had so often with her mother, for different reasons, for a mother who had less heart connection to Becca than this frail woman she'd just met.

Aurelia waved wildly. Becca breathed more easily when she deciphered Aurelia's need for a tissue in which to spit. The scene drew to a close, but not the crisis. The tissue Becca retrieved from the older woman was tinged with blood.

"Isaac, I need to talk to you." Becca's attempts to keep her voice neutral failed.

"What's wrong?" He set aside the rubber hammer he'd been using to force the metal rails of the hospital bed into their pre-arranged slots.

"Privately?"

"Sure. Where?"

Becca could see the futility of attempting a private conversation in the sunroom. It crawled with opinionated workmen. The way Isaac's eyes darted around the room, it seemed obvious he recognized the same futility.

"Do you want to go somewhere?" he asked. "We could create an excuse for another trip to the paint store without much imagination."

Even with their voices low, their huddle drew attention.

"I don't want to leave your mother right now."

"I think Ginger's still here. She said something about starting another pot of coffee before she takes off. She'd be happy to—"

"I can't leave your mom. Please."

Isaac's demeanor shifted from curiosity to concern. He took Becca by the elbow and steered her toward the library, one of the closed doors off the center hall.

She noticed but couldn't take time to care that the room boasted hundreds of leather-bound volumes. The two stepped fully into the mahogany-paneled library. Becca shut the door behind them.

Isaac leaned against the carved desk, his hands propping him up on either side of his trim form. "What's on your heart?"

Again, a simple question with a complicated tangle of answers. The one he needed now jumped ahead of the pack. "Your mother is coughing up blood, Isaac."

"How much?"

How much? Blood is blood. What does he care if it's a drop or a quart? A person isn't supposed to cough up blood. Calm yourself, Becca. It's a legitimate question. A quart would have had you screaming rather than asking for an audience with your employer's son. "I suppose about the size of a dime." She opened her fist and uncrumpled the tissue with thumb and forefinger.

Isaac's complexion emptied of anything related to color. He turned aside from the evidence.

"Sorry. I'm not . . . good with . . . medical stuff."

Becca couldn't afford two patients on her hands. She folded the edge of the tissue and closed her fist. "My fault. I'd thought you'd want to see."

"Don't apologize. You'd think I'd get better at this. One more reason why we need you around here. Caregiving is not my gift."

"Caring is."

Isaac lifted his gaze from the carpet designs at his feet. "I do care. I wish I had your talent for expressing it."

Becca drank in his admiration, undeserved or not. *More, Isaac, more!* A thirsty soul often overindulges when offered refreshment. She'd read that somewhere. "Do you think we should call her doctor?"

"This has happened before. We won't worry unless it keeps up, okay? We'll watch her closely the rest of the day. If it was a singular episode, good. If not, we'll get Dr. Lambert involved."

"Sorry if I overreacted."

"You're expected to notice things like that."

"If you're sure she's all right . . ."

"Unsure about most things these days. But I think your idea about moving her downstairs will ease our minds on many fronts. Won't you feel better when you're just a few steps away from her? Oh, I should show you what I have in mind for *you*."

"For me?"

Isaac led the way out of the library's dark-draped embrace and opened the door on the opposite wall across the hall. "Come with me."

Beyond the door, a short hallway opened into a large, sun-washed room, an appendage of the main body of the house. Its ceiling lower than the rest of the house, it appeared to have been added long after initial construction.

"It's cool in here some evenings. When it rains for extended periods."

"How often is that?"

"Gotta say there's nothing like Southern California. Not often. My point is, there's no central heat. Hence the fireplace."

She took in the stonework of the fireplace and noted how well it fit the decidedly masculine room. A fireplace for heat. Like Geneva's cottage.

"That's why I didn't suggest it for Mother. The sunroom will be warmer for her on cool days. She's always complaining about the cold, but the doctor says it's related to poor circulation more than room temperature."

"Your mom's going to want a small fan anyway."

His eyebrows questioned her.

"The air movement. Helps her breathe."

"Oh."

Becca's gaze traveled around the room. In front of the fireplace sat a pair of cinnamon-colored leather chairs with an antique wooden trunk serving as an end table between. A wall of windows on either side of the fireplace overlooked the side yard. Rich raw-silk drapes, an intoxicating shade of mink brown, framed the windows. A walnut armoire came inches short of brushing the ceiling. In its majestic shadow, a chocolate leather sleigh bed lay under a billowing down comforter.

This is what Isaac had in mind for her? The glove leather invited her tentative touch.

"My room." Isaac's voice bore no hint of awareness of her uneasiness. "I encouraged Mom and Dad to turn it into a family room when I bought the condo and moved out. I think Mom thought I'd grow out of that 'condo phase' and come back home one day. A few weeks ago she talked as if this is where I live. I don't have the heart to correct her."

Isaac tugged his T-shirt away from his damp chest. The workday had taken its toll on all of them in sweat and weariness. Becca'd never seen, much less touched, a bed like the one that now urged her to abandon her tired body to its sweet embrace. Would she, if Isaac weren't standing there?

"It doesn't make much sense," he said, "for you to stay upstairs in the sewing room after we get Mom moved downstairs. This should be yours."

Like a calf in clover. That's how Becca felt in her small but safe bedroom upstairs. The room in which she stood now offered a horizonless sea of pasture. Too much for someone clutching a dark secret to her chest. Gifts like this were for the clear conscienced, the honest. Not for her.

"Isaac, no."

"You don't like it? I guess it is thick in the Y chromosome aura. We could find some floofy stuff somewhere."

"Floofy?"

"Lace or flowers or something."

For a moment, she wondered how he handled the aesthetic details of real estate properties if his perception of feminizing a room was to add lace or flowers.

"Did I make a mistake suggesting this? I thought you'd be content here."

He'd seen her silence as disappointment? *Oh, Isaac!*

A crooked half-smile carried his apology. Then his eyes lit. "Don't decide yet," he cautioned. "You haven't seen The Outhouse."

His attempt at humor—it was humor, wasn't it?—gave her pause. Isaac's hand swallowing hers stopped her heart altogether.

"Impossible not to fall in love with this." His half smile graduated to a full grin.

Her hand in his? No, he must mean the side door to which he led her.

A cardstock quarter moon foretold the purpose of the room behind the door. Isaac's handiwork, no doubt. Aurelia didn't seem the type to create paper moons. Becca lingered on the thought of his chuckling over his cleverness while his fingers moved the scissors through the sheet of yellow paper. The Outhouse. Right.

"I know what you're thinking," he said, drawing her into the room and releasing her hand. "It's a bit over the top."

No similarity existed between this and a traditional outhouse. None. Becca remembered a "Top Ten Bathrooms of the World" program on the DIY channel. How did this one fail to make the list?

If the constant drone of the television in her mother's sick room profited nothing else, it offered her words to put to the scene. Travertine marble tile on the floor. Lavish crown molding framing the ceiling. A seamless glass shower stall with rain forest showerhead. Marble soaking tub. And an infinity sink, its smooth edge allowing water to spill over, waterfall-like, into a larger basin.

"I have to explain," Isaac interjected. "This isn't an attempt at pretense. This is my mother's kindness on display. The daughter of a friend of hers needed a location for her design school final exam. Mom volunteered my room. Well, my bathroom."

"She did a great job."

"Pulled out all the stops. It wouldn't have happened this way if the girl's mama hadn't footed the bill for the upgrades. Mom was almost embarrassed how it turned out. She kept saying, 'Children are starving in Africa and we have a bathroom with gold leaf on the ceiling trim. What's wrong with this picture?'"

"How did you feel about it?"

"It took me about half a day to get used to the idea. I'm afraid my thoughts lost all their noble threads the first time I lowered myself into the soaking tub. Man, Becca, you are going to love that."

Lord, how far are You going to let this go? Are You sweetening the pot so I'll feel even worse when it's all taken away? It's always taken away. It would serve me right. The woman who snitched on her own father and who kept the largest part of who she was—the notorious Bertram Dennagee's daughter—behind a locked door.

"You look upset about something. Mom was doing her friend a favor. If it helps put it in perspective, the lady's daughter pulled an A on the project."

Becca shoved guilt aside. Again. "An A? I'm not surprised by that. It's a beautiful room. I can't picture myself in it. You don't . . ." How would she word this? "You don't know how little luxury I've known." Her thoughts scooted off again to the luxury of people who noticed her, appreciated her, realized she was in the room.

Isaac's expression changed. The dimples in his sun-bronzed cheeks disappeared. "Maybe it's time to change that. Before all this"—he waved his hand to indicate the changes happening in every corner of the house—"my mom used to tell me, 'God delights in delighting His kids.' If you want my opinion, I'd say you more than deserve it."

13

Isaac pushed himself away from his desk and stretched out, ruler-straight. Coffee? Would that help him focus?

He poured a cup of hand-roasted Guatemalan—embarrassingly expensive, but smooth as chocolate pudding. He could live with mismatched file cabinets and a well-worn office chair, but a once-a-week pot of gourmet coffee served as spirit lifter and psychiatrist's couch. More medicine than luxury item.

Luxury. That's the word Becca had used. *You don't know how little luxury I've known.*

Becca, I don't know anything about you.

That first day, she'd cinched the job. His aunt's recommendation could have glowed in the dark. And Becca's rapport with his mother meant more than any degree or work experience.

But he knew so little of her background, her family life. Even Aunt Geneva seemed hesitant to go into detail. Why? It was no secret Becca possessed a rare gift in caregiving, as if well-practiced and stepping into a rewarding adventure with his mother.

He shook his head. *So not like me, the Slug Son. Must be my genetic makeup. I'm probably the spawn of heartless, selfish, post-prom juvenile delinquents. It's only the environmental influence of* the world's best adoptive parents that keep me from turning out completely depraved.

His phone rang, a welcome respite from himself.

With the caller pacified for now, his mind drifted again to Becca. What was happening to his flawless work focus?

He observed Becca's dedication every day. He watched her forego her own needs for the needs of others. He not only admired but also wished he could emulate her humility, her willingness to be content with simple pleasures.

The cup of black gold in his hands seemed decadent now. Or maybe it always was morbidly decadent, but he just now realized its severity.

He returned to his desk and buzzed Mrs. Gallum, reminding her to drum up the W-4 form he needed for Becca. Becca's work-for-free idea wouldn't fly. Could he wrangle a merit increase for her so soon? Isaac dug his fingertips into his temples. *Mr. Hughes, I do believe you are smitten.*

If pressed to explain himself, what would he say? *I'm captivated by her eyes, a pool of warmth and beauty with ripples of a deep, unspoken pain I wish I could soothe. Her smile feeds a hunger I didn't know I had, stingy as she is with it. She floats across a room as if it takes no effort at all to move her body. Isaac, focus! But it's her heart I see when I look at her. What is her story? What happened to strip her of the self-absorbed candy shell that covers so many other women?*

The phone interrupted, its apparent goal in life. *Oh, yeah. My job.*

"Isaac Hughes. How can I help you?"

"Hughes, my brother!"

"Tony. Hey, how's that purple thumb of yours?"

"I keep telling you it wasn't my fault. That hammer wasn't properly balanced."

"Right. I think I know who's unbalanced."

"Hold on. You may need my muscle again someday."

"Point well taken." Isaac scooted his chair to the window and propped his feet on the sill. "I appreciate your help. You know I do."

"Have I mentioned I'm thinking about getting a grand piano?"

"Tony, you and Renee live on the sixth floor."

"Uh huh."

"No elevator."

"Bingo."

"You don't even play the piano."

"But we need a place to put our family photos."

Isaac leaned back in his chair. Tony never failed to lighten his mood. He rarely called at work, though. What was up? "You bored today, Tony, or is there a purpose for your call?"

A depth-charged moment of silence. "I enjoyed meeting Becca."

Isaac's pulse quickened. "Good."

"Have you—? Are you satisfied with her references and things?"

Isaac's feet dropped to the floor. "What do you mean?" He picked up a plastic-coated paper clip and bent it straight with one hand, a holdover skill from college late night antistudy sessions. "You see a problem?"

"Isaac, I don't want to stir the waters, but I have a feeling she's not being completely honest with you. No offense, brother."

"Is this the cop speaking, or my friend?"

"Both."

"She's amazing, Tony. I have no reason to doubt her."

"I hope you're right."

"Look, I'm about a day and a half behind on paperwork. Unless you have a legitimate concern . . ."

"Did you see how she reacted when we asked about her family, her past?" The tension in Tony's voice traveled clearly through the phone line. "She looked up and to the left."

"What?"

"Profilers notice that sort of thing. If a person's eyes dart up and to the left when they talk, they may be lying. There are other signs."

"Oh, give me a break!"

"Isaac, this is the woman who's taking care of your mother."

"And doing a better job of it than most." Isaac knew he wasn't disguising his impatience well.

"That's great." Tony pressed on. "But what do you know about her? And did you notice her faux pas about her hometown being east of Duluth, then west?"

"She just misspoke, Tony. We all do it."

"Maybe."

Isaac rubbed one temple with his free hand. "I think your training has made you paranoid."

"I'm a pretty good judge of character."

"Judge this!" A simple touch of a button broke the connection.

Less than five seconds later, Isaac dialed Tony's number. "Any room in your big, paranoid, Italian heart for forgiving a friend who sometimes acts like a jerk?"

"Isaac Jerk Hughes, you have to know I don't mean any harm here. I wouldn't mention my concerns if this wasn't so important."

Tony, don't mess with a good thing. A very good thing. "Believe me, you have nothing to worry about. Becca is legit. She's so innocent it wouldn't even occur to her to lie to me."

Tony didn't answer right away. When he did . . .

"I work with innocent-looking people all the time, Isaac. And I've put more than a few in prison."

"You know I love you, my friend, but I think we'd better get off this subject if you're going to stay on my Christmas gift list."

"Just . . . be careful, okay? Don't take anything for granted. See if you can get her to open up and reveal a little more about her past. And watch for those eyes darting to the left."

Is a fierce, pounding pulse a sign of high blood pressure? If so, Isaac's was quickly reaching critical mass. "Hang up, Tony. I'll talk to you later."

"Isaac?"

His sigh drew quotation marks around his response. "What?"

"Just thought you should know that I'm praying."

How could he object to that?

The idea of past work experience reference letters rose to the surface later that day. Was he honoring Becca or rebelling against his friend's paranoia when he opened a mental trash can and dumped the idea without further attention?

By their fruits you shall know them. The ancient counsel fed his determination. The fruit of Becca's caregiving tasted of exceptional kindness. Her patience with his mother could set a standard as a fruit of the Spirit the apostle Paul wrote about in the book of Galatians.

Ginger had nailed it. Becca's shyness kept her from running off at the mouth about every detail of her life.

Still, even he was curious.

A heart-shaped face framed by caramel silk begged him to trust her. *It's not a matter of trust,* he argued with the face. *It's what a responsible son would do.*

No. He had all the information he needed. His Aunt Geneva recommended her.

What distress formed the cloud that sometimes scudded across Becca's translucent eyes? Grief over her father's passing? Loneliness? Insecurity? *I think I can help on all those fronts, Becca.*

What was happening to him? Two weeks ago he was content to drown himself in mortgage rates and escrow, closing costs and abstracts. Satisfied with an admittedly self-consumed life, he liked not having to divide his thoughts, time, or attention. Bachelorhood suited him. Any spark of loneliness fizzled in the downpour of guy friends and more than enough to do. He liked his sleek, low-maintenance condo. He didn't mind take-out or the quiet of an empty room or the label "Fifth Wheel" when in the company of two friends plus their adorable, supportive wives.

He'd been content. Or he'd convinced himself as much. Until she showed up in his outer office with a suitcase and fragments of a story.

Now he looked for excuses to stop at his mom's house on the way home from work. He sensed a foreign emptiness when he opened the door to his dark and silent condo. Nothing his TV remote offered him held any interest. His "Cooking for One" recipe collection no longer seemed a noteworthy accomplishment. Distraction sat on his shoulder, even in church. Especially in church.

Other single men his age might laugh at that. *In church? That's when you miss having a woman in your life, Isaac? Not when you notice the other side of your bed is empty?*

It was true.

And it had been more true—truer? truest?—since Becca appeared.

Mrs. Gallum waited beyond his office door for his signature on the counteroffer at Isaac's elbow. She'd have to wait another few minutes. He reached across the contract and grabbed his Bible instead. The ultimate contract, he thought. The agreement between him and the Lord. *I'll agree to help you,* God promised, *if you agree to follow Me. If you give Me your life, I'll give you everything you need to live it well, including a safe place in which to experience eternity.*

The Divine Contract, his Bible, now lay open before him. Its words offered to quiet his unsteady heart and lower his blood pressure at least a few points. Could it also give him direction on what to do about his newfound obsession?

14

"A little Mozart with breakfast, Mrs. Hughes?"

"What are we having?"

Becca hoped her answer would satisfy. "Scrambled egg, croissant bits, and peach jam."

"Then no to the Mozart. I believe a little Debussy would be more appropriate, don't you think?"

"Debussy?"

"Something French, my dear. To accompany the croissant. No unnecessary international incidents this morning, *s'il vous plait.*"

Becca saw a reflection of her own smile in the older woman. Aurelia's humor sailed in fine form today. The sound system Isaac had purchased for the sunroom filled it with a mellow sweetness now as a Debussy CD spun its magic. For the past several days, Aurelia had requested music with every meal, as a restaurant patron might ask for lemon in her water. It didn't surprise Becca to see the previously lethargic eater turn plate-cleaner, albeit a small, doll-sized plate. Music hath charms . . . and all that jazz.

She smiled again. All that jazz. She'd make New Orleans shrimp bisque for supper in hopes Aurelia might ask for something by Charlie Parker.

Vicarious knowledge. All of it. She knew jazz not from attending concerts or sitting over a mug of thick coffee in an equally dark club, but from watching public television, listening to public radio, and reading about lives unlike her own. Every recipe in her gray matter database came from the Food Channel. Every design skill from HGTV. The History Channel filled in the gaps in her formal education. And TVLand taught her that—if the 1950s could be believed—not all households operated as her father's did. Not all moms left too soon. Not all parents got lost in an illness and forgot they had a daughter.

Becca looked at the elderly woman enjoying—yes, enjoying—her breakfast. A mom who once upon a time baked cookies and helped with the PTA book fair and walked her son to school until the day he asked her to let him do it on his own. A mom who probably considered glued macaroni pictures art, who didn't miss a soccer game despite rain or hail or sleet or dark of night, who sewed school play costumes from fake fur and tree-bark camo. Hmm. The likelihood of hail or sleet were slim here. Despite . . . Santa Anas? She'd read about them, heard Isaac's friends talking about them. Would she still be taking care of Aurelia long enough to experience them?

Aurelia Hughes—a mother who sometimes considered canned soup an act of terrorism and wore wool socks to prevent frostbite . . . in Southern California.

Why did sympathy come so easily when caring for Aurelia? She couldn't manufacture any for her father and had fought to hang onto sympathy for her mother near the end.

"Becca?"

"Yes, Mrs. Hughes?"

"I'm troubled about something."

"What's that?"

"You'll think it's silly, considering all the other things I find to complain about."

"I'm a fairly skilled judge of silly. Why don't you just tell me what it is, and we'll decide together if it's worth the worry."

Aurelia lifted her arm off the bed and pointed. "What do you see when you look out that window?"

Lord, help me see it through her eyes. A grin worked its way from Becca's mouth to her forehead. "I see a problem."

"You do? Oh, bless you." Aurelia seemed relieved of a great burden.

Becca held her hand over her eyes like a visor for effect. "I see an overgrown vine blocking part of your view of the garden."

"Yes. Thank you."

"Thank you?"

Tears hugged the corners of the older woman's eyes. "I thought perhaps the fingers of green lived only in my mind."

Within minutes, Becca had cleared Aurelia's view. The offending vine lay in undistinguished repose behind the garage. If all Aurelia's distresses were so easily solved . . .

Anger management. That's what she needed. In the few weeks since Becca had met dementia face to face, she'd learned to despise it. She railed against it, hated what it did, hated how it could take the simplest task and make it complicated, the sunniest disposition and make it ornery, the brightest mind and make it pea-soup foggy.

The heart disease would probably take Aurelia's life before Alzheimer's reached the pinnacle of its evil. But a weak heart was somehow understandable. The torture chamber of a weakened mind offered no condolences. No explanations. None.

As sweet as their exchange of the morning, the afternoon was sour. Special touches Aurelia found blessings earlier in the day became irritations. Music? Nothing but noise. Food? Bah, humbug. The view of the garden? Too sunny.

The walls crawled with scorpions. The invisible, nonexistent kind.

And Becca rode into the room on a broom, according to Aurelia. Of all days for the woman not to feel like taking a nap. Becca retraced her steps to and from the sunroom twenty times or more. She gave up explaining that she'd already (a) watered the plants in the window, though high-quality silk plants rarely require watering; (b) decided against calling the police to report the theft of Aurelia's tiara; and (c) chased the troll out from under the bridge/bed on which Aurelia lay. Becca focused instead on keeping peace. No small task.

A flash of cognizance brought pain, like a metal fork touching a tooth's nerve. For a brief moment, Becca saw clarity in Aurelia's eyes. The clarity reminded the woman how far from reality her thinking strayed. "Forgive me!" she'd pleaded. But before the echo died out, lucidity retreated. The pain transferred to Becca.

If she held the power to orchestrate Aurelia's lucid moments, waving a conductor's baton to tell the mental instruments when to play and when to keep silent, she would gladly take the confusion so Isaac could experience the choicest times of day. So often it seemed he got the dregs. Sundown with an unpleasant meaning. And it took a toll on the mother/son relationship. How could it not?

Lord, would it be too much to ask You to give those two a few more sweet memories? You could start tonight, if You don't mind.

Becca found Isaac leaning against the wall in the hall near the sunroom.

"Isaac?"

His response stalled out.

She reached to rub the outside of his upper arm. "Isaac. She didn't mean that. She doesn't realize what she's saying."

He glanced her way, then returned his gaze to the crown molding. "Doesn't she? I wonder if sometimes her explosions aren't what she's wanted to express for years but kindness kept her from it."

"You can't believe that."

"Why not? How can I know what's real and what's the disease?"

Becca wanted to either slap the back of his skull, or rub his shoulders and brush the hair off his forehead, or give him a hug. She had no right to any of those responses. A display like that could only increase his distress, not relieve it. But pain demanded a remedy, didn't it? Or at least a soothing salve.

"Isaac, you have a lifetime of evidence of her love for you."

He lifted his chin in consideration. "Almost a lifetime."

"Your mother spent herself caring for you. Before her illness, did she give you any reason to think her love was anything but genuine? You never doubted the depth or integrity of her devotion, did you?"

"No."

Becca couldn't resist. She reached out a sympathetic hand again. He didn't flinch. She hoped her words would be as well received. "Then don't let a wicked disease lie to you about what's in her heart."

His lips parted but his voice stayed locked inside. Her hand warmed microwave-style when Isaac laid his over hers. He rested it heavily. Was he trying to ensure that hers didn't move from its position?

If the situation weren't framed in tension, she might hope it would linger. Like that. With his hand over hers. With appreciation in his expressive espresso eyes.

"Thanks, Becca." With an affirming squeeze, he released her hand, forcing her to remove hers or risk embarrassment. "Thank you for taking care of both of us."

For a flash moment, Becca entertained the thought of serving in that role the rest of her life. The impossibility swept over her with a sadness that stole her breath and her hope. She'd abandoned her hopes for marriage in all but her dreams. Marriage to someone like Isaac? Odds were a million to one.

A million to one? So, you're saying there's still hope! The line from a silly movie put her feet back on the ground and set her lungs working again. *Humor yourself, Becca. No one else will.*

"Do you charge double?" Isaac's question brought a welcome interruption.

"Double? For what?"

"For serving as my counselor as well as Mom's caregiver? Is this your clever attempt at wrangling a raise?"

Pink, rose, crimson. She could feel her cheeks flush. Before she could form a witty reply, Isaac spoke again.

"That reminds me of something important we need to discuss."

Becca felt the muscles in her neck tense.

"I don't know why I didn't think of this before now. I've had employees. I know how this works."

Oh, no! Something in her background check pointed to her real identity.

"Didn't it dawn on you that you haven't had a day off since you started?"

"A day off?"

"Mom and I didn't hire you to work 365 days a year. I'm pretty sure that's not even legal."

"I have time off," she protested. "When your mother is sleeping."

"And you probably use some of those breaks to cook or clean. Am I right?"

"Not the hours between eleven at night and six in the morning. I do sleep." She injected a tension-easing smile, her thoughts drifting to the glove-leather sleigh bed and its cloud-like comforter. A place she was beginning to refer to as *her* room.

Isaac looked far more at ease discussing this subject—the business side of his mother's care—than the emotional dimension of her illness. He left his wall brace and headed to the living room. "You need extended periods of time off. Two days a week, minimum."

"Two *days*?"

"Three?"

"Isaac, how could I do that? Not going to happen."

"We survived for many months using the temp agency."

"And you weren't happy with the arrangement."

"True. But it's not fair to you the way it is. You're on call twenty-four hours a day. So, in a sense, you're now working 168 hours a week. If we don't change that, some child labor law expert will be on my doorstep."

Nice one, Isaac. "I'm twenty-seven years old. I'm pretty sure the child labor laws don't apply to me anymore."

"Twenty-seven, huh?"

"Yes." She tried to read the look his facial expression communicated.

"Then your union will be after me."

The lightness was back in his voice. Becca lifted her gratitude heavenward. Maybe her brief prayer was answered after all . . . just not the way she thought.

"I don't need—"

"Becca, are you going to tell me caring for my mother isn't exhausting?"

Losing her protests to his honey-smooth voice, she admitted, "Of course it is."

"Do you have a hobby?"

"A hobby?"

His eyes asked her to trust his train of thought. "Do you ski? Bowl? Bike? Fold origami?"

"I like to read."

"How much time have you spent in the reading chairs in my . . . your room or the library since you got here?"

Some days she couldn't remember pulling back the covers before falling into bed. Reading? Laughable. "Not much."

Isaac dropped onto one of the sofas. "I didn't think so. Here's my plan. What is it now? Thursday? Tomorrow when I get to work, I'm going to call the agency and line up help for the weekend. I've got a conference in La Jolla."

"Where's that?"

"Beach resort, high-class specialty-shop town. Doesn't sound like a conference town, does it?"

Becca mentally marked another way California seemed a continent away from what she once called home. What did she know about a place called Lahoia? She was from, oh, let's say, Minnesota.

"I'm brilliant," he said, poking his temple. "You probably have never been to La Jolla."

"No. I haven't."

"You're going to love it. My favorite part of the coastline. A great bookstore. We'll have to make sure you get to that bookstore. Awesome restaurants. If shopping is your thing . . ."

Shopping? Does it look like I'm a shopaholic? She tugged at the hem of the T-shirt she'd worn too many times since arriving at his mother's doorstep.

"The beach atmosphere is perfect for a reading marathon. Becca, so many great beaches close by. You'll— I can't wait for you to see . . . The 5 will be crazy on the weekend. But if we get an early enough start . . ."

"We?"

"Here's what I'm proposing. If I can arrange to rent another cottage, why don't you come with me? We'll drive there late Friday afternoon. Catch a nice dinner. Conference starts with a late-night session Friday, then all day Saturday, so you'd have the whole day to yourself. We could do a little sightseeing on Sunday and be back here by supper or shortly after. We'd only need a sub for Mom two nights and two days."

"What if your mother needs us?"

"That's why God invented cell phones, Becca. We won't be more than an hour away, even with traffic."

The look on her face must have shouted her hesitation.

"Your own Pacific beach cottage." From the reduced pace of his speaking, she knew Isaac was tempering his excitement over his brainstorm idea. "You wouldn't have to see me at all except for the trip up and back. Don't tell me you wouldn't appreciate a breather."

"I don't know."

"What's the hitch? The expenses are on me. Granted, you'd only have a couple of days off, but it's a start. Oh."

"What?"

"Maybe a road trip with me isn't at all your idea of a good time."

He looked no more than eight years old at the moment, afraid the girl across the table from him at noon recess wouldn't care to share his sandwich.

"I enjoy your company." *Someone should just staple my mouth shut and be done with it!*

"Then what is it? I really think you need a break. I can't afford to have you suffering burnout."

So, he feared having to replace her. Aha. That made sense. And it removed all threat of a romantic undertone. Undertow. Undertone. She'd never noticed the similarity in those two words.

"Sure. It would be good to have a couple of days off. And I . . . I've always wanted to see the ocean."

He paused, as if felled by the thought that someone could have lived to twenty-seven and never seen the Pacific. "Great. I'll make the arrangements. If I can't . . . no, we'll just assume I'll be able to secure a second cottage. I've stayed at this place before. Quaint. Comfortable, though. Run by an older couple who went from starving artists in the 60s to owners of a multi-million-dollar beachfront property. Their mind-set is still firmly nestled in the 60s. Tie-dyed shirts and all. I imagine the property taxes are steep enough to eat up most of their profits. They love hosting anyway. You'll like them."

"Why's that?"

He paused. "I don't know. I guess because they're so genuine. Authentic."

Her name wasn't her own. Another batch of her father's projects—cold cases now—probably begged for her testimony, not that she had knowledge of anything other than what she'd witnessed that one night. Everything else had happened at the homes of his other victims. Day after day she pretended she knew what she was doing in caring for his ailing mother. And he thought authenticity would appeal to her?

"What?" Isaac's question pierced her thoughts.

"What do you mean, what?"

"You shook your head just now."

"I did?"

"Yes. Did I say something wrong?"

"No." *Not wrong, Isaac. Just movie-cliffhanger poignant.* "I'm still trying to figure how I deserve the weekend." *And how I'll survive an hour each way of conversation without blowing my cover and your trusting but misguided mind.*

15

If it weren't for tiptoeing around the cow pies of her half-truths, the on-road conversation with Isaac would have been refreshing. He was an easy conversationalist, like someone who quickly found horseback riding's smooth rhythm. She on the other hand bounced on her tailbone like a greenhorn. But he laughed at her attempts at humor and countered with his own.

She'd been so intent on concocting her story on the cross-country bus trip, she'd paid too little attention to the scenery. It seemed a tragic waste now as she took in the beauty of Southern California, punctuated by Isaac's running commentary on the natural and historic sights.

"I never get tired of this," he said.

"Tired of what?"

"Especially this time of year. Fewer tourists. All of this."

If he gestured toward something, Becca didn't see. Her nose was pressed against the side window, her thoughts walking the sand of every beach they passed, her emotions dipping their toes in the waters that pounded toward shore, then receded.

Isaac's window was open, as was the sunroof. She clearly heard the sound she'd imagined when the bus trip ended. Her hair wouldn't appreciate it, but she powered down her own window to get the full effect.

I want to stop here, and here, and here, and here. In three decades of having all "this" so close, he probably had. Did his high school have a surf team like high schools in the Midwest boasted championship football and basketball teams? Had he walked the trails she saw advertised on the way? Had he seen the flower fields Ginger talked about? Did he find sites with names like Sunset Cliffs Natural Park irresistible or commonplace?

"There's sunscreen in the glove compartment," he said. "I'm just guessing, but did you pack any for tomorrow?"

"Didn't think about it."

"We'll have to get you acclimated to the culture. I know a lot of people who don't even own long pants."

She smeared sunscreen on the arm she rested on the passenger door. Her skin felt warm already. Isaac pointed to the sunroof. Taking the cue, she smeared sunscreen on her left arm and dotted her nose with it, too.

After more beautiful scenes than she thought her parched spirit could bear, Isaac interrupted what had been many miles of silent reverie.

"I hope you don't mind our taking the scenic route," he said, signaling for a lane change in midtown traffic. "We'll be backtracking eventually, but I want you to see the San Diego marina. How about that shore-hugging highway? Although, I suppose you've taken the shoreline drive around Lake Superior."

"Lake Superior?"

"At Duluth."

"Right."

"I guess I figured if you came from a small town, you and your family probably headed for Duluth when you wanted to Christmas shop or find a little culture. Was I wrong?"

"The shoreline drive. It's quite something. Lake Superior water's cold enough to freeze the devil's cauldron, though." Good guess. Had to be cold sometime during the year, didn't it?

Isaac's dimple deepened. "You might be surprised how cold the Pacific is, even this far south. Granted, we don't get the ice and the nor'easters like you brave and hearty flannel-wearers. But it has to be a mighty hot day to lure me into the Pacific farther than my knees without a wetsuit."

Note to self: Get to library and check out book about northern Minnesota. Cram for next test.

"Was your dad in the armed forces, Becca?"

Yes? Not a safe answer. The obvious next questions were, "What branch? Where'd he serve? What was his rank?" Much wiser to answer in the negative, which this time happened to be the truth. "No. He had a medical ineligibility."

"Oh?"

Okay. A believable reason for a medical ineligibility. "Asthma."

"Missed out on Desert Storm, huh?"

Becca rubbed her hand on the thigh of her jeans. "Yes. Always said it was his lucky rabbit's foot, that asthma."

"So, this sort of scene wouldn't have impressed him." Isaac nodded toward the naval marina now coming into view. Mile after mile of gray steel floated in the form of destroyers, battleships, submarines, and awkward-looking albatrosses with bright red medical ship crosses painted on their sides. Sparks flew as welders worked from spiderweb scaffolding on several boats under repair. Conning towers brushed the sky and hinted at the seriousness of the fleet's purpose whether here in port or on some foreign sea. A warm wave of patriotism surged through Becca as she took in the scene.

Protected. She felt protected. But was it the reminder of her nation's military preparedness or the presence of the man behind the wheel sending the message that she was safe?

A van pulled up beside them at an intersection. She read the message on the side:

Everyone is something-less. Home-less. Money-less. Bike-less. Food-less. Everyone is missing something.—Maddox, age 7.

Missing something. Missing a lot of things. She checked out the van for a clue about its owner. A charity group? Food bank? Or simply a panel van driver with a desire to provoke thought. Becca hadn't figured it out when the van turned at an intersection a few blocks later.

"So, what do you think?" Isaac's question tore her away from wondering.

"About what?"

"About dinner."

"Oh. I'm in favor of it."

Isaac's easy laughter patched the rift in her attention. "I figured you might be. Now, as to the second part of my question, are you squawkin', hoofin', or swimmin'?"

Becca loved the way his eyebrows jousted when he found himself amusing. "Ah. Chicken, beef, or seafood. What? No pork options?"

"Sorry. I know where you can get a slab of Kobe beef, but baby back ribs? Not on the typical La Jolla restaurant menu. And I do apologize, but you'll be hard-pressed to find a deep-fried cheese curd in the whole county."

"Deep-fried cheese curd?"

"Come on. Isn't that a staple of the Minnesota diet?"

Becca tensed again. *Now I have to juggle the dietary preferences of my invented home state, too?*

Isaac stole a glance her direction. "Oh, my mistake. That's Wisconsin, isn't it?"

Hmm. Apparently it does help to hold one's breath. "Ask me about lingonberries and lefse," Becca volunteered, "and I'll give you an earful." *Don't ask. Please don't ask.*

"Now, that's a gruesome picture."

"What?"

"An ear full of lefse and lingonberries. You'd need more than a cotton swab to clean up that mess."

Becca wondered if Isaac had any idea how often his sense of humor bailed her out of trouble. Of course he didn't. For all he knew, she'd grown up a Girl Scout, cheerleader, sorority sister. The things her eyes saw, her ears heard before she met Aurelia and Isaac lay locked behind a door she could never open. Confession is good for the soul, she remembered having read or been told. Maybe good for the soul, but how could it profit her job, her reputation, her relationship with these two people about whom she cared so much?

Caring is dangerous. As bad for the soul as confession is good, she chided. Isaac's gentle ways with her didn't make it easy to pretend she didn't enjoy his attention.

Nor did his laughter. Or the warmth of his hand or the way his eyes mirrored any light in the room. His patience with her didn't help. His generosity made it almost impossible to stay neutral about him.

His attention. What an idiot she'd been! He was kind to everybody. Paying attention came naturally because of his business acumen. She'd been starved for attention and found it in her employer's son, who simply needed to make sure she didn't burn out before he no longer needed a caregiver for his mother. She'd let down her guard and been swept along by what she mistook for personal interest. It wouldn't happen again. Through the side window, she watched a wave snatch a child's sand shovel and carry it beyond reach. Point well taken.

The Pacific peeked between houses and condos, teasing Becca. Sky-high palms overhead nodded their welcome. The traffic proved less gracious. Progress slowed. They'd rolled up the windows and turned on the air conditioning. But the car air conditioner bogged down as the highway arteries clogged. Isaac apologized.

"Do you have a presentation to give at your conference, Isaac?"

"No. I'm a student. Happy as a clam in white sauce over that idea. Last year, someone got the bright idea I could serve as emcee. Sweated every joke, every introduction. Don't know how Billy Crystal does it."

"Is there a pool of real estate humor from which to draw?"

"Clever, Becca."

"What?"

A dimple-deepening moment again. " 'Is there a pool?' How often is a personal property real estate agent asked that question?"

Becca froze mid-thought. Why did it please her so much to make his face light up? At best, her cover was thin. Only a fool would think it could outlast a tough wind. She'd soon be gone, one way or another. Running or kicked out. Only a double-dipped fool would hope a relationship could germinate in such tenuous ground.

But the hunger in her soul cried out for the manna of Isaac's interest.

"Corporate real estate isn't quite as intent on 'is there a pool?' " he said. "One of the first questions is usually related to zoning or taxes." He turned his head briefly toward her, then back to the road. "Lots of comedy material there."

Isaac's phone buzzed and jangled with text messages and missed calls every few minutes. Was life like this every day for him? Is that what he wanted? That kind of pace? She wasn't the only one vying for his attention.

"Finally," he said, swinging the Buick into the left turn lane. "La Jolla."

The sign announcing the city population offered Becca her first clue as to its true spelling and history. Spanish. Maybe she'd have time Saturday to explore the tourist center or the public library for more information. As Isaac maneuvered their vehicle through the twisted, congested streets, Becca gawked at the opulence. Fancy cars. Fancy shops. Fancy restaurants. Fancy, purse-puppy-toting women with skin unnaturally taut, and just-finished-up-at-the-eighteenth-green leather-tanned men. She lost an inch or so of height as the spaces between her vertebrae shrank. She didn't belong here.

For all practical purposes, she didn't belong anywhere. Nothing new.

"Remember this spot," Isaac said. "We're having dinner here this evening, if you have no objections." He pointed to a restaurant with a line of patrons already stretching out beyond its doors. "They've got a killer lobster bisque."

"Killer lobsters in bisque form or a lobster bisque to die for?"

"You need a nap, Becca. Your humor's sagging."

She couldn't argue either point.

Goosedown must have narcotic properties. What else would explain her drugged sleep when all she wanted was a short, ten-minute siesta? She floated on goosedown through a sea of dreams, clinging to the sides of her magic carpet.

It had been all she could do to wait until the resort owner exited after showing her the cottage amenities before she kicked off her shoes and dove head first into the down. It billowed around her until its welcome engulfed her. The cloud of wonderful swallowed her and every problem lingering out there in the world. With the sound of the waves her lullaby, and the source of her deepest pain half a country away, she relaxed first one muscle, one nerve, then the next . . .

Judging by the digital clock on the rattan bedside stand, her ten minutes had ballooned into two hours. Judging by the insistent quality of the knock at the cottage door, two hours was too long.

"Becca! Please, open up!" the voice called through the door.

Why was Isaac in a panic? Ah. Dinner reservations. Paranoid about missing a reservation appointment. Guess she had to admire his dedication to promptness, although . . .

The apologetic smile with which she greeted him at the door faded like cheap drapes in a hot sun the instant she read the unabashed concern on his face. His chest heaved as if he'd run hard up the cliff from the beach to her hilltop cottage . . . pursued by Mafia hitmen.

"What's wrong?"

"It's Mom. How fast can you be ready to leave?"

Her sleep-fogged brain scrambled to climb out of its confusion. "What happened to her?"

"How fast, Becca?" He said it in a tone she'd not heard from him before. Under other circumstances, she might have drawn back from the harshness. As it was, the sting disappeared in the wash of shared fear.

"I'm ready now. Haven't unpacked." The sweetness of her hard-earned nap turned sour, milk curdled by the vinegar of self-indulgence.

"I'll bring the car around. Already told the innkeepers we're leaving."

Becca took advantage of Isaac's brief absence and used the bathroom. The mirror mocked her. "You shouldn't have left Aurelia. What were you thinking? Others might deserve a couple of days away from their duties. But you? You've got debts to pay. Big ones. You shouldn't have left her. Is that precious old woman going to have to pay with her life, too? For your mistakes?"

Odd where the mind travels in crisis mode. Becca folded the towel she had used to dry her hands and mourned, "Housekeepers are probably going to have to clean the whole cottage just because I rumpled the bed and dampened a towel. Nothing but trouble. I'm nothing but trouble."

How often had those last words punctuated the air around her?

"Dad, I need a notebook for school."

"Yeah, that's all I need, to have you sucking me dry when your mother needs help. You're nothing but trouble."

"Dad, the school nurse said she thinks I might have an ear infection. She said I ought to see a doctor."

"Well, that isn't about to happen, now, is it? I don't have all day to haul you from here to wherever just because you whined to that sissy nurse and got her feeling sorry for you. Nothing but trouble. I don't have time for this. I'll bring something home from the store."

"Can I stay at Madeline's this weekend, Dad? It's her birthday. She's having a party."

"You selfish little twit. Who do you think will help your mom while I'm at work? When does she get to go to a party? Have a little respect."

The car horn spared Becca another trip down memory lane. She grabbed her bag and shut the door on another poisoned scene.

———

Her dad had growled when stressed. No, not growled. Snarled. Like a junkyard dog. Isaac grew silent. Neither reaction made Becca comfortable.

"Did the hospital say what happened, Isaac?"

"Too few details."

Where did her boundaries lie? As caregiver, she was entitled to know about Aurelia's medical condition, wasn't she?

Isaac's polished-granite driving technique jerked and swerved now. Nothing dangerous. Nothing like that. Erratic. As much as he complained about his awkwardness in his relationship with his mother, his caring showed itself at times like this. Worry spilled out in silence and mannerisms as halting as early versions of computer cameras.

"Was it her heart, Isaac?"

"The temp aide couldn't wake her."

"Why would she want to wake your mother?"

"Thought she'd been sleeping too long."

"What's too long when a bed is your whole world?" Becca regretted the question even before her voice added the punctuation at the end.

"Whatever."

"Sorry." Her whisper died on her lips.

"What? Oh. No, I'm sorry, Becca. I . . . I don't know much about what happened. Just that she's in crisis and I'm too many miles away."

"She's blessed to have you as close as you are."

A muscle under his right eye twitched.

"I mean, right in the same town. You could have started your business in Phoenix or Colorado Springs. Then you'd have no chance of reaching her within an hour of a medical crisis. You'd have to hear about everything by phone. Now, she sees you almost every day."

"Not that she cares. She'd rather see your face at her bedside than mine."

Was this a junior high pout? Was he miffed? Or was the man bruised by Aurelia's less-than-enthusiastic receptions lately? Becca thought he'd taken them in stride. Apparently not.

"I don't know what to say, Isaac."

"It's not your fault. You can't help it that you're adorable."

He attempted a grin, but that muscle twitched again. So did the pumping muscle under Becca's sternum.

⎯⎯ ✺ ⎯⎯

Becca and Isaac entered the La Vida hospital through the emergency room entrance, unsure if Aurelia Hughes now had a hospital room to call her own or was still under the care of the ER doctors. Or . . . ?

"We're here for Aurelia Hughes," Isaac announced to the unit clerk behind the first available admissions desk. "I'm her son. This is her caregiver, Becca Morrow."

The most recent additions to the Privacy Act blocked Becca from advancing past the double doors into the treatment area until Aurelia's own physician, Dr. Lambert, waived her through the red tape.

"She'd stopped breathing," Dr. Lambert explained as he led the two past curtained treatment cubbies. "It may be as simple as apnea, although apnea's nothing to fool around with in a heart patient. We've run a series of tests. So far, nothing unusual presents itself. Nothing of which we weren't already aware."

"They told me they couldn't wake her." Isaac's voice sounded as if his collar button was a half inch to the right of reasonable.

"A little miscommunication."

"Miscommunication?" The twitching eye muscle danced.

"The aide grew disturbed by your mother's lack of breath sounds. She started CPR . . ."

"What?" Isaac choked—on his own saliva?—and suppressed a coughing fit to ask, "Was that necessary? She signed a do-not-resuscitate order months ago."

Dr. Lambert stopped walking, looked at Becca, then back to Isaac. "It was wise of her to call 911, though. Better safe than sorry. We'll put a soft cast on her wrist."

"Her wrist?"

"The aide kneeled on your mom's wrist during chest compressions. Hairline fracture."

Becca put a hand on Isaac's arm. "How long will she need the cast?" she asked, steering the conversation before Isaac could spit out something he might later regret.

"We won't know for a while. Maybe four weeks? A lot of factors are slowing her healing right now. She'll be uncomfortable, but since she's not liable to run any marathons or tackle heavy housework these next couple of weeks, we'll do little more than increase her pain medication and watch for swelling or other distress. She said she'd had some trouble swallowing. Is that true, Becca?"

"It's not as easy for her to get her oral medications down. We work at it."

Dr. Lambert frowned. "Then I think we'll switch at least some of them to liquid versions. It's probably time to do that."

Isaac's shoulders drooped as if he felt gravity's pull more acutely with every pronouncement.

Dr. Lambert's voice took on a grandfatherly quality. "I'll show Ms. Morrow what to watch for and some low impact physical therapy for the wrist once the cast is removed. Lord willing, your mother will recover from this hitch without incident or further complication."

Isaac leaned against the nearest wall. His mouth moved moments before he spoke. "I shouldn't have gone to the conference."

"Isaac, that's part of your job. I was the one who shouldn't have gone." Becca had spent more than a few minutes in the car warning herself not to attempt a self-pacifying getaway again.

"I don't think there's any point in our keeping her overnight," Dr. Lambert said. "We'd like to conduct a sleep study, but that would be a bit much at this point. Why don't you step into her cubicle and visit for a few minutes while we prepare her discharge orders and make arrangements for the pain med change. Then you two can take her home."

You two. He made it sound as if they were a couple.

If the wheels of justice grind slowly, they've got nothing over a hospital's discharge system. Very little remained of the night by the time the vehicle pulled into Aurelia's driveway. Isaac carried his dozing mother into the house, her slight frame taxing his strength not in the least. Becca stayed a handful of steps ahead of them, opening doors and flipping on light switches. She smoothed the bed sheets in the sunroom and fluffed the pillow that so seldom had any relief from its duties.

Aurelia winced as Isaac laid her on the bed despite his obvious efforts at gentleness.

Becca looked at Isaac across the bed. "Are you driving back for the conference tomorrow?"

Isaac tugged at his collar. "I suppose that depends on how she is in the morning."

"Dr. Lambert seemed to think she wasn't in immediate danger."

"Guilt or remorse has me by the scruff of the neck. I ought to be at the conference, but I should be here with Mom, too."

"Isn't that why you hired me?"

He smoothed a wrinkle in his mother's blanket. "And you still didn't get a day off."

Aurelia snored softly, underscoring the fact that she'd probably be the only one of the three sleeping soundly that night.

16

Did you have nights like that with your father?" Isaac forked English muffins for toasting. He'd canceled his trip to La Jolla but had stopped in every morning in the two weeks since to check on his mom.

Such an innocent question. Becca slid the bacon around in the pan to keep it cooking evenly. It sizzled and popped, a stray globule of hot fat finding its target on her forearm with greater accuracy than a Scud missile. She flinched . . . at the burn power of the question. Nights like that with her mother?

Few visits to the emergency room. Doctors and her father mixed more poorly than motor oil and balsamic vinegar. Physicians spewed advice he didn't want to hear.

"Stupid doctors," he'd often grinched. "What the Sam Goody do they know?"

Doctors, cops, lawyers, and ethics committees. He had no use for them. They interfered with his life's work.

For all Isaac knew, her father's problem was an alcohol-weakened heart, not a depraved heart. And all along, she'd thought her mother was the sick one.

Emergency room. It hadn't been unfamiliar territory, Isaac thought. Different this last time, though. Becca stood beside him. She helped shoulder the burden, like a friend on the other end of a heavy piece of furniture.

Isaac's stomach clenched. He'd just described his mother as if she were a bulky, awkward, hernia-spawning four-drawer file cabinet. A burden. How fair was that?

And she'd never be upright again.

Isaac Hughes—the worm of a son. The woman deserved respect, not ridicule. He would have spit in his own face if that were possible. In light of the sacrifices she'd made for him, his response? *Why don't you resent her, Isaac? That's a good idea. She's bearing the torture of this disease every day for the rest of her life. And you? You can't spend an hour in it without squirming.*

What is wrong with you, man?

"Scrambled or fried?" Becca held a carton of eggs in one hand and a fork in the other. Another day, another breakfast. The bright spot was Isaac taking the time to stop at the house before heading for work.

"What?"

She raised the carton a little higher. "Your eggs, Isaac. Fried or scrambled?"

"Scrambled, please."

"With onions and green peppers?"

Isaac's look asked the question before the words came out. "How did you know I'm a Denver Scrambled guy?"

"Your mom. Actually, I should qualify that. She said onions and green lizards. I translated."

"Good guess."

Becca tested the waters of conversation. "She's an amazing woman."

"Yes, she is."

"It must be a joy to know her blood flows through your veins." Oh! Adoption-awkward! "Isaac, I'm sorry. What I meant . . ."

"It's okay. I'm used to slips like that. It's easy to assume she's my real mom."

"She is your real mom."

He returned to checking his e-mail or texts on his phone.

"Isaac?"

No response. Not good.

"Becca?" The monitor distorted Aurelia's voice no more than her weakness did. "Becca? Please."

"It's a good day." Becca ratcheted her voice a notch in perky. "She remembered my name." She slid the frying pan off the burner and headed for the sunroom.

If she hadn't trained her ears to pick up on such things, she might have missed Isaac's soft, "She always remembers *your* name."

———

Isaac poured juice for the three of them.

Lord, why is this so hard for me? I'm supposed to be one of the lucky ones, although I hate that word. I'm blessed, right? What should it matter that I don't know who gave birth to me? I was "chosen." And that's supposed to make me all marshmallow crème inside with gratitude. Isn't it? I can't even fault my folks . . . the Hugheses . . . for anything specific. I couldn't have wanted for better parents.

Unless you count knowing my real roots. Even Becca forgets. Why can't I?

I could fix those eggs for her. Or at least wait here until she comes back and explain my reaction. The only right thing to do.

Instead, he snagged an English muffin, grabbed his attaché from its spot near the back door, and left the scene. *Work doesn't ask questions about who I am.*

"And I thought I was the mysterious one. Where did he go?"

Becca fixed a breakfast plate for Aurelia, but her own appetite no longer mattered.

What was Isaac's problem? He couldn't be jealous, could he? Of her? Because his mother sometimes forgot his name, but rarely hers? That's a laugh. That anyone, ever, in the whole wide world would be jealous of her. *I'll trade you twenty-seven years of my life for one day of yours, Isaac. One day.*

No.

She wouldn't wish that on anyone.

The dent her father's choices made on the flesh of her heart wasn't bouncing back. Was she insane to think it ever would? She'd put too much stock in the power of changing her name. It didn't change who she was or her family history. Nothing could change that.

She'd come halfway across the country and it still wasn't far enough.

It would never be far enough.

Becca focused on the breakfast tray. With the monitor hooked on her belt, she slipped out to the garden to find something to soften the harsh edges of Aurelia's existence. She found a sprig that faintly resembled the snapdragons she knew from home. Each delicate white blossom on the stem looked like it had been painted in dark lavender with the face of an angel. Not like the face of Jesus or the Virgin Mary burnt into toast, but still . . .

She bent to read the white enameled marker at the base of the plant. "Angelonia. Common name: Angel Face."

"This is the one." She snipped the sprig and a neighboring bit of greenery and headed back to the kitchen. Tucked into a narrow clear-glass vase, almost like a test tube, the flowers pronounced themselves just what the tray needed.

Funny how much lighter her heart felt as she maneuvered through the house to the sunroom. Geneva would have said it was from "looking around for a way to bless someone." Mrs. Larkin was right more often than she was wrong, if she ever had been.

Maybe that's why it was so easy to love Aurelia—because she was so much like her younger sister. Geneva's coloring was different. Dark eyes. Hair? It changed with the seasons, but it looked most natural when she had it done in a warm brown, more like Isaac's without the sun streaks.

An undertone of Geneva's voice laced Aurelia's in its stronger moments. They had to be at least ten years apart in age, but their sisterhood was clear. "Geneva, I'm partly doing this for you."

Becca bumped the sunroom door with her hip. "Ready for breakfast?"

"I . . . can't . . . get . . . this . . . to work!" Aurelia's frustration bled through her pores in beads of sweat.

"What's wrong?" Becca set the tray on the dresser and moved to the bedside of the woman waving the portable phone as if it were a sword, punching madly with her thumb on its face.

"I can't . . . make it . . . turn on the music." Her right arm—
the only one working at the moment—dropped to the bed
covers as tears pooled. "I need music."

"We all do. Let's see what's going on." Becca pried Aurelia's
bone-thin fingers from the instrument. "You need the sound
system remote, Mrs. Hughes. This is the phone."

"Oh, dear."

Becca lifted the credit card-sized remote from the end table,
clicked one button, and the room swelled with Aurelia's favorite woodwind quintet.

"I'm sorry. I don't know . . . what I'm doing."

"All is not lost." Becca checked the face of the hand-held
telephone. "I think you may have a chance to talk to Paris."
She held the phone to her ear. "Ah! Busy signal. Wouldn't you
know? Paris is always busy this time of year."

She replaced the receiver in its base and reached for the
tray. "How about breakfast?" She unfolded the cloth napkin,
tucked it under Aurelia's chin as if fitting her for a new blouse,
then held the older woman's good wrist long enough to check
her pulse. Rapid, but even.

"I'm always better when you're in the room, Becca."

"I could say the same about you." She planted a brief kiss
on Aurelia's damp cheek. "You eat. I'll check your medications.
You're running low on a couple of them. Time to order refills."

"My wrist. Someone handcuffed me!"

"It's a soft cast, Mrs. Hughes. Like a brace. It's been helping
to keep your wrist stable so it can heal."

"I don't remember spraining it. I suppose I landed wrong
in gymnastics. But I certainly can't use it to feed myself, now,
can I?"

Becca stifled a bubble of laughter. "Sweet one, you're right-
handed. You hold your fork or spoon in this hand. That one
over there shouldn't get in the way of your eating. It'll just lie

there all cozy in its brace while this one"—she nestled the fork in Aurelia's right hand—"does all the work."

"Well, I knew that. God gave us two for a reason."

Checking prescription expiration dates and amounts remaining in the pill and liquid medication bottles in the top drawer of the tall dresser kept Becca's back to Aurelia while Becca swallowed the morning's bittersweet taste of a deteriorating mind. When she'd sorted which medications were due for refills, she relocked the drawer, slid the small key onto its jewelry clip on her watch, and turned to face her charge.

Aurelia had deposited small mounds of scrambled egg in a ragged row the length of her wrist cast.

"Interesting art project, Mrs. Hughes. But those eggs belong in your tummy."

"I'm feeding the birds. They'll be here soon enough."

Becca couldn't stop the sigh that escaped. *Think!* "I have an idea. Why don't we ask Isaac or Pete to put a bird feeder right outside the window here? Right where you can see it. Then you can watch the birds eat without their leaving a mess on your blankets."

Aurelia's face registered momentary confusion, then clarity. "Excellent idea. Who's Isaac?"

"Your . . . son."

"Oh, I wish I had a son." Fork still fisted in her right hand, Aurelia pressed it to her chest as if holding the gap shut where her heart was breaking.

The tears returned.

For both of them.

—⊗⊗⊗—

Becca shoveled the remainder of the eggs down the garbage disposal, calculating only about a tablespoonful had made it into Aurelia's stomach. And even that took a kindergarten teacher's patience and imagination. She'd fix a "milkshake" supplement drink after she started the dishwasher. Did they have any ice cream in the freezer? Or yogurt for a smoothie? Maybe if Becca sipped something, too, Aurelia wouldn't feel forced to eat. They'd share a milkshake break. Worth a try.

Ginger called before Becca had a chance to find Pete's phone number. She insisted he'd be happy to pick up a bird feeder and install it after he got off work.

"Don't you need to clear that with him first?"

"I'll ask out of courtesy," Ginger said. "But I know my man. Outshines most in the thoughtfulness category."

Yes. She'd said that before.

"Would Isaac's mom appreciate a hummingbird feeder, too? They're fascinating to watch. I don't know what you have for hummingbirds in Minnesota, but the male Anna's variety out here are beautiful. A rose-red gorget."

Ginger obviously knew a lot more about birds than Becca. "Gorget?"

"That striking patch of feathers on the throat and upper chest. Almost like a bib, but so elegant."

Becca wrote a mental note to purchase rose-red fabric to make gorgets for Aurelia to wear for meals.

An hour later, Becca and Aurelia sipped their milkshakes as they listened to an audiobook. Aurelia's face crinkled.

"Something wrong?"

"Don't like her voice."

"Whose?"

"The woman telling that story."

"We can turn it off." Becca did so, then said, "Tell me about your sister."

Aurelia's eyes widened. "Oh, we don't talk about that."

Becca felt her own face crinkle. Aurelia and Geneva were obviously close. "I know your sister. She's a wonderful woman. Did I tell you she taught my girls' club group when I was younger? I didn't get to go often, but when I did, your sister always made me feel as if—"

"Hush! He'll hear you!"

"Who will?"

The woman's eyes darted from corner to corner of the room. "Isaac."

Aurelia's good days had seemed fewer in number since her trip to the emergency room. Becca wondered if the increase in pain medicine to cover the wrist fracture was having an effect. She'd call Dr. Lambert before contacting the pharmacy, in case he wanted to make any changes in dosing instructions.

"I haven't heard from her in years," Aurelia said, setting her milkshake on the over-the-bed table.

"Sweet one, she calls or writes every week. We read her latest letter yesterday. I tucked it in your keepsake box." Becca didn't know whether to dig it out and prove it or let it lie. She stayed where she was.

"Oh. Yes. Well, it's good she keeps in touch."

17

Steeled against the guilt that always smacked him in the chest when he opened the door of his mom's house, Isaac knocked twice and let himself in. "Anybody home?"

"Glad you're here," Becca said as she came around the corner into the kitchen. "I need to get to the pharmacy before it closes. Dr. Lambert made some small changes in her medication again. Are you free to stay for an hour or so?"

"I could have picked them up for you. For that matter, I could go right now. Save you the trip. I'll be back in a—" Isaac watched her shoulders slump. Not much. Just an inch. Enough to tell him he wasn't helping anything by volunteering to rob her of the opportunity to get out of the house alone for a few minutes.

"Okay."

"No, no, I think it's best if you go," he countered. "I don't have plans. Why don't you treat yourself to dinner? There's a great burger joint in the same block as the pharmacy."

He caught the crooked twist of her eyebrows. "Or, no. Not there. Two storefronts down the other way is a Thai place that has great food."

"I love Thai. I didn't get it often back in I—. I didn't get it often."

"Great. Stop there, then."

She hesitated. She did a lot of that. "Maybe I will. Thanks."

"How's Mom?"

"Sleeping at the moment."

"Good. I mean . . ."

Becca grabbed her purse from its hook by the door. "She won't nap more than another few minutes, if the current pattern holds. Did you eat yet? Want me to bring you something Thai-ish?"

"That would be great."

"Are you familiar with the menu, or do you want to call it in?"

Isaac chuckled. "Plenty familiar. Pick something. I've never been disappointed yet." He did his own hesitation step, just long enough to stop him from adding, "You've never disappointed me."

He snagged his keys from his pocket. "Here, take the car."

"I'd rather walk. Besides," she said as she stepped through the door, "I don't have a California license."

Probably because her job hadn't given her a minute to do anything for herself. He'd found someone who related well to his mom, who cared for her at a level far higher than anyone they'd previously hired. It was so easy to let her handle everything. A paintball thunk hit him in the chest. Guilt again.

"Becca?" The monitor on the counter rasped the name.

Sorry, Mom. You'll have to make do with me this time.

The pharmacy-chain-store layout seemed eerily familiar. Thousands of miles from home and it looked like the one where her dad had worked, except for the proliferation of sunglasses and Styrofoam coolers. Back in the Midwest, the snow shovel and mitten display would have taken over those spots by this time of year.

She wasn't thrilled to get a new pharmacy tech. One of his eyes pointed slightly off-center. She wasn't sure where to look when talking to him. Left eye or right eye? Flipping back and forth gave her a headache.

She read the name on his engraved plastic badge. Riggo. "I'm here to pick up prescriptions for Aurelia Hughes."

"You must be Ms. Morrow." He drew out her name as if his tongue tripped on something.

The community was smaller than she thought. "I am."

"She's still with us, huh? Tenacious lady."

"That she is."

He turned toward the racks of filled prescriptions in hook-handled plastic bags. "Here you go. I'll put it on the credit card we have on file."

"Thank you. I appreciate it."

"Wait for the pharmacist, please."

"Sure." She was used to the routine. One of the pharmacists on duty—maybe the only one at this hour—had to verify the prescriptions. *Has Aurelia had this medication before? Any questions? Have a nice day.*

Riggo didn't busy himself with other customers. He stayed there, waiting with her, as if studying her.

If she hadn't put a moratorium on unnecessary lies, she would have started a conversation with, *"Did I tell you I'm engaged to a guy I met on the Internet, Riggo? Yep. Wedding's next month. We're honeymooning in Tahiti."* No, that would be over the top. *"In Napa Valley. Now back off."*

The pharmacist broke onto the scene before she gave in to temptation. He glanced at the bottles, flew through the standard questions, and moved on.

"All set, Ms. Morrow."

"Thanks, Riggo. Bye."

She didn't linger once she had the bag of prescriptions in hand. Escaping Riggo's discomfiting stare added to her stomach rumbling and pushed her out the door toward the Thai restaurant that was close enough for her to smell the garlic.

Isaac slapped his laptop shut when he heard the door open and close. She was back so soon?

Not only back, but bearing treasures. From the aroma floating in his direction, she'd made a good choice for his meal.

"You're home early."

She deposited a bag from the pharmacy and a paper bag from Sen Thai on the counter. "Glad I took my jean jacket. It's chilly out tonight. Didn't know that happened here."

"I can start a fire in the fireplace."

She considered the idea, lips pressed together. He expected her to say, *Don't bother.*

"That would be nice."

It took him a moment to recalibrate. "Did you take time to eat?"

"I brought both our meals home. Thought we could eat . . . together . . . and talk about your mom."

About Mom. "Sure thing. She's sleeping again. Apparently my riveting conversational skills double as a sleep aid."

He helped unearth the treasures from the Sen Thai bag. Oh, this was going to be good.

Within minutes a gentle fire was flickering in the living room fireplace—it helped that it was gas. Their Southeast Asian picnic lay spread on the sleek coffee table that likely hadn't been used in years. Oversized mugs of hot tea looked culturally out of place, but culinarily on target. Becca sat across from him on a look-alike sofa. A lot to be grateful for when he said grace.

Synchronized groaning accompanied their first bites of food.

"Outrageous."

"Fabulous."

"You can imagine how tough it was to force myself to wait to get here to eat it. I wanted to sit on a curb somewhere and dig in."

Isaac felt a wave of pleasure wash over him. She took such delight in the simplest things, the smallest kindnesses.

"What are you smiling about?"

He feigned interest in negotiating a spring roll with chopsticks. "Food. My Aunt Geneva."

"Your Aunt Geneva?"

"She sent us you." *Becca will break eye contact first. She will. Any second now.*

Becca dabbed her lips with a napkin, as if she needed it. "I owe her a lot for . . . for this opportunity."

"Well, w-we're glad you came." Now they were both stuttering. *Get a grip, Isaac. You're smoother than this.* "So"—he snagged a shrimp and a tangle of noodles—"you had something you wanted to discuss?"

She held her mug in both hands and blew on her tea. "I think it's time to install a more sophisticated monitoring system, if you don't object. It will cost some money . . ."

"How much?"

"I don't know. But I think your mother needs to hear a response from me, to set her mind at ease. She can call for me on the monitor, but she can't hear me answer back. She always seems nervous when I get to the sunroom, and it's never more than a few seconds, maybe a minute at the most, before I see what she needs."

"I agree." He dug for a snow pea.

"You do?"

"Makes perfect sense."

"The problem is that I'm not sure how much longer she'll be able to call out."

The meal sat heavier in his stomach.

"I was thinking . . ." She pulled her typical hesitation step.

Isaac put his chopsticks across his plate and clasped his hands together. "What?"

"How expensive would it be to install a video camera and then have monitors in the kitchen and the bedroom I'm using?"

Why didn't she call it her room when they talked about it? It's as if she refused to believe anything belonged to her. Even temporarily. "Parents do it all the time to keep an eye on their infants, or their babysitters."

She flinched.

"Not that I'd have to keep an eye on you. That's not what I meant. And you're no babysitter. I mean—"

"You'd probably better stop talking now."

"You're probably right. I'll look into it. Check how much it would cost. And I'll find out how we'd set it up so she can either hear you or both hear and see you when she needs something. It might make her feel more comfortable just knowing where you are."

"I always tell her where I'll be."

"But the words don't always stick."

"Right." Becca looked at her plate of food. She reached to push it away. He pushed it back toward her.

"If you don't eat it, I will."

She glanced at him without raising her head. "I can put it in a container so you can warm it up tomorrow."

"Or you could eat some more right now and enjoy a few minutes of peace and quiet in front of this lovely, oh-so-natural fire, in the company of a guy who doesn't tell you often enough how much he appreciates you."

He saw it, the smile that teased its way out despite her attempts to suppress it.

"Thanks, Isaac Hughes."

"You're welcome, Becca Morrow."

Okay, so now what was wrong? All he did was say her name and the light went out of her eyes.

18

The phone rang a little after ten the next morning. Becca caught it after the first ring. It hadn't been a good night. The fewer noises that disturbed Aurelia, the better.

"Yes?"

"Hey. Good morning."

"Good morning, Isaac." Becca stood on her tiptoes to extend the duster handle far enough to reach the cobweb that had been bugging her for two days.

"Aerobics?"

"Excuse me?"

"You sound out of breath."

"Housework. Same thing."

He chuckled. They were back on safer ground today. "I have a favor to ask."

"Go for it."

"Would you mind if our men's group met at the house tonight? Tony's wife had foot surgery, so she's laid up for a while."

"Not a problem. So Tony won't be here? How many, then?"

"Tony's coming. Her sister is staying with them for a couple of weeks to help out."

"Okay. How many, then?"

Isaac mumbled as he counted. "Eight. Maybe nine if the new guy joins us. You met him two or three Sundays ago. Brent. Widower. Three little kids. He said he'd come if he could find a sitter."

"Do you want me to set up the dining room?"

"No. We don't need the big table. We'll push some of the furniture around in the living room. But leave that for us. And Tony's sister-in-law is sending treats, not that any of us need them."

"So what do you need me to do? Coffee? Soft drinks?"

"That'd be great. I mostly wanted to make sure you didn't mind the invasion. I'd say we'd try to keep the noise level down, but I'd be lying."

Lying. Ugly word. "Your mom didn't sleep well last night."

"Oh. Not good. Maybe I should tell Tony we can't do it this week."

We. Nice word. "It'll be okay. I'll turn her music up. What time?"

"Start at six-thirty. Done promptly by eight. Some of the guys have kids in school and don't want to miss tucking them into bed."

"Good daddies." The thought was out before she could reel it back in.

"Yeah. The best. But if you think it would agitate Mom . . ."

"There's no telling what her mood will be, Isaac."

"We can always move it outside to the backyard if it bothers her."

"That's true." Becca set aside the duster and jotted a note about brushing off the patio furniture when she got a chance. She'd spent too little time out there since arriving, but it was a great spot for entertaining . . . or men's grouping.

"Let's forget it. I'll call Tony—"

"No. I think it's a good idea. Your mom enjoys those 'boys,' as she calls them."

"You were quiet there for a while. I thought—"

"Already two tasks ahead of you."

"Not surprised. Okay, then. See you shortly after six. Pete will come early with me so we can toss sofas and chairs. He says he has a bird feeder to install, too."

"Oh, good."

"I could have done that. You could have asked me."

And added one more thing to your ink-filled planner? She wasn't reading petulance in his voice, was she?

"But," he continued, "if it needs to be plumb and level and all that stuff, Pete's your man."

"Pete it is."

"See you later."

The idea fed an emotion she'd hadn't acknowledged for a long while—anticipation.

⁂

Becca couldn't wander far from Aurelia's side before the woman called out. She seemed restless, but claimed she wasn't in pain.

"How can I help you, Mrs. Hughes?"

"I don't know."

"Does your wrist hurt?"

Aurelia patted her tummy. "No."

"Stomach ache?"

The older woman scowled. "Why would my stomach hurt?"

"You patted your belly. I thought that meant—"

"Oh, for goodness sake. You don't know anything. The people they send from that temp agency never have a bit of sense to them."

"I came because your sister Geneva asked me to come. I'm not from the temp agency."

Aurelia's countenance calmed. "Geneva? I wonder how she's doing now. Poor thing. Such a shock."

"What's a shock, Mrs. Hughes?" Becca drew a chair near the bed and lowered herself into it without releasing the hand she held.

"We did the only thing we could."

"Who did?"

Her eyes seemed to look through the ceiling. "I'll always carry a little pain right here"—she tapped her heart—"because the thing that gave me joy brought her so much sadness."

"What thing, Aurelia?"

Her eyelids slid shut. She drew an artificially deep breath that staggered out on the exhale. Her chest rose and fell in sleep's rhythm then. Becca stroked the back of Aurelia's hand with her thumb.

The afternoon sun inched its way from the foot of Aurelia's bed toward the head. Becca stood and lowered the shades to keep the room from warming too much or the light from waking her.

She stretched her back. How long had she been sitting in the wooden chair at Aurelia's side? Her watch told her Isaac would be there in two hours. She gave the top dresser drawer a tug—habit—and, assured it was locked, left the room for the one she was borrowing. If Aurelia caught up on sleep she lost the night before, Becca could take a soaking bath. Maybe she'd read in the tub. Something to take her mind off the swift decline of Aurelia's.

Pear soap and matching shampoo. A woman's best friend. Becca toweled off, enjoying the light fragrance the soap left on her skin and in the room. She dressed in her good jeans and a cotton sweater with three-quarter-length sleeves. Her hair had grown just long enough to pull into a respectable twist, which she secured with a clip.

With one ear to the monitor, she took the time to apply foundation, concealer, mascara, and lipgloss. She needed more sun. If Aurelia rallied at all, maybe the two of them could spend some time in the garden. The wheelchair Isaac had rented sat idle in a corner of the garage, waiting for a day when his mom felt strong enough to use it.

She had less than an hour to get Aurelia fed before Isaac and Pete arrived. Aurelia could use blusher, too. Becca grabbed her blush brush and an unopened tube of rosy lipgloss. It wasn't every day Mrs. Hughes entertained guests.

Aurelia liked bits of hard-boiled egg in her asparagus soup, added at the last minute as a garnish. Becca had grown to like it that way, too. She chopped the egg as fine as she could without making it unrecognizable and sprinkled some on Aurelia's sauce-dish-sized bowl. Her own soup mug fit onto the tray. She could do this in one trip.

"The cavalry has arrived!" Pete burst into the room, chest first, barely catching the door before it slammed into the corner of the counter.

Isaac followed a few seconds later, his sharp-looking shirt and crisp pants a testament to how much of the muscle for furniture moving was going to come from Pete.

"Out of my way, Pickle," he told Pete. "I have to change. Upstairs bathroom okay, Becca?"

"Sure."

"Down in a minute."

It was *his* house. The house he grew up in. He didn't need Becca's permission. She wondered if he found that as curious as she did.

"Good to see you, Pete. How's Ginger?"

"Gorgeous as ever. She says hi."

In a world of broken marriages, it was refreshing to see so many healthy ones among Isaac's friends. What was their secret?

Maybe nights like this. Men not afraid to support one another, laugh together, hold one another accountable. She heard the thump as Pete dropped a book on the kitchen island.

"Light will be gone soon. I'll get that bird feeder set up for you. Bought some birdseed. Who knew there were so many flavors? Hope what I picked will be okay. I figured 'for song-birds' was a good option?"

Becca warmed at the idea of Pete standing in the birdseed aisle, scratching his head over the choices. "Perfect. Thanks so much. I know Aurelia will appreciate it."

"The feeder hangs in a tree, so I don't have to dig a posthole. Oh, hummingbird thing too. There's a recipe on the box for the sugar stuff they drink. I'll be back before Isaac gets into his work duds."

He scooted out the door before she could add another "Thank you."

Becca cupped the bottom of Aurelia's soup dish. Still warm enough? Might need a minute in the microwave.

"I got it," Isaac called from the entry in response to the front doorbell.

Tony and Isaac jostled each other through the doorway to the kitchen. The microwave dinged.

"What is that smell?" Tony bent over Becca's mug. "Phew!"

Becca snatched it from under his nose. "Asparagus."

"It's a vegetable." Isaac elbowed his friend.

"Nasty stuff."

"Hey!" Becca protested.

"This is real food," Tony said, planting an insulated tote on the island next to Pete's Bible. He pulled out a tray of smoked meats and cheese sliced the thickness of a deck of cards. "And for the sweet tooth—"

"Isaac!" Pete's call echoed through the garage and pierced the fun. "Isaac!" Face pale, eyes wild, Pete half-fell into the house. "Your . . . mom. Saw . . . through . . . the windows . . ."

Becca dashed toward the sunroom, pressing the monitor to her ear. Nothing. Isaac and Tony were two steps ahead of her, feet pounding as hard as hers.

Aurelia Hughes had left the room.

In her place was a cold, fragile shell of a spent existence. Eyes open but unseeing. Mouth gaping. Unlike the graceful woman she'd been in life. Gone.

Tony took over at the bedside when Becca collapsed into Isaac's arms. Confusion wracked her from hair follicles to toes. How did it happen so soon, so unexpected? Why wasn't she there by Aurelia's side? It was Becca's fault. She'd somehow cheated Isaac out of the opportunity to be with his mom in her last hour.

Last hour. Aurelia had been sleeping a little more than an hour earlier. Sobs shook her. Only half of them were hers. Isaac claimed the other half.

"Something's not right," Tony whispered into the tension. He stood, stiff, eyes wide. "Everybody out."

Isaac released his grip on Becca. "What do you mean, man? Tony, come on."

"Don't touch anything," Tony barked. "Call 911."

"She's DNR. She didn't want to be resuscitated. Signed the paperwor . . ." Isaac's voice crumpled before the consonant.

Tony's demeanor said he was not prepared to argue. In full professional mode now, he stepped back from the body. "We don't need EMTs. We may need the homicide team."

"Who's been here today?" Tony the Cop asked when they'd retreated to the living room. Tony the Friend had gone into hiding.

Becca's mind whirled. Thoughts jumbled. What happened? Isaac looked her way. "Becca?"

"Me. Just me. I was in her room most of the day. Let me see her. I haven't said good-bye."

"Sit tight."

"Tony, you're scaring her." Pete stopped pacing to speak but resumed after the words were out. Becca and Isaac sat on one sofa. Tony on the opposite. His pen scratched notes in a black flip-top notebook.

"Becca, I have to ask these questions."

She fought for enough saliva to swallow. "I understand."

"I don't," Isaac said, stiffening and leaning forward. "What's going on? Mom was dying. We all know that. Oh, Lord God!" He sank against the back of the sofa, his forearm over his eyes.

Tony flipped the notebook closed. "I am so sorry, Isaac. This is rough, no matter how you look at it."

Voices on the front porch sent a jolt through Becca's numbness. Laughing voices. The men's group. "Pete!"

"I got it." He bolted for the front door.

Someone had already opened it, judging from the jostling and noise. "Hey, Isaac, there are a bunch of cop cars pulling up. Lights and everything. What'd you do, brother?"

Becca didn't recognize the voice. She recognized her fear.

19

The pan at the bottom of life's toaster had somehow worked loose. All the crumbs were falling out.

Isaac's pulse pounded in his ears. He couldn't think. Couldn't breathe. What a nightmare! Pears. He smelled pears. How odd was that? Becca. She smelled like pears. Her tears had stopped, but she trembled beside him on the sofa. He should put his arm around her.

She stood to her feet.

Tony pointed at her. "Where are you going?"

She wrapped her arms around her middle. "Make coffee?"

"Yeah. Okay." Tony glanced around the roomful of people, singling out one of the female detectives. "Lisa B. Go with her."

"Tony!" Isaac's fingers dug into his knees.

"Sorry. Protocol."

Lisa B. followed Becca from the room with an arm around Becca's shoulder. Finally, someone with a little sympathy.

Isaac turned his attention to Tony. "You have to tell me what's going on. This is craziness."

"You know I can't divulge details of an open investigation, Isaac."

"Could you stop being a cop for a minute or two and just be my friend? My mom died! And you're acting as if Becca had something to do with it. Are you out of your mind? Have a . . . heart." He sat down. Shaking. He didn't remember having stood. He knew his mom's death was inevitable, but he hadn't envisioned anything like this.

Tony was beside him now. "I hate this as much as you do."

Impossible. He shrugged off Tony's hand.

"I hope I'm wrong."

"Of course you're wrong." Isaac worked hard to keep his voice even. "Mom is gone. It was her time, I guess. Doesn't it always seem like it's too soon?" He clawed his fingers through his hair. *Dad, I wish you were here right now. You'd handle it better than I am. No. You wouldn't survive this bizarre scene.*

"That's not what the evidence is suggesting."

"What evidence?"

Tony's right knee bounced like a jackhammer. "Let the CSIs finish up in your mom's room and we'll—"

"Crime? *Crime* Scene Investigators. Do you hear what you're saying?"

"It's a hunch."

"A hunch? You're putting us through all this because of a hunch? Call off the hounds, Tony. This is ridiculous. Worse than ridiculous. This is cruel."

"Mr. Hughes?"

Isaac's neck crunched as he swung to face the person who'd called his name. A gloved investigator stood in the archway.

"Yes?"

"The locked drawer in your mother's room. Are her medications in there?"

"Yes."

"Who has the key?"

"Becca. She's . . . she was Mom's caregiver."

"Who else? We'll need to get in there."

Isaac's insides clenched. "Just Becca."

"You have no access?"

"No. She handled all the medicines. She can get you the key. She keeps it on a clip on her—" He fought for control. "On her watch."

The investigator nodded, lips pressed tightly together.

"Miss Morrow's in the kitchen," Tony added.

"I'm right here." She stood with a tray of coffee cups. Behind her, Lisa B. carried two carafes.

Isaac jumped to his feet, hurdled Tony's nervous knees, and took the tray from her hands. "I'm so sorry, Becca. This is . . . I can't even . . ."

She laid her pear-scented palm along his jawline. "It's okay. They have every reason to be suspicious. It'll be okay."

She slid the watch from her wrist, the tiny key jingling against the watchband. "You'll need this." She unclipped the key and handed it to the CSI. With gloved hands, he held it by the clip and headed back to the sunroom.

Becca glanced from Lisa B. to Tony but avoided eye contact with Isaac. "Can we do this downtown?"

Do what?

Tony rubbed his hands over his face as if scrubbing away a thought. "That would be best."

"Let's get this over with." She asked Lisa B. to get her purse from the hook in the kitchen.

"Becca, what's going on?" Isaac searched her eyes for a hint, her eyes now intent on him.

"They want to question me. That's all. I haven't done anything wrong."

He drew her in to a hug. "I know that." The twist in her hair had come undone. He buried his face in it, eyes squeezed tight, jolts of sharp pain shooting through him at wild angles like the web of a laser security system. "I know that," he whispered again.

She pulled out of the hug, palms pressed against his chest. "Don't say that with such confidence." Her sea-glass eyes glistened. "You don't know who I am."

The department could save money if they didn't have the air-conditioning cranked so high. Becca sat on her hands to warm them, then thought about who else might have been in that vinyl chair before her and slid them out from under her.

She needed to wash up. They hadn't arrested her. But it was clear from their demeanor she wasn't free to go wherever she wanted without permission.

"Ask a few questions," they'd said.

So far all that had happened was that they'd stuck her in a cold, stark room and left her alone long enough to relive the nightmare a dozen times.

Aurelia. Gone. Becca closed her eyes against the memory of the vacant, flushed body, the lamp Becca left on at Aurelia's insistence making grotesque shadows of what had once been a beautiful face. Those empty eyes, mummy-dry.

And Tony's suspicions that turned the thwap of grief to a twisted, thorny labyrinth of confusion.

What made him think anything but Aurelia's diseases had taken her life? The woman wasn't well. They should have been sitting at her bedside after the news, holding her hand one more time, kissing her hollow cheeks, thanking the Lord for taking her quietly.

Taking her. Quietly.

Saliva pooled in her mouth. She was going to throw up. Becca searched the room for a trash basket. Nothing. She held an arm across her stomach and pressed the other hand over her mouth as she retched.

"Use this!" someone said, sticking a plastic waste can under her chin.

They'd been watching her. She should have known. She wretched two more times, but nothing came out. The toxins of the scene stayed inside, churning, eating away at the lining of her organs.

"Feeling better?" the voice asked when Becca settled into the chair again.

Shaking. Still cold, but sweating. She wiped her eyes with the back of her hand and focused on breathing, slow and deep.

The detective lowered himself into the identical chair on the other side of the slate-colored table. "Would you like a sip of water?" He slid a bottled water toward her.

She shook her head but reconsidered and reached for it. One small sip. She couldn't trust her stomach with more than that.

"This has been rough on you, huh? Understandable."

Ah. The good cop of good cop/bad cop.

"I'm Detective Jansky. Need to ask you a few questions, if you don't mind. I'll be recording our conversation." He pushed a button on a hand-held recorder.

If she'd done anything wrong, this would be the moment to say, "I do mind. I'd like to speak with my lawyer, please."

But Aurelia's death had nothing to do with her.

Did it?

"When did you last see Mrs. Hughes alive,"—he tilted his head back to use his bifocals to read the top part of the report he held—"Ms. Morrow? Miss or Mrs.?"

"Miss. Four o'clock."

"You're certain? That was a quick response for something unrehearsed."

Becca took another sip of water. "I looked at my watch when I left her and knew I had two and a half hours before Isaac and his men's group arrived."

"So, they planned to arrive at six-thirty."

"Yes. No. No, Isaac and Pete planned to come early, at six, to rearrange furniture and things. They got there a little early. It must have been five-thirty when they arrived, because I was fixing Aurelia's supper so she could eat before the boys came."

"The boys?" He scratched something onto a legal pad and looked up over the top of his glasses.

"That's what Aurelia—Mrs. Hughes—called them. The boys. Isaac's men's group. They usually meet at Tony's but his wife had foot surgery and—" She took another breath and relaxed the tension in her shoulders. "And these are details you don't need to know."

"Anything might be relevant, Ms. Morrow. Where were you then between four and five-thirty 'or so' when Isaac and—"

"Pete."

"—when Isaac and Pete arrived?"

"I can't remember." Realization dawned. "I took a bath."

"Could you speak up for the recording?"

"I took a bath and read a book." She'd leave out the part about dawdling with makeup and choosing a sweater she thought a good color for her. The one she still wore. The fluorescent lights in the interrogation room made it look sickly. She could imagine what they did for her complexion.

" 'Took a bath and read a book.' " Detective Jansky said the words slowly, as if it were an alibi he couldn't buy.

That's exactly what it was—her alibi.

"And no one else was home at the time?"

"Correct."

"No one can verify where you were or what you were doing?"

"I . . . bathe alone," she said, instantly regretting the sarcasm. *Jesus, help me!*

Was that it? Was that what divine help felt like? She wasn't teleported out of the room, but fear retreated a degree or two and a little sliver of calm sneaked in to replace it.

"Of course you do." Jansky's eyes wandered in a wholly inappropriate way.

She stiffened her arms and planted her palms on the surface of the table. "I loved Aurelia. I would never do anything to hurt her. I took care of her."

"We're all aware of your position."

Becca let her hands drop into her lap. "It wasn't just my position. I took care of her because I wanted to. She's a . . . she was a beautiful soul."

"Nice." Jansky leaned back. "That little hitch in your voice at the end? Work on that. If this goes the way I think it will, you'll need that in court. A real jury-pleaser."

Her mouth watered again. No stopping it this time. Where was that waste can?

She should apologize. Detective Janksy was going to need a new legal pad.

"Is it decaf?" Isaac asked.

"Guaranteed," Pete answered.

"Not that it matters." How long were they keeping Becca at the station? "What time is it?"

Pete checked the mantel clock, the same one within Isaac's line of sight.

"Never mind. I can see. Almost ten."

"Anybody else you need to call?"

Aunt Geneva. Almost midnight her time. Could news like this wait until morning? No. "I have to call my mom's sister. I don't know what to tell her. She says she adores Becca, so this will hit her doubly hard."

Ginger took Pete's hand. That's what he should be doing right now. Taking Becca's hand. Sitting beside her. Praying for her to get through whatever questions they were asking her. How could Tony suspect Becca of knowing anything? The whole world was crazy.

"Do you want us to call?" Ginger's question hung in the air for a moment before Isaac made the connection to Aunt Geneva.

"I need to handle it."

"Not alone, though." Pete's words dovetailed with Ginger's. Same thought. Same heart. One flesh.

"I'd better get used to alone. With Mom gone, I'm an orphan again." The truth of his statement hollowed his ribcage. "I thought only little kids felt like this." He leaned his elbows on his thighs and held his head.

Two hands—one large and one smaller—rested on his shoulders. He couldn't hear their words but knew the Jarrs were praying for him.

And he was praying for Becca.

What did she mean when she said he didn't know who she was?

Geneva Larkin's phone rang four times before her voicemail kicked in. Isaac hung up. He was not leaving a message like this on a machine.

Fifteen seconds later, his cell phone rang. It was her.

"Isaac? Did you just call here?"

"That was me."

"I'm sorry, dear. I couldn't get to the phone fast enough. But I saw what I thought was your number on caller ID just as you must have been hanging up. Is everything all right out there?"

Isaac leaned into the soft leather of one of the armchairs near the fireplace in the room he once thought of as his. He had needed a quiet spot to make the call. And he had needed to feel closer to Becca. "Nothing's right, Aunt Geneva. Mom's gone."

Geneva's gasp traveled well over the phone. "Oh, honey! So soon? I thought we had more time. I was going to fly out there for Christmas to see all of you. How's J— Becca handling it? Isaac, honey, I'm so sorry. That dear woman. Nobody loved Aurelia more or had more to be grateful to her for than you and I."

Isaac's tears had been few until now. He heard traces of his mother's voice mirrored in Geneva's, traces of her heart in his aunt's compassion.

"Isaac?"

"I'm here. Processing."

"What a shock! I mean, we all knew her days were numbered." Her breaths were short, audible gulps of air. "I can hardly think straight. What can I do? Do you need me to help with the funeral arrangements? Sure you do. Tell me what you want, Isaac. I'll get a flight out tomorrow if I can."

"I won't know anything about arrangements for a day or two. Mom talked to the funeral director more than a year ago. Filled out all the paperwork when she was more lucid."

"Can I talk to Becca? She must be so upset."

The barrenness in his chest cavity returned. "She's not here right now." How much should he say? Pete and Ginger told him the Lord would let him know how far to go, how much to tell.

"Becca's not there? Where did she go?"

Pears. He stared into the cold fireplace. "They've taken her to the police station for questioning."

"What? What did you say?"

He could almost see the shock on her face from six states away. "Remember my cop friend Tony? He saw something. We don't know what. But it made him . . ." Trying to explain it heightened the ridiculousness. "Whatever he saw made him suspicious that something or someone . . ." He couldn't say the words. A shudder raked through his body. "That someone helped Mom along."

"Isaac! No!"

"It's insane. I know. Becca will be back here as soon as they get her story. She's the only one with access to Mom's medications, so they're drawing unfounded conclusions and—"

"Isaac, don't you let them at that poor girl!"

He hadn't ever heard her so animated. Her protective nature had ramped up several notches when it came to Becca, apparently.

Always loving and attentive, Aunt Geneva had kept a lid on her emotions when he was around. This was her grief talking. His was a few hours old. Hers, only a few minutes.

"It's out of my hands, Aunt Geneva. But don't worry, really. She'll be home soon and it'll all work out. Right now it's a mess. Nobody knows anything. And if they do, they're not telling me."

"Are you alone?" Her words sputtered, muffled sobs forming the spaces between them.

He surveyed Becca's room. Her touches had hardly left a mark, as if she'd never completely settled in. But her fragrance was there. "No. Pete and his wife are here at the house with me. I'm not ready to head over to the condo yet. Somebody should be here when Becca gets back."

"Don't leave her. Believe her."

What an odd thing to say. "I'm not going to leave her. She's very special to me." Sounded like a cheesy Valentine card from the discount rack.

"Isaac, please. Believe her."

Why wouldn't he?

20

They moved Becca to a different interrogation room while a custodian attended to the first one. They switched out detectives, too. Still no sign of Tony. He kept his distance. Becca didn't want to see him, but Tony was her link to Isaac. Still no sign of Isaac.

"Am I a person of interest?" she asked Detective Sanchez.

"You know the lingo." His dark eyes danced under caterpillar eyebrows. "Been here before?"

"TV."

"Ah. Such a rich source of education."

She needed to behave herself so she could be dismissed before their database revealed the obvious, disturbing, incriminating connection. "When will I be able to get back to the house? I haven't eaten." Bad choice of conversation points, considering the need for a custodian. "And I'm sure Isaac— Mr. Hughes—would appreciate it if I made up the rooms for family coming in."

Family. Geneva Larkin. Isaac would have called her by now. *Oh, Geneva!*

"A few more questions, Ms. Morrow."

She hadn't flinched, had she? *Get control of your breathing, Becca. Don't give them anything to pounce on.*

A tap at the door drew Sanchez away. Becca used the break to make a mental list of chores that might ease Isaac's burden over the next few days. She'd seen his church respond to others in need with a semi load of casseroles and cakes, gas cards, restaurant gift cards . . . Food wouldn't be an issue. But she could set up the bedrooms to look like rooms at a bed-and-breakfast—matching towels at the foot of the beds, a basket of toiletries for travelers who forgot something, scented candles in the bathrooms.

Assuming Isaac would want her to stay now that Aurelia was—

Sanchez closed the door and returned to his side of the table. He gripped the back of his chair. "So." No further comment.

He couldn't remember where he'd left off?

"You said just a few more questions?" she prompted.

His stiff brows lifted. "Preliminary lab results are back. Interesting. And we did a little background check. Maybe more than a few questions, Ms. Dennagee. Jayne."

"Isaac?"

"What?"

"Hate to wake you, buddy. Ginger and I are going to head on home, if that's okay with you. My mother-in-law's a saint, but she's going to need help getting the kids off to school. And I really should show up for work in a few hours."

Isaac blinked, hoping the words would make more sense if he could see better. "What? What time is it?"

"A little after four."

He bolted upright. Becca's chair. He'd been asleep for hours? "Is she home?"

His two friends exchanged too brief a glance before turning their attention back to him. "Not yet."

"I'm going down there." He scrubbed his teeth with his tongue. Not good enough. "Look, guys, I really appreciate your staying." Blinked again. "You should have gone back to your kids hours ago. I never dreamed it would take this long. I'm going down there."

He tripped over his shoes, bent to pick them up, and edged around his friends on his way to his en-suite bathroom. No. Becca's en suite. He pivoted. He kept a toothbrush in the duffle in his car. Still wore his work duds. He should change back into his office clothes.

"We'll let ourselves out, Isaac. But we'll be back anytime you need anything. Let us know, okay?"

"Yeah, thanks. Thanks for everything, for being here."

Ginger stepped close enough to grab one wrist. "Isaac, you have Becca call me as soon as she's able."

"Sure. Will do."

"We're all going to miss your mom. She was an amazing woman."

"Thanks, Ginger. I'm glad you knew her before she got sick."

Pete put one arm around Isaac and one around his wife. "She was amazing to the very end."

"I wish I'd been better at telling her that."

"No regrets. She loved you. You loved her," Ginger whisper-spoke. "She's not fighting for breath or fighting for a grip on reality either. Peace. Sweet peace."

He nodded. That's all he could manage.

—⋙⋘—

Her father's past clung to her like a grease stain on an old recliner.

"Why did you change your name, Jayne?"

Innocent. She'd done nothing wrong. Jansky and Sanchez were double-teaming her now. Her eyes were gritty. Teeth worse. Sanchez had offered her a stick of gum. She wished she'd taken it. How long had they been at this? Sleep deprivation made a great torture technique. She rested her elbows on the table and propped her head in the V formed by her hands.

"I changed my name because I'm *not* like him."

"Who?" The two detectives traded hits as if they were playing doubles tennis against the skinny single girl with no racket.

"You know." Becca's neck cramped. She had to sit up. Trust her muscles to hold her head.

"Tell us about him."

She ground her molars. "I'd rather not."

"Tell us about this photo, then."

She glanced at the full-color image on the 8½-by-11 printout. Wait. What? "Those are the flowers I picked for Mrs. Hughes's breakfast tray."

"Interesting. Do you know what kind of flower?"

Where was this going? "I can't remember the scientific name. They're called Angel—. Angel Face."

"Jansky here is a gardener. Did you know that? Recognized them right away."

A bubble of righteous indignation worked its way up from her belly. They'd been snapping photographs while Aurelia's body grew colder! The woman deserved honor, a hymn or something, not this.

"And Jansky recognized the green sprig, too."

"What?"

"This little bit of greenery. You picked that, too, didn't you?"

"Y-yes."

"Hmm. Little sprig of Angel Face. Little sprig of hemlock. You don't find that at all symbolic?"

Dolts. "Hemlock is for suicide. Not mercy killing." She clamped her mouth shut four seconds too late.

"Is that what it was, Jayne? A mercy killing?"

"No!"

"Then what was it?" Jansky leaned halfway across the table, his index finger sliding the photograph closer to her.

"I'd like to talk to a lawyer."

"Plenty of experience with mercy killings in your background, huh?"

She shook like a fevered child with chills. "Lawyer. Please."

⁂

"What does she need a lawyer for?" Isaac stood his ground with his hand on the front door. Tony was not coming in this time, not by invitation anyway.

"Why do you think?" Tony's face held none of last night's rigid professionalism. He looked like Isaac felt—drained. "Let me in, man."

Isaac released his grip on the door and turned toward the interior of the house. If Tony followed, so be it. "Two minutes later and I would have been on my way to the station."

"I've been there all night."

"Did you talk to her?" He didn't face him. Couldn't yet. His numb legs steered him to the kitchen with Tony on his heels.

"Not my job. I'm not the lead investigator. I'm rarely pulled in on homicides."

He whirled at that word. "What gave you the insane idea there'd been foul play? You've seen Mom lately. She was at the ER a few weeks ago. Talk to her doctor. He knows what she's been through, how close she was to her last breath." The injustice boiled inside him. How cruel to taint his mother's passing with this circus.

"We did. We talked to her doctor."

"And?"

"He said she was failing, and there was no way to predict how long she would have lasted."

"See?"

Tony pulled out one of the island stools. "He also said Becca—we'll get to that later—called him to have one of your mom's medications changed from what had been prescribed earlier. He said she thought it was making your mother excessively sleepy."

"What's your point? He agreed, didn't he? He made the adjustment. Blame him, if anyone."

Tony clasped his hands together. "We're exploring every avenue, Isaac. It's what we do."

"You saw something in the room. It made you instantly suspicious. What was it?"

The clenched fists pounded lightly on the island countertop. "Some details I can't reveal yet. I would if I could, Isaac. Believe me."

Believe her. Aunt Geneva asked him to believe Becca. Why wouldn't he?

Tony splayed his fingers on the surface. "There's something else you should know, though. About your mom's caregiver."

"I don't want to hear it." Isaac pressed his index fingers to his tear ducts. His sinuses ached.

"How long have we been friends?"

"A long time." About a hundred times longer than he'd known Becca. But right now, math wasn't the issue.

"You have to know I have your best interests at heart."

"I used to think so." He picked a knot of fuzz from his slacks, tossed it into the trashcan, and let the lid slam.

Tony pulled a piece of paper from his shirt pocket and handed it to Isaac.

"What's this?"

"Becca's real name."

"Jayne Dennagee?"

"She did everything legally. Filled out the forms. Paid the fee. She's legally Becca Morrow."

"Then what's the problem? What are you fishing for?"

"Flip it over. That's a picture of her father. Look familiar? Made every headline from here to Bangor, Maine."

"The assisted suicide turned mercy killing turned is-this-really-mercy guy?" Isaac felt behind him for the edge of the counter near the sink. A cold dread snaked down his spine.

"She needs a lawyer, Isaac." Tony's expression held warning and concern in an oil-and-water mix. "And you need to decide if you're going to help her with that or not."

<hr />

As muddled as if talking through a scuba mask twenty feet below the surface, Tony's voice droned on about Isaac's need to protect himself from any hint of implication and other non-sensical garbage.

"Stop it! Stop talking!" Isaac pressed his palms to his temples. His brain hadn't exploded yet. It was only a matter of time. Her father wasn't dead. Becca had lied to him.

"I know this is hard," Tony said, sliding off the stool. He took a step toward Isaac but came no closer. "I know you care about her. You just lost your mom. I am so sorry you have to go through this. You should be, like, picking out your mom's songs or talking to Pastor Nick about the eulogy, choosing flowers . . ."

Becca was so good for his mom. The last months, hard as they were, had been the happiest she'd been in more than a year. The happiest he'd been, too. He couldn't lose them both on the same day.

"Is she okay?"

"Becca? It's been a little rough, from what I hear."

Lord God . . .

"She's okay, Isaac. But I . . ."

"What?"

"I don't think it's too soon to start praying for her."

"You're the one who got her mixed up in this farce."

"I was doing my job."

"You didn't trust her from the beginning."

"I'm trained to be observant. Things didn't add up. *East* of Duluth? Never says the name of her hometown? Any time we ask her anything about her life, she changes the subject. Come on. You must have wondered about that."

Isaac looked at the man's image on the piece of paper Tony had given him. Yes, he'd seen it before. Made his skin crawl. "You need this back?" No wonder Becca faked her story.

"Nah. We have more copies."

He ran water in the sink and fed its shreds into the garbage disposal. As soon as he flipped the switch, he regretted how it might gum up the blades. The least of his concerns. Life was messier than it had ever been and all he could do was snap at the people he thought were his friends, stiff-arm the mourning he should have been facing, and admit that he was probably well on his way to loving a woman with a past he'd fed down the disposal.

Ginger must have done the dishes. Or Lisa B. and Becca took care of that when they made coffee a lifetime ago. The kitchen was spotless. That seemed so wrong. Order should have stabilized him in the middle of the chaos.

And when I'm gone.

A distant memory of his mother's voice made him turn. She wasn't there.

But the gossamer phrase drew his thoughts to the picture on the wall in his mom's old room upstairs. He'd commented on it several times. A photo from the "healing" trip he and his mom had taken with Aunt Geneva six months after his dad died. Inside Passage cruise to Alaska. Sweet.

Traveling with the two sisters—one of them only living in reality part-time—provided its share of comic moments. Lots of memories, though. His mom was right. The scenery held soul-healing properties—the vastness of the sea and mountains, the glaciers calving—ancient ice sloughing into the strange-colored, milky, aqua water, reminiscing about Dad, watching his mom and Aunt Geneva laugh together . . .

One of the many photos they'd taken hung in his mom's room. Every few months she'd tell him, "And when I'm gone, Isaac, you'll see it for what it really is."

He'd brushed it aside. "Yeah, Mom. Alaska. Healing. Life goes on. I get it."

She'd squeeze his hand. "And when I'm gone . . ."

The sentence rarely ended. It hung there in space.

Isaac checked on Tony, who'd moved to the living room. Still on the phone with his superiors. Isaac gestured that he was going upstairs. Tony nodded that he got the message. Isaac noted the grandfather clocked had stopped ticking again. Tupping, as Becca called it. Ornery clock. He reached to start the pendulum again, then paused. His mom was gone. Who cared whether the clock worked or not?

He hadn't been in his mom's old bedroom, the one she'd shared with his dad for just shy of fifty years, since he and Becca moved his mom to the sunroom. He saw the contrast even more clearly now. The room was dark and stuffy compared to the light and—his breath hitched—life in the sunroom. No music here. No easy view of the garden. So far removed from the center of everything. Even with the sun now over the horizon, the room still seemed too gray to support life.

Becca had suggested redecorating in brighter colors, lighter fabrics, before he sold the house, if he ever chose to do so. Staging, she reminded him.

He moved to the windows and pulled the drapes open as wide as he could. If Aunt Geneva got an early enough flight, she'd sleep in this room tonight, unless it made her squirmy. Sissy and Bud and the kids, plus a bunch of other relatives awaited his word about which day would work for the memorial service.

Isaac turned to the photo that had drawn him to the room. It was on the wall opposite the bed's headboard. His mother had it constantly in her line of sight. He lifted it from the nail in the wall. Not a speck of dust. Becca was meticulous in everything she did.

Then how did she get caught?

Where did that come from? He chased the thought with a low growl. She couldn't have had anything to do with this. Impossible. That's not who she was.

He ran his hand around the frame as if subconsciously trying to rub it awake, like a genie's lantern. "Tell me your secrets," he said aloud. "'And when I'm gone . . .'"

In the photo, he stood between his mom and Aunt Geneva—a younger, darker-haired version of his mom—with an arm across the shoulders of both women. In the background, the deck rail was all that separated them from an endless sea and sky. The expression on his mother's face—serenity. Geneva's—joy. His expression? Peace. The trip had been a good idea, no matter how much maneuvering he'd had to do to free his work schedule. His dad would have loved it.

"'And when I'm gone.'" He flipped the picture. Nothing on the back of the frame. Had she hidden a message to him under the backing?

"Isaac? You done up there?"

"Down in a minute." He bent back the clips holding the photo in the frame. No slip of paper tucked behind. No message written on the back of the photo. What had he expected? A poem? Her favorite scripture? Maybe the message was as simple as the look of serenity on his mom's face. A priceless gift.

"Thanks, Mom." He drank in the reminder that no matter when or how she left this earth, her soul retained its sense of serenity, a look that now would never leave her.

He needed to deliver the picture to the funeral director. *Make her look like that. And if you can't, then keep the casket closed and put this nearby.*

As they walked from the parking lot toward the entrance to the precinct, Isaac pumped Tony for answers.

"Tell me what I should do. My corporate attorney isn't going to handle something like this. Who does Becca need?"

"You're sure you want to—?"

"She needs legal counsel, doesn't she?"

"I wouldn't recommend the lawyer who defended her dad." Tony stopped walking. "Sorry, man. That was low."

"We all have some apologies to make when this is over, when the truth comes out. You'll see."

"When the heart gets involved, it's hard to see things for what they are." Tony picked up the pace again.

See things for what they are. "And sometimes we can't see clearly *unless* the heart gets involved. You know what I mean?" What did a collapsed lung feel like? The pain under his ribcage, sharp and relentless, wouldn't let him draw a full breath.

Tony had no comeback.

"Give me the name of a good lawyer, Tony. I think I'm supposed to do this. If I'm wrong . . ." He shivered despite the sun already heating the pavement. "I can't be wrong."

21

She'd been told someone was contacting a lawyer on her behalf. *I'd rather talk to Isaac.* Until the lawyer arrived, she was to sit tight. In a windowless room. Great way to make a sane person lose her religion. Or make her consider getting more serious about it.

She wouldn't stoop to negotiate with the Almighty. "If you get me out of this, God, I'll—"

She had nothing with which to bargain. An odd sensation swept over her. The first wave of sympathy for her father. He'd sat in a room like this. He wasn't evil. He was horribly, horribly misguided. How had her mother's illness warped his thinking? Did anyone listen when he tried to explain how far his thoughts had wandered from an ethical center, or why?

He had no excuse for what he'd done, or for making decisions only God had the right to make. Bertram Dennagee deserved his sentence. He owed his victims and their families so much more than that. He owed her.

But for the first time, Becca wondered if anyone had listened to him.

And more clearly than ever, she connected with the idea that the kind of grace Geneva talked about, the kind she kept stumbling upon in the Bible in her borrowed room, had nothing to do with what we deserve and everything to do with an irrepressible love in the heart of God, a God whose haunting "Come to Me" sounded so different from her father's attempts to push her aside.

Crumbs from the vending machine breakfast burrito they'd offered her dotted the table top. It had helped a little with the headache. She needed to stay hydrated. The churning in her stomach subsided as the hours ticked by. Curious, since the tension continued to crescendo as she sat in the black hole of uncertainty.

Some "persons of interest" probably use their waiting time to get their story straight in their mind. Timing. Actions. Alibis.

She relived the progression of events, not to cement her story—to try to make sense of it. Not fabricating a story this time. Trying to get to the heart of the truth. The irony caught her by the throat.

Had she heard any unusual noises during her bath? She never let the monitor out of earshot. She'd double-checked after Pete stormed into the house with the news that sent them running. It was on. Batteries good. She'd heard nothing.

Maybe she wasn't completely innocent. What would have happened if she'd checked on Aurelia before heading to the kitchen to warm the soup? Was she alive then? Could she have—?

Done what? Becca was well aware of the do-not-resuscitate order.

Someone beyond the closed door laughed. Beyond the *closed* door. She held the paper coffee cup to her breastbone and let the aroma fill her nostrils. *Breathe in. Breathe out.* The coffee long cold and reminding her of a burnt marshmallow flavor from months ago, it still served a purpose, rooting her to a normal smell in an abnormal world. The surface of the liquid shivered. Earthquake? No. Becca-quake.

Isaac, I need to talk to you, to tell you the whole story. It won't change anything and won't bring back your mom. But I'm not my father's daughter.

Did she hear him? It almost sounded like Isaac's voice somewhere in the din.

She would pound on the door and demand to see him except for two things. She'd lost her energy for anger and demanding years ago. And she didn't want him to see her here. Not like this. Not for this reason.

It wouldn't have to be across a candlelit table in a five-star restaurant in La Jolla. She'd settle for a grilled cheese sandwich and tomato soup with him in the kitchen back h—

Home.

⸺∞⸺

Damp on her cheek. Hard and damp.

Becca opened her eyes. Cold gray walls tilted at an odd angle. She'd fallen asleep with the left side of her face stuck to the table, her hands in her lap. And she was drooling. Nice.

She wiped the corner of her mouth with a fist and glanced at the surveillance camera in the corner near the ceiling. Someone saw that. She flicked the hair off the back of her neck. Bracing herself on the table, the center of her world, she pushed herself to stand. It took thirty-four steps to circle the room, but she intentionally took them at a slow pace, so the camera didn't see a guilt-ridden caged animal, merely a woman needing to stretch her legs.

On her third lap, the door opened, letting in a rash of noise and a Kevin Bacon lookalike with better hair and a leather briefcase with teethmarks on the corners. She must have been staring. The man closed the door and set the briefcase center-stage on the table. He nodded toward it.

"Bite marks make me seem tougher than I am," he said, extending his hand. "Damon Todd. For now, I'm your attorney."

Becca shook his hand. Warm. Solid. Not what she expected. "For now?"

"It's up to you. I was asked to offer my services. We agreed on my fee. But it's your choice, ultimately."

"You're not court-appointed?"

He laughed as he dug in his briefcase. "With fine luggage like this? Actually, it was my wife's miniature dachsund's teething toy, so . . ."

How could he be so cavalier? Didn't he know what they suspected her of doing? "You said, '*We* agreed.' Who agreed?"

"Friend of yours. Geneva Larkin. Sister of the deceased."

Becca's breath caught in her throat. "I can't let her do that."

"Suit yourself," Mr. Todd said, sliding his papers back into the chew toy. "I'll go have a talk with the second in line."

"Excuse me?"

"Mr. Hughes called me thirty seconds after my conversation with Ms. Larkin. Can't say I've seen that often, considering what they've lost. They must believe in you." He held her gaze an extra moment. "Take your pick."

Becca tapped her feet together, as if that would help her think. "I can't repay either one."

"If we get you out of here soon, and if we can find another explanation for the evidence they have against you . . ."

". . . and since I'm innocent?"

He smiled. "Exactly." His suit jacket pulled a little across his abdomen. He seemed visibly relieved when able to undo the button. "Let's chat a little."

"I don't even know what they're calling evidence."

"We could start at the beginning, or right here. Okay. Obviously, your fingerprints are all over the room."

"Of course." She pressed both hands to her middle. "I was her primary caregiver."

"The numbers aren't adding up in the lab work."

"What do you mean?"

"I asked for clarification. Toxicology isn't aligning with the physician orders for her medications. Lots to sort out there. We'll give it a few hours before I rattle a cage or two."

Someone must have fiddled with the air conditioner setting. The room was no longer icy.

"And there's the hemlock/Angel Face reference, but that wouldn't—"

"—hold up in court."

"Right. *Perry Mason* reruns?"

"*Hawaii Five-O.*"

He put down the pen he'd been clicking. "Then there's the San Diego Zoo full of paternal elephants in the room."

"My dad."

"Again, that's not enough to convict anyone."

"Am I being arrested?"

"Not yet. I'm going to do my best to keep that from happening. But your father's history isn't helping. I'll be honest. It'll keep law enforcement digging. All the makings of a TV drama, you know?" He resumed clicking his pen, then seemed to notice it might annoy her. He reached into his briefcase and withdrew a drinking straw. His thumb closed over one end, then opened, then closed.

"Recently quit smoking?" she asked.

"Earlier today."

Wonderful. "About my dad, I don't now nor have I ever approved of his actions. He and I have widely differing opinions about what he did."

"He considered it a public service."

"I know."

"Acts of mercy."

She sighed. "I'm not my father. I came out here to put as much distance as I could between my life and his."

"Sold."

"Really?"

"Everything they have so far is circumstantial. Unfortunate, but circumstantial. You say nothing more without clearing it through me, though. Got it?"

She nodded, mouth shut to underscore the depth of her understanding.

"We'll know more after the autopsy."

A small cry slipped out.

He angled his head, his eyebrows asking the question before his words came out. "You worried about the autopsy?"

"No. I didn't think about their having to cut her open. I loved her."

"Wish love were a good enough defense, Ms. Morrow. FYI, it isn't."

———

They wouldn't let Isaac see Becca. Once they knew the attorney was with her, Tony and Isaac parted company. He couldn't go home.

Isaac closed the door to his office, expecting to find it a sanctuary. Every project file, every sticky note, every phone message screeched, "This isn't what's important right now."

The tasks he'd thought so necessary to life and livelihood showed their true, bleached-out colors in light of his mom's death and what was happening to Becca. How long could he turn his back on his job before it all fell apart? But how long could he turn his back on his grief before *he* fell apart?

He sank into his office chair. Had the leather grown stiff over the last couple of days? He arched his back. Why didn't it fit him like it had in the past?

His laptop kept him updated away from the office. It seemed an annoyance rather than a convenience lately. Of the "must-do" items on his desk, only two needed immediate attention. A phone call and a signature. The rest could wait.

He swiveled his chair to look out the window. What if he'd said, "The rest can wait. Mom needs me," months earlier? What if he'd found a way to better balance what happened in this office and what happened at home?

Poorer bank account. Richer life.

The thought came to him as if texted to his brain.

The phone rang. Mrs. Gallum had taken the morning off for a podiatrist appointment. Hammer toes. It was up to Isaac to answer.

"Hughes Commercial Realty. This is Isaac Hughes."

"I hoped I'd catch you there."

"Aunt Geneva?" He checked his cell phone. Three unanswered messages. All from her. When had he muted the phone?

"I'm here."

"At the airport?"

"You didn't get my messages? When I couldn't reach you, I rented a car."

Isaac flicked his cell phone. It skated across his desk until it hit a stack of folders. "I'm sorry you had to do that."

"I think it's actually better. I'll have my own wheels to come and go. Although the traffic was enough to scramble my nerves."

"How long can you stay?"

"How long do you need me here?"

The first word that came to mind was *forever*. But he knew better than to count on forever anymore. "You're amazing. This whole mess is . . ."

"A mess."

"Did you know you retained a lawyer for Becca minutes before I tried?"

"You did?"

"How did you choose Damon Todd?"

She hesitated an uncomfortable half second. Like Becca sometimes did. "I have connections."

"I guess you do."

"Oh. You have a delivery out here. Looks like envelopes."

Why would FedEx deliver envelopes to the house? "Where are you?"

The office door opened. The darker-haired, younger version of his mother stood in the doorway, holding a cell phone to her ear. If he couldn't have his mom, this was the next best thing.

The chair might have grown stiffer, but his Aunt Geneva's embrace hadn't. His footing felt solid for the first time in days.

"You've lost weight," he said when they'd broken the long-awaited hug.

She smiled and struck a model pose. "A quarter of a pound. Thanks for noticing."

The chuckle—brief as it was—felt good. His mom would have approved.

"So, you're staying at the house," he stated.

"I assumed that would be okay."

"Definitely."

"I buzzed out there first. Sobering to see it all locked tight."

Isaac grabbed his briefcase and directed his aunt to the outer office. "I've been thinking about moving some things from the condo to the house for a while. Setting up a command center. Crisis Central, we could call it."

She winked or flinched. "Why don't you just call it *home?*"

━━━

Two hours later they'd eaten and gotten his aunt's luggage moved to a room upstairs. She'd chosen the smaller back bedroom. He didn't blame her.

"Do you think we can see her now?" she asked, her traveling clothes exchanged for something more friendly to Southern California temps.

He doubted the mortician would even have his mother's body yet, considering the time he'd been warned it might take for an autopsy. "She's changed so much. So thin. Frail. Hardly anything left of her at the end."

"I meant Becca. Aurelia's dancing with Jesus. We'll pay respects to the body that housed her in due time."

"Her diseased mind thought she could, but Mom couldn't dance."

"Not before now."

She was so good for him. Kept him rooted. Both in the physical—*You have to eat, Isaac*—and in faith. "About Becca. To my knowledge, they haven't tried to charge her with anything. Can you talk to Damon Todd? I could ask Tony, but contrary to popular assumption, he doesn't live at the station. And . . . he's . . ."

Aunt Geneva leveled her gaze. "You are aware he was doing his job that night?"

"I understand that, factually. But his ridiculous suspicions are costing a lot of people a lot of grief." He poured himself an iced tea then offered her one. "Did you know about Becca's father?"

She slid onto a stool by the kitchen island and accepted the tea. "Yes. I knew."

It was his turn to pause before answering. "Why wouldn't you mention a thing like that when you told us she was looking for a job?"

"You don't have to know everything about a person's past to know who she is right now." Her words ricocheted around the room.

He took a long, thought-gathering drink. "When this is over, when things are back to—"

"What is it, Isaac?"

"No. I shouldn't have let myself consider it right now."

All the contours of Aunt Geneva's face softened. "Tell me what's on your heart."

"I want to know about my own past." He scratched at an itch on the back of his neck. "I want to find my real mom."

Tears gathered in her eyes. Isaac could always count on her to sympathize, but he didn't want to make her cry more than she probably had since her sister died.

"She was your real mom, Isaac."

"I know. I mean . . . It's not wrong for me to wonder, is it? So many unanswered questions. Health history. Genealogy. Someday, I'd like to find out where I really belong."

Aunt Geneva turned her face toward the windows. He should have known better. Lousy at caregiving, he was even lousier at grieving.

"I need to qualify that, Aunt Geneva. I loved Mom and Dad."

"And they loved you." She didn't turn her gaze from the windows.

"I would never have wanted to hurt them by searching for my birth parents while they were still alive." He couldn't find the right words. Never could. "Please forget I said anything.

We haven't even set a date for Mom's funeral yet and it's as if I'm already thinking six months ahead to when it might be appropriate for me to—"

"Isaac." She lifted her chin as she faced him, the look of a thousand griefs pooling in her eyes. "Here. You belong right here."

He'd apologize for disrespecting his dead mother, her dead sister, later. After he hired someone to help him figure out how to say how sorry he was for thinking of himself at a time like that.

Maybe it was his own ache, his own longing for his mother—the Aurelia Hughes version—that reignited that old, familiar tug. An adoptive mom like his didn't deserve that. He'd loved her as fully as anyone could. Together, Aurelia and Douglas Hughes had parented him so well, most of his friends were jealous. For good reason.

Okay. New plan. Focus on celebrating their lives for now, on grieving how much he had lost with their deaths. Plenty. He might be fifty years old before he allowed himself to think about the faceless woman out there somewhere—if she were even alive—who felt she had no choice but to give him up for adoption.

She'd felt remorse, hadn't she? She had no other option?

Isaac David Hughes! When Dad died, I thought I knew what it was like to lose someone and not be able to think straight. It's worse than that. I've become detestable. His mother lay halfway between a morgue and a funeral home. Becca was stuck at the police station. And he couldn't force himself to think an unselfish thought.

Aunt Geneva had excused herself to freshen up but now seemed more eager than ever to talk to Becca. "I called Mr. Todd's office," she said, her mood as sweet as if he hadn't been a jerk. "He's in court. His assistant will give him our message."

"Great. Thank you." He set his empty tea glass in the sink. *No, that wasn't right.* He rinsed it and stuck it in the dishwasher. "What now?"

"Have you seen the answering machine? It's blinking like it's about to explode. I'd say you have some calls to return."

"You talked to Bud and Sissy?" Isaac's eyes itched. He blinked. Rubbed. No better.

"Yes. They're still waiting for word about the funeral arrangements. Do you need a nap? Want to tackle the answering machine later?"

"I slept a little last night. Don't know how, but I did."

"Good," she said. "It probably wasn't enough. Some is better than none."

He snatched two frozen Hershey bars from the freezer.

She shook her head. "No thanks. That quarter pound I lost is begging to come back."

"Tell me what you know about Becca."

"On second thought, a frozen candy bar sounds divine right now."

He tossed it to her and waited while she peeled the wrapper and took her first crunching bite. She fully swallowed but still didn't respond.

"About Becca?"

"She is the sweetest thing."

"I know." Must have been the caffeine in the chocolate. Heat crept up his neck. Caffeine will do that.

"I've known her almost all her life."

"You knew her as Jayne."

Aunt Geneva bit off another hunk of chocolate and chewed slowly. She closed up the wrapper around the remaining half and crossed the room to stick it in the freezer. With her back to him she said, "All those years as Jayne. Yes."

"Do I have to start from scratch to understand who she is?"

Aunt Geneva closed the freezer door, but didn't turn. "Do you have to start from scratch to know who you are?" She paused, then added, "Digging into the past turns up as many dead relatives as it does heirlooms."

22

You're free to go. Not free to leave town." Damon Todd patted her hand as if that were all Becca needed in order to sleep soundly tonight.

"That's it?"

"Not the end of . . . this." He swept his hand toward the now open door of the windowless room, toward the noisy, suspicious squad room.

"So, what do I do?"

Todd put a hand on the small of her back and pushed her toward the door. "Go home. Rest up. And, as I tell all my clients, stay out of trouble."

Really?

"Seriously, Becca." He leaned close to whisper in her ear, "Any comment about your father right now would not be in your best interest." Then, straightening, "Do you have a ride home?"

Home. Did she have a ride? Did she have a home? "I don't think . . ."

"Easy fix. One moment." He pointed his cell phone in her direction, then keyed something with one thumb. "Geneva. Damon."

He paused, listening.

"I'm here with her now. And the lady needs a ride."

Another pause.

"Yes. For the time being."

Becca imagined Geneva Larkin on the other end of the discussion. Nothing about Becca's life was her own anymore, if it ever had been.

"Great. I'm heading back to my office. Going to be a late one tonight. We'll talk again. Good to hear from you. Yes, you too." He slid his phone into his jacket pocket and smiled a Kevin Bacon smile at Becca. "There you go."

<hr />

Almost Thanksgiving, and the air rested sweet on her skin like late June in the Midwest. She sat on a bench at the far edge of the property while she waited for Mrs. Larkin. The last time she'd climbed into a car Geneva drove, the woman had just come from Becca's/Jayne's father's sentencing.

Would the day ever come when every experience wasn't somehow linked to the ugliness of the past? She knew better than to expect life to be one giggle after another. But every story, every sentence ended with a unique conclusion with her dad's name embedded in it.

Add another so they don't end that way.

Lack of sleep strikes again. She was talking to herself.

Try it.

She retraced the offending thought. What would it sound like if she tacked on another sentence? " . . . *had just come from her father's sentencing. But she now sat half a country away, with a new name, a new life, and a fragile hope that her future could be different from her past.*"

Becca stopped there, refusing to cave to the temptation to bookend the positive with another patched-on sentence about the night she'd just spent as a "person of interest."

She needed a shower. Her head hurt. But she was breathing sun-warmed air. The impossibly tall palm trees reminded her how far she was from now-barren cornfields that abutted the small town on the edge of insanity.

Isaac had been through grief before. He'd be okay on his own.

She'd get a job out here, once the police mess blew over. It would blow over. It had to. Her job prospects would be slim in this town if the press twisted the Dennagee connection, even once the truth came out about Aurelia's death, whatever it was. She could move to Northern California. How hard could it be to disappear into the fabric of an overpopulated state?

Once this storm blew over. Once Aurelia was properly honored. Once she knew Isaac was going to be okay without her.

What was she thinking? After all this, his life would be far less stressful without her in the picture. *"Let me introduce my friend Becca. The police accused her of being involved in my mother's murder, but then later found out it wasn't her. Lucky for us, huh?"*

Great foundation for a relationship.

Who lived on the edge of insanity? After all they'd put her through, Becca couldn't stop herself from praying for the law enforcement officials, that they'd discover what really happened.

"Becca!"

The call came from a neon-blue compact car at the curb. Geneva Larkin waved wildly through the passenger window. That meant . . .

Bent at an odd angle to fit behind the wheel sat Isaac Hughes.

Becca held her breath and slid in behind Geneva, where there remained legroom for more than toddlers. "Thanks for coming to get me."

Isaac waited for her while she buckled her seatbelt, then signaled and pulled into traffic. "How are you doing?"

Lousy. "I'm okay."

She saw him flick a glance at his Aunt Geneva in the passenger seat.

"How about you two?" Her throat pinched the words on the way out. She could feel a good cry brewing.

"We're hanging in there." Geneva answered for them. "Good to see you, Becca."

"You can call me Jayne if you want. He knows."

Geneva faced forward. "I would, but that's not your name anymore. You'd have to go back to court again if you wanted to change it to something other than Becca Morrow."

True. How had Geneva managed to get her smiling with all that had transpired?

Geneva craned her neck to talk over her shoulder. "How was it in there, honey? The truth."

Isaac repositioned his grip on the steering wheel. Becca could see him better than she could Geneva from this vantage point. Truth. About everything. He deserved it. Lies backfire.

"I survived. It went a lot smoother for me after Mr. Todd showed up. Thank you, by the way."

"You're welcome," the two said in unison.

Isaac explained, "We're still wrestling over who writes his checks."

"I don't know what to say."

"You already did. Thank you is enough."

As the palms and intersections marked their progress, Becca pondered the awkwardness of the unspoken. She broke the silence with, "It will take me a few minutes to pack."

Geneva and Isaac exchanged glances again. "You're not leaving." Another duet.

"Not leaving town. I'm not allowed to at this point. I can find a motel with long-term rental."

Isaac tugged his seatbelt away from his chest. "No one's taken over your room, Becca."

"I'm upstairs in the rear bedroom," Geneva added. "It will be good to have you there at the house. We have some catching up to do when we get a minute."

"But Isaac—"

"My condo's not that far, if you need anything. I'll be at the house a lot, I'm sure. For the next few days, at least. But there's room upstairs for the rest of the family coming in. No need for you to move right now, Becca."

She didn't understand. How could he not be creeped out by her presence in that house, even if he was clinging to a shard of hope she was innocent? Hadn't it occurred to him that with Aurelia gone, she was no longer employed?

"The Hughes kindness factor."

Awkward. Awkward, awkward, awkward. She'd said it aloud. Now no one was talking.

They stopped at a fast-food drive-thru—In and Out—saying they understood why she didn't want to go in anywhere, why she just wanted to get home.

The onions sat heavy in her pulverized stomach. She closed the wrapper of the sandwich after the first bite. Geneva had suggested a fresh strawberry milkshake as advertised to go with the chicken Caesar sandwich. Becca had taken three sips before it registered that the last shake she'd had was when she'd attempted to get Aurelia to eat.

She nested the cup in the holder on the narrow console between the two back seats. Eating—overrated.

"Do we need any groceries?" she ventured.

Geneva chortled. "Oh, dear child, you should see the warehouse of food that's been brought in! The sign of caring friends, I always say. The casseroles and ham sandwiches start showing up before the coroner pronounces 'time of death.'" She looked at the other passengers in the car with her, her head tilted down apologetically. "Just an expression."

Isaac glanced in the rearview mirror. "Ginger volunteered to come organize it all. She's recording who gave what and where it is—fridge, freezer, the big freezer in the garage. That will help when it's time for us to write thank-you notes."

Us? He'd looked at her, too. Not just his aunt. They acted as if she were a family member rather than The Accused.

"That's what we should have done, Isaac," his aunt said. "Pick up some thank-you notes."

"Add it to my list," he said.

He didn't need one more thing to do. "Add it to mine," Becca said. She must be talking in her sleep. What would possess her to act as if she were part of the solution, not the lion's share of the problem? "If you . . . if you tell me exactly what you want."

Geneva's "Flowers" burst out concurrently with Isaac's "No flowers."

Flowers and a sprig of greenery had been part of the detectives' discussions with her.

If Isaac ever looked at Becca seriously again, the way he had started to before his mom died—in a way that stirred her soul—it was a sure thing he wouldn't call her *Angelface*.

Uncertainty hung in the air like fog over a swamp. Isaac watched Becca pour herself into any hands-on labor—dishes, meal prep, laundry—but she stayed in the shadows when others were around, as if wishing her superpower were a cloak of invisibility. She refused to answer the phone or the door, at first finding excuses why she was needed elsewhere. After a few days, it was assumed she'd disappear.

Isaac ached for what she'd been through. He prayed for her. But it didn't seem appropriate to force her to talk or to engage with guests and family. The situation would read "weird" on anyone's scale.

Nothing functioned normally. Isaac's work had been put on hold, except for the essential. Funny how *essential* meant something different than it had a few months ago. Between the two of them, he and Geneva pooled efforts to keep the place upright, doing most of his work from the condo or the house, trusting the "Family Emergency" message that his secretary had rehearsed would make adequate apologies for him.

Becca moved her things to the sewing room. Was she more intent on distancing herself from the sunroom crime scene or was she stuck on the ridiculous notion that she didn't "belong" in his old suite? He couldn't argue. Neither point would chalk up a win.

A closed-casket memorial service had been his mother's wish. It seemed the best choice. The photo Isaac loved so much would show her true self.

They felt their way through the planning, relying heavily on the notes his mother left with the funeral home director, notes created shortly after she'd become aware she battled not a single disease, but two. She said she wanted her "acceptance speech" ready, no matter which disease won.

It pained him not to include Becca in the preparations for the service. She'd been present for the most intimate and the sweetest conversations with his mom in the last days of her life. But that was the problem. She'd been present. No one could deny that. Some couldn't forget.

If asked to chart the details of the last few days, he'd be hard-pressed. One meal blurred into another. One task into another. Aunt Geneva had to remind him who he'd just talked to or where they were headed when running errands related to his mom's service.

Isaac had insisted his aunt and Becca ride with him to the church. They needed to be together. Becca opened her mouth to object, but Aunt Geneva put her fingers across Becca's mouth and spoke for her. "We'd be blessed. Thank you, Isaac."

The money he'd spent on a classy black suit for his Dad's funeral meant he was spared the discomfort of shopping for one now. It fit well and was relatively comfortable, as far as funeral attire goes. After the line of mourners he expected prior to the time of the memorial, it would boast hug marks and maybe a smudge of makeup from an overzealous but well-meaning woman among his mom's group of friends. Right now, it still looked crisp. Sharp. He'd chosen a Monterey-blue shirt and a tie a shade darker to keep from looking too funeral-like. He'd watch Becca's expression to see if the combo worked.

It must have. Her eyes widened and the faintest of smiles teased her lips.

Aunt Geneva twirled for him. "Will this do?"

"You look great."

She persisted. "You're not looking at me, Isaac. You're looking at the young one."

He snapped his attention back to his aunt. "I meant it. You look great. Becca looks . . . stunning."

Her blush offered her pale cheeks just the right color. Her black dress was simple, elegant, with a stripe of black sheen—satin, maybe?—running from shoulder to where the dress ended just at her knees. She looked . . . polished.

"Your aunt insisted on taking me shopping." Becca's facial features read almost apologetic.

"I approve."

Aunt Geneva took his arm. "I knew you would. Let's head to the church. It'll be a long day. Time to collect some memories to hold us."

Isaac pulled his keys from his pocket. When had his heart ever been this heavy heading to church? He stepped back to let the women precede him to the car. Unmistakable—that heady scent of pears.

23

Hard as it had been, Becca cherished every minute she'd spent at the Hughes home, even after her release from questioning. She'd stayed in the background as much as possible to avoid making things even more difficult for their family. But the faith that permeated the atmosphere in their home intoxicated her. With all the distress, they floated on an invisible undercurrent of peace.

The faith that bookmarked Aurelia's Bible bookmarked Isaac's and Geneva's lives as well. Becca's was just emerging from "without form and void" by comparison. She'd said as much to Geneva as they fixed breakfast one morning.

"I know the words, Mrs. Larkin. You taught me well in girls' club all those years ago. I know what faith is supposed to do— what it's doing for you and Isaac and the others."

"What's that?" Geneva had asked, dicing mango slices into small bits.

Becca fought for the word. Rejected several. "Sustain."

"Hmm."

"Your faith sustains you. No matter what. You love no matter what. You give no matter what. You trust God no matter what."

"That's the definition of faith, Becca. Trusting no matter what."

"Even when it doesn't make sense?"

"Especially when it doesn't make sense. Especially then."

She'd landed her point by lowering her voice, of all things. Becca had paid attention.

How much should she reveal? "I have a feeling . . ." No.

Mrs. Larkin had laid her knife on the cutting board beside the chunks of mango and waited for Becca to finish her thought. If she couldn't feel safe around Geneva . . . She owed her honesty. "I've had a feeling lately that if my faith were stronger, I could have handled my dad's situation better."

"Better in what way? Not caring about what he did?"

"No! My faith makes me care."

"Then, by 'handling' you mean . . ."

Becca hadn't had an answer at the time. She did now as they rode to the service. She should have said, "I wouldn't be broken." She considered reaching from the backseat of Isaac's car, tapping her on the shoulder, and letting her know she had found the word. *Broken.*

Until a few days ago, the sight of the two people in the seat in front of her had served as Steri-strips for the broken places, holding the bits together so they could heal. Now the two she loved most represented a new pain.

Did she mean that? Love? Both of them?

In order for their grief fissures to mend, she'd have to leave. Becca was a constant reminder that Isaac's mom had died under "suspicious circumstances." Sure, they said they believed she had nothing to do with it. But their imaginations wouldn't stay on vacation forever. They'd have to suspect she'd done something, even if unintentionally.

She read it in the faces of the mourners who parted to let them into the church. Sympathetic toward Isaac and Geneva.

First surprised, then either mortified—whispering behind their hands—or fidgety at Becca's presence. Geneva said she was imagining things. Despite her companions' invitation to sit up front with the family, she would find a spot behind a potted plant or a column, in the back row or the parking lot.

A few attendees made it a point to talk to her. Pete. Ginger. Others of Isaac's friends. She couldn't tell if the resistance in the air came from her or them. She'd been an outsider so few months ago. Aurelia's death—no, the connection to her father—made her an outcast.

"How are you holding up, Becca?"

"Fine."

"What are your plans now?"

No good way to bring that conversation to a satisfactory conclusion. It seemed more ridiculous than ever to talk about returning to nursing school. She feigned a need for the restroom so many times, she feared someone would offer to give her a ride to the clinic.

Surrounded by their church friends, Isaac, Geneva, and the rest of their family members surfed the unique waves of grief for the death of a saint. Those waves could flatten a person unprepared for them. If ridden well, the experience could be exhilarating.

That's what Aurelia had said the afternoon before she died.

Becca found a spot near the exit from which to watch the surfers.

—◦◦◦—

As she expected, the service celebrated a life well lived, a faith well lived. She dabbed at tears through the songs and the eulogy. She fought an almost irrepressible urge to run forward and wrap an arm around Isaac when he fought to get through the good-bye letter he'd written to his adoptive mom. Not Becca's place. Not the right time. Not culturally acceptable considering her recent stint at the precinct and the name with which she was born.

The sanctuary had filled quickly. Becca and a young mom with a newborn occupied the last row. Becca scanned the crowd, marveling that so many cared about the woman who hadn't been in her right mind or her right health for more than two years. She'd seen some of them visit, knew others would have, if they'd known what to say.

The back of one figure drew her attention. The bald spot and collar-brushing curls reminded her of someone she couldn't place. If he turned his profile to her, she might be able to tell.

As if listening to her thoughts, the man rested his elbow on the back of his chair and slowly swiveled his upper body to face her. Misaligned eyes. Half a smile and a head nod shot through her like a shard of ice. Riggo? What was he doing here?

He faced forward again at the pastor's words, "Let us pray."

She closed her eyes but heard only snatches of the prayer. Riggo was a member of the community. He had every right to be here. Is this where he attended church? She'd never seen him.

Why did his presence make her uneasy? Perfectly wonderful people had misaligned eyes.

But . . .

But none of them except Riggo had touched Aurelia's medications.

Prayer or not, she looked up. He was gone.

Tony. She had to find Tony!

As the pallbearers stood to escort the casket from the sanctuary, Becca slipped out to the large, high-ceilinged, skylit foyer. The funeral procession, the casket, all the people would file right past her if she stayed there. Where had Tony been sitting? She hadn't noticed. Oh! He was one of the pallbearers.

She wouldn't have opportunity to talk to him until after the graveside service. She ducked down the hall toward the restrooms, her favorite haunt. She locked herself in a stall, pressed her hands on either wall, and let her face wail without making a sound.

"Becca, you in here?"

Ginger.

"I recognize your shoes, Bec."

She sniffed and clicked the toes of the sleek black pumps together. "You should. I borrowed them from you."

Ginger giggled. "Hon, we're heading out to the cemetery. Do you want to ride with us? Isaac wanted me to ask you."

"Sure." She fake-flushed and exited the stall. "Give me a minute to wash my hands."

Becca hurried through the pretense of handwashing and followed Ginger from the restroom.

"You okay?"

Ginger, could you ever once be a little less perceptive? "Fine. Just, you know, touched."

Ginger gave her a quick hug as they made their way down the hall toward the waiting caravan of vehicles.

Like a Marine at attention, Tony stood rigid, face forward during the short graveside ceremony. What would she have done if she could have caught his eye? Exonerating herself, or at least throwing some suspicion another direction, would have to wait.

The gentle words of the committal service—simultaneously sad and soothing—seemed as fragrant as the sweet casket spray that perfumed the air, air hinting of the endless stretch of ocean not so far away.

Her one glimpse of the Pacific at the beginning of Isaac's and her aborted retreat in La Jolla was enough to convince her tides weren't the only magnetic force of the sea. Could she ever live landlocked again?

Aurelia or Geneva would tell her that question had two meanings.

She drew a deep breath of floral sea-not-far air. Isaac stood near the casket. He looked above the flowers at her. His head tilted slightly, his brow furrowed, he seemed to ask her a question she couldn't decipher without words.

How could he not have doubts about her? Any thinking person would. She'd shown him a façade she'd invented, a persona even she wasn't completely comfortable adopting yet. She'd grow into it. Could he wait that long?

As he opened the car door for her, he'd ducked his head toward her ear and whispered something that sounded like, "I love you." Like he'd tell Pete, "I love you, man," if Pete brought hot wings to a party. He'd change his tune if Pete had killed his mother.

She hadn't. Not intentionally. No amount of rehearsing the events of that day showed her where she might have erred. But the woman was gone. What could Becca have done wrong? What did she miss?

Unless Riggo . . .

Now who was the one letting her suspicious mind run wild?

⸺⊰⊱⸺

It was late afternoon before Isaac, Becca, and Geneva were alone in the house. Isaac had looked for Becca several times to talk to her, and found her sequestered in the kitchen.

"Come sit with the family," he'd urged.

She shook her head and busied herself with coffee, dishes, and what looked like supper preparations.

As the last of the guests left, Geneva headed upstairs to change. Isaac entertained the same thought—getting out of his suit and tie. But a trip to the condo was a mountain-climbing expedition and winds weren't favorable for a climb. He sat on the third step in the entry. The grandfather clock ticked its flawless rhythm, a steady reminder of the childhood he'd spent in this home. Endlessly ticking the seconds of a life that would never be the same. Hadn't he left the pendulum silent the night his mom died?

"Isaac?"

Becca stood in the kitchen doorway, twisting her hands then interlocking her fingers to keep from appearing as nervous as she felt.

He scrubbed his fingers through his hair then loosened his tie. "Yes?"

"Did you have plans for supper?"

"No. It looks as if you do."

"Where was your mom's favorite beach or park? Where did she like to go when she was more active?"

A favorite? She celebrated everything, found joy in everything. A favorite? "Oceanside."

Becca unclasped her hands. "Could we—the three of us—take a picnic there and watch the sunset together? I thought—"

He straightened. "Brilliant idea, Becca. That's— What a great way to honor her, to end this day."

"You don't mind my tagging along?"

Why was it so hard for her to grasp what she meant to him? "It wouldn't be the same without you."

Her chin lifted as she sucked in a breath. "Great. I'll have things ready in a half hour or a little more."

"Just enough time for me to go to the condo and change. I'll hurry."

"Watch for traffic," Geneva called from the top of the stairs.

How did she do that? How did Becca think of the small things that made such a difference? His legs had felt as heavy as tree stumps a minute earlier. Now he bounded out to the car, infused with a pulsing hope, a "tupping" hope.

The condo echoed more each time he entered it these days. He ignored the hollowness and changed quickly. Another layer of deodorant.

He'd brought one box of items from the memory table at church in his trip from the car. It sat just inside the door now. He'd deal with it later. Except for the photo of his mom, the one from their Alaskan cruise. He pulled it from the box and stood it against the lamp base on the entry table. Beautiful picture. The two—scratch that. Two of the three women who meant the most to him.

He lifted the picture again and drew it toward his face. Where was the hidden message, the clue that his mom had said would make everything clear? He looked at the wispy clouds for a symbolic shape that should mean something to him. The patterns of their shadows.

That serene face of his mother. The look of joy on Aunt Geneva's face. Both with their arms entwined with Isaac's.

Aunt Geneva stood a step closer to him than his mother. Almost as if his mom knew she'd soon be gone.

Or . . .

He looked into the mirror above the table. He mimicked the look on Aunt Geneva's face—head tilted slightly, full-mouth smile, eyebrows raised, dark eyes dancing.

Dark eyes. Just like his.

The women were more than ready when he pulled up. Becca toted an insulated bag. Aunt Geneva carried a handled jug of what looked like iced tea, ice cubes rattling against the interior as she walked. Isaac grabbed both items and the old tablecloth slung over Becca's shoulder, deposited them in the trunk of the car, and resumed his position behind the wheel, the women already having strapped themselves in for the short ride.

He guessed the sun to be four finger-widths above the horizon. They had an hour before sunset. He could have looked it up on his smartphone. His dad would have used the finger-width method.

Skirting main thoroughfares, they wound their way to the destination without the annoyance of rush hour traffic all the way to the park. They left the vehicle in a designated lot and walked a wide stretch of sand with the lure of ocean waves in the near distance.

Becca's sharp intake of breath matched Aunt Geneva's. The sun was an inch away from belly flopping into the water. Isaac moved the three and their gear to an unoccupied stretch of sand not far from the distinctive Oceanside pier. After jockeying for appropriate positions, they all opted to sit facing the water and the sunset.

"I can see why she loved this spot," Becca whispered.

"We used to come here when I . . . when I visited," Geneva added.

Isaac listened but the scene didn't need his response.

Becca dug in the insulated bag and withdrew three covered mugs and three napkin-wrapped forks. They each removed the covers.

"What's this?" Aunt Geneva's quizzical expression must have mirrored his own.

A tear slipped down Becca's cheek, glistening with the last rays of the sun. "Mashed potatoes. Just . . . mashed potatoes."

Isaac's heart caught in his throat. How fitting.

They ate in silence. The same sun that rose the day Aurelia was born now eased itself into the Pacific in a grand, color-splashed farewell.

24

A perfect way to end this day, Becca. Thank you." Geneva set the tea container on the kitchen island and smothered Becca in her embrace.

Isaac deposited the tablecloth-blanket over the back of a kitchen chair. "I agree. Perfect. Thanks."

Becca warmed at the thought of having brought a small measure of joy to the two.

"I guess I'd better be going." Isaac rubbed the thighs of his jeans.

Fast enough to make her dizzy, Geneva turned to him. "You're not going to work tomorrow, are you?"

"No," he said. "Not ready for that. I thought I'd come over after church and . . . do some . . . paperwork. Clean up in the garden. Pete's coming to help me get the hospital bed disman-tled so we can return it."

Becca's heart clenched. "Is Tony coming, too?"

A vein along Isaac's jaw tightened. "No. You don't have to worry about that."

"I need to talk to him," she said, fully aware of how the statement must have startled the others with whom she shared the room and the moment.

Judging by their silence, she wasn't wrong. Then it occurred to her what they might be thinking. "Not to confess!"

Isaac frowned and exchanged glances with Geneva. "That's not what we were thinking."

"I don't have his phone number."

"I'll call him right now if you want me to." Isaac's frown hadn't left. "Can you tell us what it's about? I mean, if you don't mind?"

Geneva stepped in. "None of our business, Isaac. She's a grown woman. None of our business." She took the tea container to the sink and started the process of rinsing it out as if she'd had the last word.

This would be so much easier if she weren't still living at the house, Becca thought. Tomorrow she'd dip into the money she'd squirreled to restart her nurses' training and instead start the process of finding another place to live. No. Tomorrow was Sunday. She'd wait until Monday. These two needed to get on with their lives. Isaac needed to decide what to do with the house or his condo. Geneva Larkin would head back to the Midwest and her normal life. Becca needed a plan, too. First order of business: Get her name cleared, if that were possible.

"You really need a cell phone of your own, Becca." Isaac pulled his from his pocket. "I'm happy to let you use mine. It's not that. But we'll make sure you get signed up for a cell plan before—"

Geneva coughed. Isaac stood with his mouth open. Apparently all three of them caught his faux pas. A *cell* plan.

Not if Tony's imagination could stretch far enough to consider a new person of interest.

Isaac and Geneva sat at the other end of the diner, sipping decaf and looking disinterested in the pair seven booths away. Becca sat facing Tony, whose back was to them. She leaned out farther than Tony and waved at them to show she was okay.

"They have to come along?" Tony asked, stirring artificial sweetener into his coffee.

Her tea too hot to drink, she folded her napkin as if preparing to cut snowflakes. "They insisted."

He looked up at that.

"I know. I wonder about their faith in me, too, Tony."

He rubbed his chin with his forefinger. "Look, Becca, I understand why you'd change your name. I get why you'd want to start fresh somewhere else. But the deception is a huge complication when a thing like this happens and then you want people to trust you're telling the truth."

She stopped folding and clasped her hands in her lap. "I know. I should have told the truth from the beginning. I'm paying for that now."

He stopped stirring.

"And I understand your loyalty to Isaac. You're a good friend for him."

"He doesn't think so right now."

Becca offered a sympathetic smile. "We might be able to change that."

"You and me?"

"Obviously I don't know all you and the other investigators found in the room or in the autopsy."

"You haven't been charged."

"Which means there's still some question in your mind that it might not be foul play."

"Oh, we're sure there—" His mouth twisted.

"Or," she went on, "it might not be me."

"I'm not allowed to discuss details of the case with you, Becca. If that's why you asked me here . . ."

She leaned in to the table edge. "No. I have a theory."

He sat back and folded his arms across his chest. "I'm listening."

She stole another look at Isaac and Geneva, both of whom were turned toward her. Keeping her voice low, she said, "What if someone—not me—tampered with Aurelia's medications *before* I touched them?"

"We've considered that. Who? And why? Is there anyone else with a family history like yours?"

Punch to the gut, Tony.

"Sorry. That was unwarranted," he said. "Do you have someone in mind?"

Becca's second thoughts were now fourth and fifth thoughts. But she plowed ahead. "Did you notice that Riggo, the pharmacy tech from Medi-Now, was in the crowd at Aurelia's funeral? Does that seem normal to you?"

Tony stirred his coffee again, although it doesn't take that long for sweetener to dissolve. "Ernest Riggo seems a decent enough guy. He has a real way with the elderly customers, his boss says. Cares about them."

"How long has he lived here?"

Tony removed his spoon from his coffee and set it on the table. "Not long. Why?"

"Riggo would have been the only other person who had access to Aurelia's prescriptions."

Tony tapped his fingers on the tabletop. "But a licensed pharmacist checks every prescription before it's released to the customer."

"It was busy that day."

"Did the pharmacist talk to you?"

Becca had relived every moment. Some details were fuzzy. This, she knew. "He did, but he didn't look at what was in the bottle. It was a lick and a promise."

"What?"

"Midwestern expression, I guess. It means doing something half-heartedly, just to say you did it." Midwest? Old West?

"So, now you're accusing the pharmacist of playing a role in this?"

Becca's heart rate responded as if her tea were super-caffeinated. "No. All I'm saying is that it's possible Riggo did something. That he made a mistake. Or switched something. Possible. Isn't it?"

"A mistake you wouldn't have noticed?" Tony glanced over his shoulder at his friend. "I know you want Isaac and his aunt to believe you had nothing to do with Aurelia's death."

"I *had* nothing to do with it. I want them to believe it because it's true."

Tony finished his coffee, spending an inordinately long time on the final sip. He set the cup in its saucer. "Your theory would take some attention off you."

He said it as if that were a less than honorable intention. Becca's heart sank.

"And I don't have anything to go on to even investigate."

"Don't you guys always talk about motive and opportunity and alibis?"

"You watch too much television."

"I used to."

"What motive, Becca? What would possibly be his motive?"

She could feel the lines between her eyes deepening. "I don't know. But he had opportunity."

"You're reaching."

"Tony, wouldn't you reach if you were in my position?"

How many minutes ticked by? "For Isaac's sake, I'll do some checking around."

"Thank you." Her breath hitched on both the inhale and the exhale. But she could breathe.

"So," Aunt Geneva said after Tony left the diner, "what did he say?"

"And what did *you* say?" Isaac interjected. "Can you tell us what this is about now?"

Becca cringed. These dear people. And she was still keeping things from them. "I wish I could. Not yet. But Tony listened and he's trying to help."

Isaac's skepticism clouded his face.

"Don't lose your friendship with Tony over me, Isaac. He's a good man and a good cop doing what he believes is the right thing. He cares about you and your mom. Cared about your mom."

Isaac shifted from one foot to the other. "I wish he were more interested in what this is doing to you."

"How is it you so easily dismiss where I came from, my family history?" She'd made an awkward conversation more so with that question. Time to go back to pondering things in her heart rather than spewing them.

He tucked his hands into his jean pockets. "She told me to," he said, elbowing his aunt.

"As if you've always listened to what I say," Geneva jostled back. "Let's go home. It's been a long day."

Long days. The norm. When Becca wasn't working on restoring the house to its prefuneral state—washing sheets and towels, rearranging donated food items in the fridge and freezer, clearing away the evidence of a houseful of mourners, she retreated to her small bedroom upstairs to read or worked in the garden, letting her pores inhale the Southern California climate. The landscape service the Hughes family hired to tend the garden once a month wouldn't have much to do when they came in December at the rate Becca pruned and swept. And deadheaded.

The underground irrigation system functioned without much attention. So she narrowed her efforts to trimming, tidying. The hemlock, an invasive weed in every sense, was gone.

As she worked, she kept her back turned to the sunroom as much as possible. One day she'd have to face it. Maybe not until the moment she left the property forever. How long could she legitimately postpone that farewell?

Was there any point in filling the bird feeder or mixing sugar-water for the hummingbirds? If Isaac intended to sell the house, the presence of birds could help or hurt, depending on the preferences of the prospective buyer. She should talk to him about it. What did he want to do with the house? Not that it was any of her business.

Geneva agreed to stay through Thanksgiving weekend. Two days away. The two women plotted a menu. Did Isaac want to ask a few friends to join them? He said he preferred just the three of them. Neither woman objected.

Becca carried a bundle of pruned twigs to the refuse pile behind the garden shed. When she turned to head to the house, she caught sight of a lone figure standing in the sunroom. A shadow. But an unmistakable one. Isaac watched her move through the garden toward the entry at the back of the garage. Home early. Home, where he belonged.

Her pulse quickened. Her determination to remain neutral about someone she dared not picture in her future failed. It would take her a long time to get over the thought of him.

Ginger's lasagna and a tossed salad had the trio groaning with satisfaction at the dinner table. What a friend. She'd left two pans—one in the refrigerator and one in the freezer. Lasagna the day before Thanksgiving, the holiday celebrating calories? Maybe not the best plan.

The flurry of funeral-related phone calls having dwindled, Becca—and no doubt her companions, too—waited for one that might offer hope.

Instead, it was the doorbell that interrupted their lasagna meal.

Isaac answered the door and returned to the table with an armful of bright autumn flowers and a quizzical expression. "These are . . . for you," he said, extending them toward Becca.

"What for?"

"I don't know." Isaac's discomfort was obvious. "I didn't send them. Look at the card." He resumed his seat at the table, but left his food untouched.

Becca lifted the card from its forked plastic holder. It fell into the sauce on her plate, face-up. Its one-word message stared back at her: JAYNE.

Geneva reached to pick it up from where it landed, but Isaac stopped her. "Don't touch it. Tony should see this."

Her plate was no messier than the confusion in her brain. What did it mean? Someone knew her birth name. Had the press spilled details she hadn't seen? Did someone from her past read about— No. They wouldn't know the address.

"Maybe my lawyer sent them?" Becca's question sounded ludicrous to her ears.

"Easy way to find out," Geneva said, thumbing her cell phone. "I thought you told me he always called you by your legal name."

"He did. He does."

Isaac pushed away from the table. "Was there a note inside?"

"I didn't look."

He held the back of her chair, as if expecting her to want to move from the scene, too. "Let's call Tony, okay?"

"Okay. I'll go . . . put these in water. No, that's not right."

Pulling her chair out for her, Isaac said, "Let's leave them on the table. If Tony can't come right away, we'll call the precinct."

Geneva put an arm around her waist. "Come on, honey. We'll go make a pumpkin pie for tomorrow."

Because that would solve everything.

25

Isaac would care about anybody falsely accused. But it wouldn't rattle him like this deal with Becca. Tony asked him to leave room in his mind for the possibility that the accusation wasn't false. Even thinking about it now made him frown, made him itch, made his throat feel swollen. He couldn't swallow the idea. But he also couldn't explain why he held that conviction so firmly.

He knew so little about Becca. But didn't he know her heart? She seemed more real than any of the women he'd dated in the last half dozen years. He had no trouble buying the reason she'd changed her name. His aunt's caution to believe Becca wasn't contrary to what landed like a stamp of approval on what he'd already decided.

And yet . . .

Three half-finished plates of lasagna waited on the dining room table as if a television drama had been paused for a bathroom break.

Aunt Geneva and Becca found something to do while they waited for an expert to look at a marinara sauce–soaked piece of paper. All Isaac could do was shake his head.

Within minutes, an entourage of Tony's coworkers filled the dining room. They tweezered and bagged the curiosity/evidence. Becca's eyes darkened when they confiscated the bouquet of flowers, too.

"We can get you more flowers," Isaac whispered.

"That's not it," she whispered back.

"Then what is it?"

She paused. Tony opened his black notebook and stepped toward them.

"Anything else to report? Suspicious phone calls?"

"The flowers," she said, her brow furrowed like the beach after a storm. "They're the same as the ones in Isaac's mother's casket spray. How could that be a coincidence?"

"Already noted," Tony said, nodding.

Isaac's stomach tightened. Why hadn't he noticed that? The possibility of something sinister behind the delivery loomed grotesquely large. The shadow it threw crawled across the room.

"So," Becca said, "doesn't that mean whoever sent these must have been at the funeral? Or at the graveside?"

"*Hawaii Five-O?*" Tony asked.

"*CSI Miami.*"

Isaac watched the interplay between them, baffled that Becca could remain calm. His insides churned like the surf at Big Sur.

Tony planted himself between them and the other investigators, as if what he had to share wasn't formed enough to share with the professionals. "Becca, before you even ask, yes. We'll trace who ordered the flowers. If it's who I think it is, we'll have reason enough for a warrant."

Becca trembled. Isaac would have put an arm around her, but Tony beat him to it.

"Have you found anything else on him, Tony?" She looked both hopeful and scared out of her mind.

Him, who?

"Not much. Not enough. Nothing so far that can't be explained away. We'd need that warrant to take a look at his web activity, phone calls . . ."

"Him, who?" Aunt Geneva asked what Isaac had been thinking.

Tony drew them into a huddle. "Until we know more, it isn't wise to speculate openly, guys. I'm sorry. If something were to slip, we might blow an opportunity to uncover evidence that could exonerate Becca and get to the truth. We have to be able to prove it."

His answer rankled Isaac. Becca wouldn't need exonerating if Tony hadn't fed the suspicion pool. Why couldn't he see that? And why was she acting as if Tony were an ally rather than the original finger-pointer?

"Isaac, can you describe the delivery person?"

He parked his frustration to answer the question. "Wendy."

"You know her?"

"Not Wendy. Lindy. That's it. Lindy Callison. The owner's daughter."

Tony wrote in his notebook. "That goes along with the logo on the cellophane wrap around the flowers. Callison Floral. Legitimate delivery. So we trace back to who ordered the flowers and hope he or she used a credit card or wrote a check. Or ordered in person and was caught on security video."

Tony's train of thought had drifted off into a world outside of Isaac's business decision making. He'd always admired Tony's dedication to his job. The respect his friend showed Becca now thawed some of the frozen ground between them. Becca trusted him. Aunt Geneva looked like Isaac felt—confused.

"Give us a day to check into this. Oh. Thanksgiving's tomorrow," Tony said. "Give us a couple of days to see if we can secure a warrant. If we find out anything solid, we'll bring you in on it. Sound okay to you, Becca?"

She nodded.

"Now, I have to get back to work. Why don't you three go for a walk? Or to a movie. Let us get this processed and see what we find out."

His house—his mom's house—had become a movie set. No need for more drama. Where had the serenity gone?

It rested on his mom's face. Like the photograph from their cruise. Serenity and joy. His mom and Aunt Geneva.

"And when I'm gone, it will all be clear," his mom had said. *Right now, Mom, it's about as clear as San Francisco fog.*

⊸●●⊸

He'd offered his culinary expertise to the women Thanksgiving morning. They took him up on it, assigning Isaac the task of opening the jar of cranberry salsa and slicing the brick of Baby Swiss cheese Aunt Geneva had brought from Iowa.

By ten, the kitchen smelled the best it ever had. A small turkey but enough for leftovers, he hoped. Spices and herbs. Sweet and savory. The debate about whether it was stuffing or dressing raged in sage, all good-natured. He didn't care what it was called. The smell was *dee*-vine, as Pete would say.

Football games didn't hold his interest this year. Pete texted to ask, "Did u see that interception?" Isaac texted back, "Helping in kitchen." Pete's reply: "Don't worry, dude. Taping it 4 u."

Isaac thought about responding that his presence in the kitchen was by choice, but let it go.

By mutual consent, the three kitchen dwellers avoided all talk any more serious than salt in the gravy and the advantages of letting the turkey rest before slicing into it. The women discussed how strange but wonderful it felt to have a cup of coffee in the garden on Thanksgiving Day during a much-needed break, to open the windows to temps in the low 70s, to prepare the meal in sandals.

Becca seemed at home with the California temperatures. Aunt Geneva seemed eager to get back to a four-season routine. And she would. All too soon.

He and his aunt set the table in the dining room while Becca made crudités.

"I didn't even have to tell you that the silverware is laid from outside to inside, Isaac." His aunt smiled.

"I did pick up a few things in my business travels."

"What are you going to do about Mrs. Gallum?"

"I don't know. I can't say I was disappointed she's, leaving. The timing's lousy, but . . ."

"Maybe not." She folded a crisp crease in the pumpkin-colored linen napkin in her hand. "Maybe it's excellent timing."

He let the sentence hover. "Do you think Becca would agree to work for me? Isn't she still interested in nursing?" As soon as the words were out of his mouth, he saw the picture they created. Her dream had been nursing. First her father, now this. No matter how Tony's investigation ended, who would have the courage to keep pursuing that path? Maybe Becca. Maybe she was the one who would.

"Do you have any doubts about her work ethic, Isaac?"

"None."

"About her . . . character?"

"No." He answered without thinking, as if fully convinced. Was he? "Maybe she has no intention of remaining around here."

She moved a water goblet an inch to the right. "Have you asked her? What did you think she was going to do?"

Six chairs around the table. Three place settings. What a great meal it would have been if his mom and dad and his birth mom occupied the other three chairs. As an afterthought, he mentally pulled up an extra for his birth dad. He rarely thought about that. Some psychologist would have fun toying with the fatherless anomaly. Right now, he couldn't imagine the table without Becca. "I don't know what I thought. I guess I hesitated to think anything until the legal part is settled."

"They don't want her leaving town right now."

"I heard." His tension headache was back.

"So . . ."

"What if she doesn't want to work for me?"

Aunt Geneva crossed her arms. "Isaac, are you kidding?" She stepped toward him and reached up to ruffle his hair. "What's not to love?"

———⁂———

"And thank You, Father God, for the healing that's on its way, for the company of these two beautiful women, and for sustaining us through this difficult week and the ones to come. We are grateful. In the Name of Jesus, amen."

It didn't escape Becca's notice that Isaac used the word *sustaining*. It was as if he'd overheard her conversation with Geneva.

"Isn't there something you wanted to discuss with Becca, Isaac?" Geneva picked up her napkin and head-pointed toward her.

He followed suit and said, "Yes. Please pass the turkey."

Both women snickered. Becca handed him the platter of turkey. He held it so she could fork a piece of dark meat for herself first.

"Annnnddddd . . . ?" Geneva drew out.

"And graaaaaaaaaavy?" Isaac mimicked.

"Oh, for the love of—"

"I'll get to it," he said, pouring gravy on his mashed potatoes, his meat, and the mound of stuffing/dressing he'd dished out.

His reticence could have been a game he played in an attempt to lighten what had been a very heavy-mooded several days. Or the subject might have made him genuinely nervous. If it were the latter, Becca wasn't sure she wanted to hear what he had to say. It could well mean she was eating her last meal in this home. She stabbed a garlic roasted brussels sprout and concentrated on chewing it.

Isaac set down his fork. This was serious.

Geneva laid hers aside as well. Becca did the same.

"Becca, what are your plans?" he asked as if a principal grilling a delinquent student. He must have realized how it sounded. He swallowed and asked again, lowering both his chin and his voice. "Have you made plans for what comes next?"

Geneva sighed.

"What I'm saying is that I have a sudden and unexpected but not altogether unpleasant need for a receptionist at the office."

Geneva sighed again, deeper this time.

Isaac's eyes widened as if trying to communicate something to his aunt without using words. He turned back to Becca. "I don't know if you'd be interested in receptionist work."

Becca recalculated where she thought the conversation was headed. "You're offering me a job?" A reason to stay around?

"Two jobs, really." Isaac resumed eating, talking carefully around bites of food. "I also need someone to stay here at the house until I can sell my condo."

"You're taking over the house? Giving up the condo?"

Geneva scooted her chair forward. "You hadn't told me that."

"I know it seems like too much for me," Isaac said. "But it's . . . home."

He only needed her in the house until he sold his condo. As soon as the sale was complete, Becca would be homeless again, her own place to belong still elusive. Maybe it would take a while for someone to buy his condo. Would it be wrong to pray for that?

"Isaac, I may be unavailable for either request. If the court decides I—"

"Nonsense!" Geneva interjected.

"We have no reason to believe that will happen," Isaac added. "And if it does . . ."

Geneva lifted her napkin and snapped it fiercely before repositioning it on her lap.

"If it does, we'll deal with it at the time." Isaac snapped and repositioned his own napkin.

Becca drank in his words. He was offering her an opportunity to remain in La Vida, to remain in his circle, to stay connected, to work with him. To work. "Yes."

"Yes, you will, or yes, we'll deal with it at the time?"

"Both. But you don't really need me to stay here at the house. That's just your charitable spirit talking."

Geneva poked her in the arm.

"Are you opposed to staying here?" Isaac paused before lifting another forkful of food to his mouth.

"Not at all."

"Even with all that happened?"

How different this atmosphere felt from the home where her mother had died. "I'd be working at the office a lot, wouldn't I?"

Isaac laughed. "Oh, yes."

Geneva leaned forward. "And, Isaac, you'd come over from time to time, wouldn't you? To check up on things? Maybe host your men's group? Have friends over? Much easier here than in your condo."

"We'd have to talk about that," he said. "I wouldn't want to interfere with Becca's life."

Interfere away! Becca chewed a bite of turkey to cover the smile teasing her lips. She swallowed and said, "That would be nice."

"One thing, though. You'd have to move back into the suite downstairs. It only makes sense."

"And then when the condo sells . . . ?"

Geneva and Isaac exchanged glances. He half-winked. "You're talking to two real estate people."

"It could take a while," Geneva said.

"Could be a long while." Isaac focused on his plate again.

"How much for rent?"

Isaac chuckled. "Free? Is that within your housing budget?" He picked up his fork again. "You'd be doing me a favor. House-sitting. Kind of."

She leaned back a couple of inches. "Free is right in my price range."

"And the receptionist position?" Geneva asked the question this time.

Becca used her knife to draw a figure eight in her mashed potatoes. "I may not be qualified."

"You'll learn fast," Isaac countered.

"That's not the issue," she said. "I'm not particularly fond of fire-engine-red nail polish."

Isaac lifted her free hand and kissed it. "Bless you."

Doing the dishes would be extra challenging since now she couldn't get that hand wet.

"You don't intend to put your condo up for sale, do you?" Aunt Geneva asked him when Becca disappeared out of earshot into the kitchen after the last bite of cranberry salsa.

"I will. Eventually. The holidays are a lousy time to sell a condo."

"Sure, they are."

"Maybe in the spring."

"Isaac, out here, it's always spring. When it isn't summer." The chiding look on her face couldn't outshine the quirked smile.

"I'll get to it."

"I'm sure you will."

Becca poked her head around the corner. "Whipped cream or ice cream with your pumpkin pie?"

"Whipped," they said in unison.

Becca grinned and disappeared into the kitchen again.

Aunt Geneva patted his hand. "You're a good man, Isaac. I'm proud of you, son."

It felt good to be called son again. Just an expression, a term of endearment from his aunt. But it sounded . . . right. "Why are you crying, Aunt Geneva?"

She sniffed back tears. "Everything. Aurelia. The mess with the suspicion about Becca. My flight leaves the day after tomorrow. I don't want to leave you."

"I don't want you to leave either."

"But I know I have to. It's always hard. Always hard to say good-bye to you."

Becca entered bearing three dessert plates with whipped-cream-topped slices of pumpkin pie. He stood to help her distribute them.

The first bite melted in his mouth. The second bite stuck in his throat. Always hard to say good-bye to *him*?

26

Isaac slipped the photograph from its frame and fed it through the scanner in his office at the condo. He made a 5-by-7 print and tucked it inside the cover of the book he'd picked up at the "Book-in-the-Hand" bookstore. A thank-you gift for his aunt. A small gesture of gratitude. He wrapped the book in tissue paper and tucked it into a gift bag.

The package accompanied him when he picked up his aunt to take her to the airport.

"What's this?" she asked, slipping out of her California sandals into shoes more fitting for a late November trip back to Iowa.

"A little thank-you for all you've done."

"That's so thoughtful of you."

"Don't open it until you get home, okay?"

She looked deeply into his eyes. Hers misted. His probably were too. He gave her a Hughes-sized hug.

"Hey," she said, wiping her eyes, "save that for the airport. We can't start the good-byes this early or I'll run out of tissues."

Becca opted to brave the Saturday after Thanksgiving madness at the stores and find herself what she called suitable clothes for the office. Isaac and his aunt would be alone for the airport run.

"She's stronger than she looks, Isaac," Aunt Geneva offered when the conversation about La Vida traffic and the perpetual need for sunglasses waned. She pulled her seatbelt away from her shoulder and angled herself toward him as much as the constraint would allow. "You won't find another like her."

"If you're matchmaking, Aunt Geneva . . ."

"Who, me? No. Generously sharing my observations for the benefit of all humanity."

A quick glance her way told him she wore her coy face. The twinkle eyes showed she could let her sense of humor out to play even in the middle of life's messes. Just like her sister.

Another rogue wave of grief splashed over him, threatening to knock him off his feet. He suspected the season of rogue waves would last a long time.

They talked real estate and gas prices and debated what to do about Geneva's nonrefundable airline tickets that had been purchased months ago to spend Christmas with her sister.

Isaac signaled for the airport exit marked "Departures." "You could still come."

He heard the small hitch in her voice. He had them, too, these days.

"That's less than a month away." She fished in her purse for her boarding pass and ID as Isaac steered the car toward her carrier's drop-off point.

"You won't get your money back."

"It's not that."

"You know you're welcome anytime."

Aunt Geneva turned her face toward the curb. Isaac pulled between two other vehicles that left him an inch more room than he needed. He grabbed his aunt's luggage from the back while she exited the car and double-checked that she had everything.

"It wouldn't be right without you there," he said, pulling her into a bear hug he hoped communicated all he couldn't say.

Others waiting for a spot along the curb voiced their protests, forcing Isaac to separate from his aunt so she could grab the handle of her wheeled bag and with a final blown kiss turn to enter the terminal.

He called after her, "Do you have the gift?"

She nodded and lifted her tote-bag-sized purse to shoulder height, but didn't stop and face him. Her torso rose and fell as if drawing a deep breath and exhaling something heavier than air.

Yeah. I'll miss you, too.

Becca surveyed her purchases. They lay across the bed as if she were packing to leave rather than preparing to stay.

A step or two up from her casual wardrobe for caregiving, her new office attire consisted of a small collection that, shuffled into dozens of combinations, would serve her well. Nothing fancy. Nothing expensive. Nothing dry-clean-only. Utilitarian . . . with flair. A gray pencil skirt she could pair with the teal sleeveless shirt and gray featherweight jacket or with the claret short-sleeved ruffled blouse. A black mid-length skirt that looked good with the gray jacket, the ruffled blouse, or the short-sleeve cotton sweaters in butter yellow and blush pink.

She'd chosen inexpensive but artsy jewelry and two sweet pairs of shoes—deceptively easy on the feet—that turned what could have seemed matronly into Southern California–worthy fashion. Or so she hoped.

Ginger approved. She'd raved over the possibilities when she stopped in with a turkey-celery salad she'd made from Thanksgiving leftovers. They hadn't talked long. Pete waited in the car with his golf clubs. Golfing two days after Thanksgiving. Becca could get used to the climate. And the people. The prices, on the other hand . . .

She mustered her courage and snipped the price tag from the cobalt-blue sleeveless sheath. Ginger wouldn't let her return it, despite Becca's second thoughts. It was perfect, she'd said, and added that it would definitely impress Isaac.

She could have argued that wasn't her goal. But she'd taken a vow of a deception-free life in the last few weeks. She discarded the tags and hung the dress on a padded hanger in the closet. The rest of her purchases joined it, bumping the closet contents to another stratosphere in color as well as volume.

The shoes found a home on a rack built for that purpose and had hardly settled in when the phone rang. Becca scooted to answer it. A ringing phone in an empty house isn't a calming sound.

"Becca?"

"Isaac." A wave of warmth slowed her breathing into sweetness, like high-quality butterscotch melts on the tongue.

"Everything okay there?"

"Yes." *Except the house seems vacant without you.* "Did your aunt's flight leave on time?"

"No glitches. I hope her whole trip home is as smooth."

"Me, too."

"How did your shopping spree go?"

Becca lowered herself into the oversized chair nearest the window. "Good. Thank you for the advance."

"You're the one who used that word, Becca. I said, if you'll recall, 'Take the money and get thee to a mall-ery.'"

"That's really not necessary. I—" She heard his groan. He wanted to be generous. She knew enough about him by now to realize he took uncommon joy in giving, a remarkable trait for someone with a strong business drive. "I'm grateful. Thank you."

If a pause could smile, his did. "Do you have plans for the evening?"

She snorted, wholly unladylike. "Sorry. No. I believe my calendar is empty."

"Do you feel like having leftovers? And before you answer, I don't."

Becca relaxed deeper into the chair. "No. Not really."

"Seafood?"

"Where?"

"Cute, Becca. I mean, do you like great seafood?"

"I'm from an area so far removed from fresh seafood that the snails in the dentist's office aquarium started to look good."

His laughter reverberated through every cell in her body. "I'd like to introduce you to a cuisine decidedly more upscale than aquarium snails, Becca. Can I pick you up in an hour?"

"Casual? Fancy? Paper baskets and plastic forks?"

"Does it matter? It's great food."

"I need to know how to dress for the occasion, sir."

"Ah. Medium?"

"Big help. Are there paper placemats or linen tablecloths on the tables?"

He cleared his throat. "Linen tablecloths. Candles. And an ocean view."

Definitely the blue dress.

Geneva Larkin listened to the odd harmony of jet engines and her seatmate's gravelly snore. A ping signaled the plane had reached cruising altitude. Isaac had asked her to wait to open his gift until she got home. Close enough.

She unlatched her seatbelt and wiggled her way into a position to reach the handle of the purse tucked under the seat in front of her. The onions on a sub sandwich a row or two away smelled especially strong. A bag of roasted almonds and a small container of dried apricots rested somewhere in the depths of her cavernous purse. She'd fish them out right after she tore into Isaac's present.

The ribbon slipped off as if waiting for her. She dug a fingernail under the tape on the tissue paper. She was right. A book.

A *children's* book?

The tissue paper trembled in concert with the flutter of Geneva's heart. Tears blurred her vision, but the title was clear enough: *Are You My Mother?*

<hr />

Becca grabbed a fine-gauged knit throw from the back of the chair when she heard the doorbell. It wasn't exactly a wrap or shawl, but it would do if the temps turned cool before the end of the evening.

She'd never feel right about Isaac having to ring the doorbell of his own home just because she lived there now. But she appreciated the courtesy. She peeked through the sheer on the window panel beside the front door. He stood on the porch rocking back and forth on his heels. He wore black slacks and a cobalt-blue shirt. Not just blue. Cobalt blue. She debated bolting for her room to change. Too late. He saw her eyeing him through the curtain and waved.

She opened the door but he didn't enter. He stood beyond the threshold with his mouth open.

"I know," she said. "Coincidental, huh? I didn't get the memo you were wearing blue. Isaac? Isaac?"

"You look . . ."

"Like a copycat? Overdressed? Ridiculous?"

Deep breath. "Wow. Yeah. Like . . . wow."

"Well, thank you." Her cheeks warmed. Too tame a word. They heated.

"Are you . . . is that . . . will you wear that to the office?"

"No."

"Good. I mean, it looks very nice on you."

"But . . . ?" She hadn't thought the cut of the dress inappropriate in any way. Had she missed something?

She backed up to the full-length mirror in the foyer. What was his problem? Perfectly reasonable skirt length. She turned to catch the view of the back. Zipper secure. Yes, her arms could use some strength training to tighten up some of the chicken-wing flapping, but—

Isaac was standing too close when she turned back to face him. He had to grab her arms to keep her from stumbling into him. "Becca . . ."

"What?" The question started off with a whine then softened before the end consonant. The way he was looking at her . . .

"You look radiant. With all you've been through, I don't know how—"

All *they'd* been through. She hadn't thought about their layered crises for almost a full ten minutes. A new record.

"May I?" he asked.

"May you what?" *Breath, don't fail me now.*

The kiss she thought might land on her lips, maybe her nose, dusted her forehead. Like a blessing.

"I hope you know how beautiful you are."

She didn't dare glance in the mirror again and find out his words were exaggerated. She opted instead to focus on his Adam's apple. It moved up and down several times before he spoke.

"I suppose we should get to the restaurant."

"Do we have reservations?" Good. A safe topic.

"None at all." He backed up a step. "Oh. Yes. Yes, we do." He glanced at the face of the grandfather clock. "Let's hope traffic isn't bad tonight."

Yes, Isaac. Let's talk about the traffic. Or the weather. "Should I bring a notebook?"

"A notebook?"

"To take notes. About Hughes Realty? I start Monday, right?"

He opened the door for her then pulled it shut behind them. "Monday will be soon enough to discuss work."

It was official, then. He just wanted to be with her.

Or maybe he didn't want to be alone. Two different things.

27

The hostess led them through a maze of tables and a short arched hallway onto a wide concrete balcony.

"You might need that later," Isaac said, nodding toward the wrap draped over her arm. "It'll get cool out here when the sun goes down."

Becca noted the lamppost-like heaters stationed around the perimeter of the balcony.

The hostess directed them to a table near the far railing. Wave sounds told her this part of the balcony hovered over the water, no doubt supported by massive columns driven deep into the sand. She ought to know the real word for the columns. Pilings? If she stayed on the West Coast, she had more than a few things to learn. *God, please let me stay. Somehow.*

Isaac held her chair for her, an upholstered rattan on casters, comfortable enough for a nap when the meal ended. She reached for the arms of the chair as she lowered herself into it, unable to tear her gaze from the ocean as it readied itself to welcome the sinking sun into its embrace. She snatched her sunglasses from her purse. Isaac grabbed his from his breast pocket, where they hung by one earpiece.

"Some evening, huh?"

She searched for an adequate descriptor and came up empty. "Mmm." A light breeze teased her hair. She held her hand toward the sun. Two fingers between the bottom of the sun and the horizon. It would set in about a half hour. She didn't want to miss a minute of it.

In addition to ice cubes, their water goblets held a cucumber slice and a strawberry. They declined the wine steward and focused attention on the silver-haired waiter, who listed the menu items from memory.

"Anything appeal to you?" Isaac asked her.

"Everything." He couldn't know she meant every menu item, the setting, and him.

"May I make a recommendation?"

"Please."

Bailey, the waiter, smiled as Isaac described the succulence of the roasted Dungeness crab over herbed rice with mango salsa.

"I've never had Dungeness crab."

Bailey and Isaac exchanged a knowing glance. "If I may," Bailey interjected, "you won't be disappointed. And might I suggest our lobster bisque for your soup course and our champagne vinaigrette grilled hearts of romaine salad with seared scallops and hearts of palm?"

"That's three meals right there."

The two men seemed to enjoy her naivete, not in a demeaning way, but as if they couldn't wait to introduce her to this new culinary experience.

With no paper menu in front of her, she was at a loss. "How much is the—?"

Isaac's eyes widened. He shook his head and pressed a finger to his lips. Leaning in, he whispered, "It's considered rude to ask the price here."

Bailey shrugged his shoulders and arched his brows as if to communicate, "What can I say?"

She swallowed her concern and answered, "Everything you suggested sounds wonderful. Thank you."

Isaac's joy at her decision lit his face. "And I'll have the same."

"Very good, sir, miss." Bailey retreated and left the two alone at the table by the sea.

A few days earlier, she'd choked down a vending machine sandwich at the precinct. A week from now, she could be eating worse fare. Nothing was tidy. No plan solid. Life shifted like the color of the water.

The buoyancy in her heart grew heavy. She pushed back against it, determined to enjoy this one glorious moment.

"Are you thinking what I'm thinking?" Isaac asked, positioning his cloth napkin—cobalt blue—in his lap.

Not a chance.

"I'm thinking we may have to get dessert to go and eat it later."

She shook her head at the thought of ever being hungry again.

Music drifted over the scene from speakers hidden among the plants or rocks. But the sound that fascinated was the rhythm of the waves. She'd never tire of sea music.

Isaac seemed equally fascinated. Content to listen rather than speak, they sat silent as the sun sank lower. The bisque arrived, smooth and rich and perfectly seasoned. Becca stifled her instinct to groan her appreciation for it.

She drew her spoon through the bisque in a figure eight.

"I was the real estate agent on this project," Isaac said, dipping his spoon in the bowl in front of him.

"Seriously?"

"I had aspirations of . . ."

"Of what?"

"Turning it into a residential property. Buying it. Living in it. Here. Right here."

"You could do that?"

He shook off the idea. "No. Can you imagine the taxes on this piece of property? And the zoning nightmare would have given me—"

"Nightmares?"

"Ulcers."

She took another spoonful of the bisque, imagining a living room that opened onto the scene in which they sat. Imagined waking to that view, those sounds . . .

Isaac set his spoon aside. "The one and only piece of poetry I ever wrote was scratched out while sitting on this balcony."

"I didn't take you for a poetry kind of guy."

His mouth tilted. "I'm not. Just that one time."

"Do you remember it?"

He dug back into the remaining thick goodness in his bowl. "You don't need proof I'm not a real poet."

"I'd like to hear it."

His eyes searched hers. "I only remember the first line."

"And that line is . . . ?"

"If you mock it, you're fired, you realize?"

Becca leaned her elbows on the table and her chin in her hands. "I'd like to hear it."

He coughed deep in his throat, stared toward the place where the sun had been moments before. " 'These waves sound like the womb of my beginnings.' "

How had her throat knotted itself? When she finally untangled it, she said, "That's truly beautiful."

"In a sappy sort of way."

" 'The womb of my beginnings.' " She let the words ride the air. They settled like dew on her heart.

"I was born here, Becca."

"I assumed so. A private adoption. Right?"

"But . . ." Isaac drew a deep breath, then another. "I think I was conceived in Iowa."

❧

The salad looked delicious. And seared scallops don't like to be kept waiting.

Bailey hovered too close for Isaac's taste. Didn't he have other customers? A half dozen other tables on the balcony were filled. Maybe it was the subject matter of their conversation that made Isaac squirm. He'd used the words "conceived" and "Iowa" and "womb" in the same paragraph. He couldn't trust his mouth anymore.

Becca's salad sat untouched, too. Isaac picked up his fork and knife and sliced into one of the delicacies. Butter soft. The scallops were perfectly cooked. He stabbed a piece and raised it to his mouth, pausing long enough to gesture with it to Becca, as if to say, "Eat first, talk later?"

She removed her sunglasses, the reason for their need having slipped below the horizon. Her eyes asked questions he wasn't sure he could answer. She pointed to his face. Ah. His sunglasses still shaded his vision. But little cleared up when he tucked his shades into his shirt pocket.

"All I have is suspicions, Becca."

She stiffened. "Which can be wrong. Suspicions can be wrong."

He'd stirred the stewpot of pain again, had brought up burnt pieces from the bottom. Not his intention.

She searched his face. "Tell me what you're thinking. What did you mean about your life not starting here?"

251

Isaac attacked his salad. He'd talk about it, but casually, not revealing the amount of time he'd spent on the subject in the last week. "What if Aunt Geneva were my birth mother?"

⁂

So he felt it, too. An almost umbilical connection between Isaac and Geneva Larkin. Becca thought she'd imagined the way their features seemed to mimic each other. No one would expect Isaac to look like his adoptive mother, Aurelia. But who would expect he'd look so much like his aunt?

He'd felt it, too.

"Did she ever say anything to you, Becca?" His eyes—her eyes—begged an answer.

"No. The resemblance is obvious, but—"

He brightened. "You think so?"

"Not just in your facial features. Little habits. The way she tilts her head sometimes when she's thinking. But, Isaac, you've been around her all your life. It wouldn't be unusual for you to adopt some of the traits of a much-loved aunt. You admire her. She's meant a lot to you over the years."

He turned his attention to his salad, slicing through a scallop, but leaving it on his fork. "Maybe I'm projecting what I wish were true." He lifted his face to the sky. "No offense, Mom."

Becca's eternal ache thundered. What must it be like to not know your birth parents' identity and long to connect? Her life's ambition had been to disconnect from the people who acted as if forced to call her their daughter. Did they know she'd overheard them talking about not wanting to have had kids? About making sure a mistake like Becca didn't happen again?

252

How could her yearnings be so different from Isaac's? "The Geneva I know wouldn't be offended if you simply asked her."

He raked his fingers across his forehead. "I kind of did."

On some women, tears make their faces streaky and pinched. Becca's tears sparkled in the candlelight. She'd hidden her fear too long. She couldn't hide her compassion. It made her all the more beautiful. She dabbed at the corners of her eyes with her linen napkin. He almost asked her to stop and let the tears glisten.

"I wish we could be there when she opens the package." She pressed her palm to her heart.

"Yeah." He glanced at his cell phone. Her plane would land soon. He hadn't asked Aunt Geneva to call him when she got home. Maybe she wouldn't open the gift until she'd unpacked. Maybe not until morning. It was almost ten her time. Then the ride home from the airport. If he were wrong about his suspicions, the book wouldn't make any sense to her. She'd call in the morning, maybe, but only to check on his sanity.

"It was a dumb idea." Regret dumped a truckload of bile into his stomach.

She reached her hand across the table. "Isaac, it was one of the most tender things I've ever heard. Either way, you can't lose."

"I could be embarrassed to death."

Becca's soft smile blessed him. There was no other word for it.

"If she is your birth mom, your search is over. If she isn't, you still have her in your life. The world's most caring aunt."

"You're good for me, Becca."

She tilted her head. Just like his Aunt Geneva when she was thinking.

"Finished with your salads?" Bailey stood at Becca's elbow.

"Yes, thank you. They were delicious." Isaac laid his fork upside down on his salad plate.

Bailey quickly cleared their places and returned with steaming platters of goodness. Becca's eyes saucered. She pressed her lips together as if stifling a giggle. He didn't stifle his.

"Looks like we need to apply ourselves to the task at hand."

"May I just—? No. Never mind." She bent to breathe in the best the sea had to offer.

"What? What were you going to ask?"

"Bad idea. Forget it." She picked up a grilled lemon half and squeezed it over the seafood.

"Becca, I think it's obvious by now that my curiosity is not easily assuaged."

"*Assuaged*? Your word-of-the-day calendar?"

"Coll-idge ed-jee-cation. Dad would be so proud. Don't change the subject. What were you going to ask?"

The color in her cheeks deepened. "I thought it might be good if we prayed together about your aunt's reaction when she opens your gift, that I could . . . could pray for you."

He slid his hands across the table, palms up. She slipped hers into his. He'd remember most of her sweet, heartfelt prayer. He'd remember all of what it felt like to hold onto her.

The patio heaters flickered to life. Had the air cooled? He hadn't noticed. But Becca drew that thin knit thing over her shoulders as the two addressed the food in front of them.

Perfect meal. Perfect company. Perfectly horrible time for his phone to ring.

He snatched it up with the intention of silencing it, but a familiar name on the screen punched him in the gut. Tony. That could only mean trouble.

Isaac pointed the phone face toward Becca so she could read what he saw. She leaned in and squinted in the low light. He knew the moment her vision focused. Desperate hope curled her into a question mark.

He glanced at the other diners on the patio. Between the music and the waves, his phone conversation wasn't likely to disturb anyone. But as he hit the talk button, he pushed away from the table and headed for the abandoned hallway that connected the patio to the body of the restaurant.

"What's up, Tony?"

"You busy?"

"Yes, frankly."

"I tried calling Becca at the house. She's not there."

"She's here. With me." Not that it should matter to Tony.

"Good."

Good? Had he changed his tune about Isaac's interest in her?

"How fast can you get to the precinct?"

"Tonight?" Isaac glanced back toward the outdoor patio.

"This is important. We may have something. How soon?"

Isaac calculated the distance, took into account the traffic they'd likely encounter and how hard it would be to tame his lead foot. "We can be there in forty minutes."

Isaac pocketed the phone and flagged Bailey for their check and boxes for their leftovers.

"Becca, I'm so sorry to cut this short. You deserve better. Tony's got a lead. He wants us at the station as soon as we can get there."

"The check?"

Bailey handed it to Isaac before she finished asking. Isaac slipped his credit card into the holder.

"Very good, sir. I'll be back in a moment to box the remainder of your meals."

"We can take care of that," Isaac assured. Then, noting the expression Bailey wore, he added, "Family emergency."

"So sorry, sir. Understood." He left them to scrape enough food for two more meals into the take-out boxes. Isaac's heart rattled unnaturally. He pulled out Becca's chair for her and helped her adjust the shawl around her shoulders. He stood behind her for a moment, rubbing his hands on her upper arms as if he could keep her warm enough and protect her from whatever lay ahead. He bent to whisper in her ear. He meant to say, "We'll get through this." What came out was, "I love you, Becca."

She didn't flinch. Instead, she leaned back against him and turned her head toward the ocean they were leaving too soon. "'These waves sound like the womb of my beginnings.'"

So much better coming out of her mouth.

28

They had no trouble finding a parking space at that hour of the night. Becca had seen more of this building than any of the charming tourist destinations in the area.

"Nervous?" he asked her as they half-ran from the lot to the entrance of the precinct.

No longer chilled, she balled her wrap in one hand. Isaac gripped the other. She inventoried the emotions coursing through her. Nervous? Her heart pounded like mallets on tympani . . . at the climax of the *1812 Overture*. Whatever Tony had found in the investigation could go either way for her. Why were they running? She slowed her pace. Isaac matched hers.

"What's wrong? Is it your shoes?" He pointed toward her footwear.

"My shoes?" An unexpected explosion of laughter erupted and doubled her over. Of all the things that could be wrong at that moment, blisters from new shoes were the least of her concerns. Was this the definition of insanity? The laughter cackled out of her despite her attempts to suppress it. Bent in the middle, holding her stomach, she had no choice but to let it spend itself, exhaust itself. The tears this time rode waves of the ridiculousness of it all.

"What did I say? What can I do? Are you okay?" Isaac's warm arm across her back added to the tragicomic scene—half tragedy, half comedy. He must have felt every outburst through the fabric of her cobalt dress.

Stand up straight. Deep breaths. Bite your tongue until it bleeds if you have to. A glance at the precinct entrance sobered her. Tony stood in the doorway, watching.

"I'm fine, Isaac. Let's go."

Like a drop of bleach on silk, laughter's color instantly blanched.

"You planned this, right?" Tony said, pointing from Isaac's shirt to Becca's dress as he held the door for them. "Adorable. Matching outfits."

Becca didn't trust herself to speak. She clamped her lips together. Isaac caught the signal.

"What do you have for us, Tony? It must be important or . . ."

"Detective Hahn is waiting in his office. This way."

She'd escaped from this building and these interrogators a short time ago. It made no sense, but scenes from *Dead Man Walking* flashed through her mind.

Hahn's office, blistered with fluorescent lighting and a decided lack of décor, lay at the end of a too-long hallway. Detective Hahn didn't stand when they entered but pointed with a pencil toward two straight-backed chairs that faced his desk. Tony introduced them then stood off to the side.

Becca didn't expect an ice-breaker of small talk, so it was no shock when Detective Hahn blurted, "We've been watching Ernest Riggo. It's confirmed he sent you the flowers."

A shiver inched its way up her arms.

"And we've seen enough to make us want to dig deeper. But it's not enough for a judge to grant a warrant."

"For his arrest?" She'd found her voice and a thread of hope.

"Hold on. A step at a time. We need a warrant to dive into his personal records, computer activity, search his apartment, his workplace."

She reached for Isaac's hand. Tony cleared his throat. She pulled her hand back and laced her fingers in her lap. "How does that involve us? Me?"

Hahn shot a glance at Tony then drummed his pencil on his Just-the-facts-Ma'am desk blotter. "You've spoken with Riggo a number of times?"

The extravagant meal congealed into concrete in her stomach. "Only when I picked up that last . . . that last set of prescriptions for Isaac's mom." The loss still fresh, speaking her name tightened her throat. *Relax, Becca. If they smell fear . . .*

Hahn stopped drumming. "We need you to engage him in conversation. See how he reacts. He knows details he shouldn't. We need to know why."

Isaac's posture stiffened. He leaned toward Hahn. "If he's dangerous, you're not suggesting Becca put herself in harm's way." Becca watched his brow furrow like a newly turned field.

Tony stepped into her field of vision. "We wouldn't send her in without protection, Isaac. Our guys will be there. And if Riggo's done what we're beginning to suspect, he doesn't fit the profile of someone who would act out in any spontaneously violent way."

The whole room tensed.

"I don't know if I could pull it off. Wouldn't he suspect something? He creeps me out." She sounded like a middle school girl whining about her assigned lab partner.

Hahn's first of several chins lifted. He looked at her through the bottom of his glasses. "You successfully hid your true identity from"—he gestured toward Isaac—"people you care about for how long?"

"Point taken." Somewhere inside, she waved a white flag.

Isaac leaned forward. "Wait. Wait a minute. She doesn't have to do this, right? Does her lawyer know about this?"

Tony interjected, "We've spoken to him, Isaac. He's in New York this weekend but said you could call him if you have any questions about this procedure."

"And no. She doesn't have to do this," Hahn said. "But if she's truly innocent—"

"Which I am. And I'm right here. I can hear you." *Tame it, Becca. You want to stay on their good side.*

Hahn sighed. "This could go a long way toward clearing your name. We're not pressuring you into this. But we'd appreciate your cooperation."

This is not what she'd signed up for when she'd agreed to hire on as Aurelia Hughes's caregiver. She thought back to that first day they met. The instant connection. The light rekindled in Aurelia's pale eyes and the way Aurelia—sick as she was—managed to rekindle Becca's faith.

She owed it to the woman's memory to be braver than she felt at the moment. "What is it you want me to do?"

"And I can walk out if I sense he suspects something?"

The tiny earbud, hidden by her hair, answered back. Tony's voice. "Absolutely. But you're good, Becca. I mean no disrespect here, honestly, but you had most of us fooled for a long time. You'll do great."

Most of them. Not him. And, she wanted to add, she hadn't lied about her name. She'd paid good money for it.

She zipped shut the blinged denim vest Tony suggested to further camouflage any outline of the wires taped to her torso. She'd always walked to the pharmacy, so the team had let her out three blocks away. She paused at the two-block mark to check her makeup.

"Becca, what are you doing?" the earbud buzzed.

She barely moved her lips in reply, whispering to the hidden microphone, "I got zero sleep last night. If I don't make sure these circles under my eyes are covered and that I have a sun-kissed blush in my cheeks, he'll be suspicious before I say a word."

She swiped gloss across her mouth and willed her lips to stop trembling. Deep breaths. A prayer on every exhale. Heart of a lion. Heart of a lion. Heart of . . . a lioness, she told herself. Every story Geneva Larkin had told her about finding uncommon courage by leaning into God tumbled in her mind.

Becca patted her soft-sided purse, reassuring herself the pepper spray was there if she needed it. Like that would help.

"Keep walking, Becca," Tony said.

"Will I recognize the undercover cops inside the building?"

"No. We don't want you to notice them and react. They have their shields of invisibility raised."

"Cute, Tony. Why wasn't I issued one of those?"

"Becca?"

"What?"

"Isaac isn't the only one praying for you."

Her racing heart slowed by several beats per minute. "Thanks."

"Now, let's do this."

One more block. The frail appendages she used to call her legs took her nearer her destination. An adrenaline headache wrinkled her scalp. There. She had a reason to start a conversation with Riggo. "What's a good headache remedy for trauma-induced distress?" That wouldn't raise any suspicions. She swallowed her sarcasm and the last of the moisture in her mouth.

The script she'd been given played out in her mind as she gripped the steel door handle and walked into the scene that would either free or doom her. *Aurelia, when you said God would be with me wherever I go, did you mean here, too?* Her imagination was as ripe as her nerve endings. She thought she heard the word yes.

Fingers of shelved items beckoned her attention. Retractable canes and industrial-strength dandruff shampoos had grown fascinating overnight. She'd picked up one of the plastic shopping baskets at Tony's suggestion and now chose a few items to line it as if shopping were anywhere on her priority list.

Facial tissues. Who doesn't need more of those? A new brand of exfoliating facial wipes safe for eye-makeup removal. Nice find. Throat lozenges. A sick grin tugged at the corners of her mouth. If Riggo slit her throat, at least she'd have lozenges handy.

She drew a breath that shuddered on the way out. Humor wouldn't change the inevitable. She sauntered toward the pharmacy counter at the rear of the store. Her eye caught the security camera aimed toward the spot where customers stand when talking to the pharmacist.

"Make contact, Becca. Let's go."

Becca startled at the sound in her ear, as if the whole store could hear.

"Ms. Morrow. Didn't think I'd see you here . . . so soon." Riggo's enthusiasm read decidedly false. "Earache?"

"Pardon?"

"You held your hand to your ear. Thought maybe you had an earache. We have a few good over-the-counter options for that."

She erased the opening line of her script. "Must be water in my ear. Swimming. Or from the shower." *Not good. None of it. Can we start over?*

He continued shelving cold medications, pulling older inventory to the front and placing new inventory behind. "Ever try a little peroxide on a cotton ball? My mom swears by it for drawing out water."

"Have to try that. Thanks."

"Sorry to hear about Mrs. Hughes passing."

The sound in her earbud cautioned, "Careful."

"Yes. What a wonderful woman."

"I thought so, too." Riggo sighed and stopped stocking the shelf. "Good woman. People like that shouldn't suffer."

Bingo. *Okay, Tony. Tell me what to say next.* Silence. "Hard to understand why some do."

Ernest Riggo stared at her. She stared back, unblinking. *Give us something, Riggo. Anything.*

A soul-deep darkness fixed his stare. She couldn't flinch. If she smiled knowingly, would that encourage him to spill? Barely perceptible. As if she understood his thoughts. How long had it been since she'd drawn a breath?

"I admired your father's work."

Her peripheral vision darkened. The room listed like a sailboat in a fierce wind. Riggo said something else, but the sound seemed far away, too far, yet not far enough. She blinked but held her gaze on the evil one.

"I . . . I didn't realize you knew my father."

"Worked with him a few years ago," he said, returning his attention to decongestants. "Read everything he wrote. He said I didn't understand what he was trying to do." Riggo pivoted to face her. "I could have talked him into taking me on as his assistant, if I'd had enough time. The man shouldn't be in prison."

His statement brought the tunnel vision back. She shook it off without moving her head.

"He shouldn't?"

"You ruined everything. So now . . ." His eyes darted. "If you'll pardon the expression, you're getting a taste of your own medicine."

His chuckle scraped her nerve endings.

"You weren't easy to find. But someone has to pay for a good man going to prison. I found a way to make that happen. I'm surprised you're out on bond. Guess my job isn't done yet."

A shudder worked its way from scalp to soles.

"You'll pay, though. Clever how I could end Mrs. Hughes's suffering and start yours with the same act, wasn't it?"

Becca forced an unfelt calm and leaned slightly forward, as if interested in his story rather than petrified of the man with uncoordinated eyes. "Excuse me. I need . . . restroom." She steadied herself on the shelf nearest her as the undercover detectives swarmed in, guns drawn.

⁂

Lisa—the detective who'd helped Becca kill time on the night Aurelia died while the crime scene investigators scoured Aurelia's room for evidence—helped rid her of the wires and microphone.

"Do you think they got enough to get a warrant to search his apartment?" Becca asked, still shivering, still fighting off the dizziness she feared would never leave after that encounter.

"More than enough, sweetie. Hahn already heard back from Judge Forsythe. The process is started."

"What if Riggo bolts? What if I blew it by stopping the conversation with him so suddenly? I couldn't . . . I couldn't go on."

Becca tugged her blouse back into position but left the vest off.

"No worries. The team brought him in for questioning. We can hold him long enough for his apartment and computer hard drive to be thoroughly searched. If my guess is right, he's as eager for the publicity as we are to convict him."

Riggo. There. In the building. She had to get home where she belonged.

"Tony said to say thanks for your help. He'll catch up with you and Isaac later. I must say, I haven't seen him so determined in a long time."

"Thanks, Lisa. You've been a breath of fresh air through all this."

"I'm glad for your sake it's almost over."

Becca stopped herself from correcting the woman. Her lineage would never be over. Her grief over the way Aurelia died would never be over. Her guilt would never end. If Becca hadn't moved here, if she hadn't taken the job, if Riggo hadn't found her, Aurelia might still be alive. Barely. But alive.

Lisa closed the lid on the storage box for the monitoring unit. "Free to go. Oh, one more thing before you do."

What could that be? More paperwork?

Lisa opened the door to the prep room and let in Isaac. As she exited, she closed the door behind her with a wink.

All the dizziness drained out through her feet. His presence in the room righted what had been tilting. "Isaac."

He drew her into his arms and held her wordlessly. She drank in the scent of him, the strength he loaned her, the wonder that he was there, with her, had been there all along, just offstage.

They hadn't moved, hadn't broken the embrace when a tap-tap-tap a few minutes later preceded Lisa opening the door a crack. "Guys? You're going to want to get in on this."

Detective Hahn's office was no more inviting than it had been the night before. He hung up his phone as they entered. "Glad you're still here. Thought you might appreciate an update." He nodded toward the phone. "That was Tony. They're drowning in evidence over at Riggo's apartment."

Becca's chest tightened.

"Everything we need and more. We already have enough to open three cold cases and will probably find more that had been labeled 'natural causes.' We'll be busy for a while."

How could this news both relieve and devastate? Others, too? *Oh, Daddy! What did you start?*

Isaac must have recognized the implications. His knees buckled as he slid into the chair nearest him.

She stood behind him, one hand on his shoulder. It didn't matter who was standing, who collapsed. They pulled comfort from each other.

"And Riggo's chatting like a jaybird," Hahn said, his glee appropriate for law enforcement but disturbing to those still in mourning for one of Riggo's victims. "Tony will never let me hear the end of it. He kept insisting 'God wouldn't let him' stop looking for some other explanation than you, Ms. Morrow. I say it was good investigative work. He put in a lot of extra hours on this. More to come. I think you owe him a steak dinner."

"We'll take care of that, Detective," Isaac offered. "Right now, if it's okay, we just want to go home."

"Sure. Sure. Lisa, you'll see them out? Thanks again for your patience and your help."

Isaac leaned against the headrest after starting the car and cranking the air conditioning to high. He heard the click when Becca buckled her seatbelt. Neither said a word.

The cords in his throat hadn't relaxed yet. He stretched his neck against the headrest. Eyes closed against the swirl of emotions, he listened to the rhythm of his heartbeat. Or was that hers?

"Isaac, thank you for believing in me."

He turned his head to face her then. "Mom told me to."

Her smile complemented the mist in her eyes. "That was your Aunt Geneva's line, if I remember correctly. Your mom wouldn't have known to suggest it."

He fished his cell phone from his pocket, punched up the text, and showed it to her. "A text from 'Aunt' Geneva."

The dawn of recognition on her face was as distinct as the moment the sun clears the horizon in the morning. "Oh, Isaac!" Breathless. Like he felt. "When did this come?"

"When you were getting wired. Before you confronted Riggo. I couldn't say anything until now, not without it serving as a distraction, even subconsciously."

The sun came from over his shoulder. It made her squint. She used her hand as a visor, but this wasn't the place for further discussion on the subject anyway. He backed the car out of its parking space while Becca stared at the screen of his phone and the ten-word message he'd memorized. "Yes, Isaac. I'm your birth mother. When can we talk?"

29

The hospital bed was gone. Once the crime scene had been cleared, Isaac returned the bed to the rental place, along with other reminders of Aurelia's illness and death. The sunroom was vacant in every meaning of the word.

Becca made iced tea and turkey salad sandwiches while Isaac dragged a small, round patio table and two wrought-iron chairs from the backyard into the sunroom. His idea, not hers. It still took courage to enter that room once beautiful because of the soul that spent her last days there.

Isaac insisted. For a man with a business mind, tradition and setting ranked surprisingly high on his priority list. Maybe it was the real estate agent in him. He envisioned scenes, not just buildings and rooms.

"I need to be here, in this room, Becca," he said by way of explanation as she entered with the tray with their salads and tea. He took the tray from her hands. She arranged the table and place settings and tried not to think about the ugliness that had tainted Aurelia's final breaths, Riggo's deadly, desiccating Atropine drops in one of her liquid medications, the absence of moisture in the lifeless eyes, grossly dilated pupils, hot, beet-red skin that had set off alarms in Tony's mind.

Becca's grief grew exponentially with the horror of how Aurelia had died, despite Dr. Lambert's assurance it would have been quick for a woman with a fragile heart.

The garden—Aurelia's garden—danced in the midday sunlight. Isaac and Becca sat in its soundless music, separated from it by a wall of windows that had afforded Aurelia her last glimpses of earth.

"When are you going to call your aunt? Your mom?" Becca used the side of her fork to cut off a chunk of honeydew melon. "I'm sorry, Isaac. I don't know what words to use for these women who meant and mean so much to you."

"You're not alone. Until we talk, I don't even know if Aunt Geneva is ready for me to call her Mom. Or if she wants things to stay the way they've been."

"You are so blessed. Two incredible women loved you with all their hearts."

He cupped her chin in his hand. "Two?"

"I would say three, but I'm wrestling with the word *incredible*."

He leaned to touch his forehead to hers. "The timing's all wrong, Becca. But someday, I hope you'll call Geneva Larkin your mother-in-law."

So this is what joy feels like.

———

"Is it okay if I put you on speaker phone, Aunt Geneva? Becca's here with me."

She must have answered in the affirmative. He grinned and set the phone on the table between them.

"Can you hear us?"

"I hear you fine, Isaac. Becca?"

"I'm right here, Mrs. Larkin."

"Isaac texted that you've been cleared of all suspicion. Praise God."

Becca wished she could have been with them for that moment.

Isaac leaned toward the phone. "I know it's going to be hard to talk about all this long distance. And I don't want to make it any more awkward than it is."

The phone on the table stayed silent too long.

"Aunt Geneva?"

"I would never have dishonored your mother, Isaac. She raised you. She had every right to consider herself your true mother. I wouldn't have told you if she were still alive unless you asked outright or she insisted on it. We made an agreement when you were born. Both of us kept our word."

Isaac pressed his fingertips to his eyes. Becca rubbed his back with one hand.

"Was I born here? In California? You've lived in the Midwest since you got out of college, I was told."

"I stayed with your parents during the pregnancy. They were at the hospital with me when you came into the world. That's why they have so many pictures of you just hours old. Your birth certificate is accurate."

"And my father? My birth father?"

A long pause punctuated the awkwardness of the question. "I don't know, Son. I can't tell you his name or anything about him."

Isaac frowned at the phone. "Someone . . . assaulted you?"

"No." Another impossible pause. "I was a different person then. Heading into my last year of college. Tired of being . . . It sounds ridiculous now. I was tired of being good. You know the kinds of things parents worry about when their kids go on spring break? For good reason."

Isaac rested his head in his hands, elbows on the table. Eyes closed. Becca touched his arm and nodded toward the pitcher of tea. He shook his head and sighed.

"I know that's not what you wanted to hear, Isaac. I'm so sorry. And I don't blame you for feeling ashamed of what I did."

He started. "I'm not ashamed of you, Aunt Genev— Mom. How could I be ashamed of you? I know who you are *now*. I've always admired you."

"Your mom and dad were the ones to be admired. They loved you so well. How could I have asked for anything more for my son? And they allowed me to stay in touch, to visit as often as I wanted. They sent photos and cards and included me in everything. They didn't want you not to belong to me in order for you to belong to them. I know that probably sounds strange. We shared the task of making sure you knew you were loved. I couldn't be more grateful that they allowed me that privilege."

"I want to know the whole story."

"You deserve to hear it. I know it will take some getting used to."

Isaac's fingers traced the perimeter of the phone. "I think God was getting me used to the idea long before I knew."

"Becca, are you still there?"

"I'm here." She scooted her chair closer.

"Will you hug my son for me?"

"It'll be a sacrifice, but for you . . ."

"Hey!"

"Isaac, I know we kept you on a fruitless search for where you truly belonged," his newly revealed mother said. "Son, you were already there."

Geneva's Christmas plans held more significance than ever. A mother-son reunion. Becca determined to do everything in her power to make sure it felt like a celebration but allowed the two all the time they needed to be alone.

And somehow, that would fit around her new job.

Because of the chaos of the last weeks, Monday dawned before they'd had an opportunity to get Becca a valid driver's license. So Isaac swung by to pick her up before work. He looked more relaxed than she'd seen him in weeks. She checked her mascara in the visor mirror. She looked more relaxed, too.

Training for her job under Isaac's supervision revealed two disadvantages. The nearness of him was a complete distraction. And he wasn't exactly sure what Mrs. Gallum did at the reception desk, other than screen his calls and take messages when he was out of the office.

She'd learn, but most of it would be by trial and error. Isaac insisted he wasn't disturbed by her unending stream of questions. She thought it best to assume everything was important, unless told otherwise. The next best thing to taking care of Aurelia was helping Isaac with his business.

Riggo's story hit the news her second day on the job. Becca knew the routine. A week or two of penetrating press, then relative silence during the interminable wait for the trial, when the press would buzz back out of their hives again. She prayed the early stories would fade before Christmas. It would be close.

Bud and Sissy had made cruise reservations long before they heard about Aurelia's death. Isaac and Becca agreed that as good as it would have been to see them and the kids, this Christmas was the perfect time for Geneva and Isaac to have a smaller, quieter holiday.

Sales naturally slumped in commercial real estate in December. Isaac begged off all but the unavoidable holiday obligations. He used the time to catch up on office work that had grown appendages while they'd dealt with their layered crises. Becca used the time to familiarize herself with the computer system at Hughes Realty and to compile a menu and decorations that would do justice to the reunion.

After Isaac dropped her off at the end of the day, on the nights he headed straight for his condo rather than staying for supper, Becca pored over the photo albums in the library, choosing a dozen or more that would mean even more to mother and son now that the truth was out. Pictures of Christmases past with toddler Isaac on his "Aunt" Geneva's lap. Her presence at all the important events in his life. High school and college graduation. The ribbon-cutting ceremony for Isaac's business. Snapshots of their famed cruise to Alaska.

The framed picture Isaac had borrowed from Aurelia's room upstairs now hung in the living room, above the fireplace. He'd pointed out to Becca the clues the photo offered him—joy and serenity surrounding him. Aurelia standing a few inches farther away to allow Geneva a photographic, at least, oneness with her son.

Joy, serenity, and peace.

What if she'd been born into a family like that? How might her life have played out differently?

The stray thought caught her unaware. She might never have met Isaac.

Becca tensed. "You're annoyed with me."

"A little," Isaac confessed.

"I'm sorry."

"Don't apologize."

"But you're annoyed with me." Becca held her palms up and out as if asking, "What do I do with that except apologize?"

He took the vacuum cleaner from her and deposited it in the hall closet. "Why would you think you had to ask if I wanted you with me when I pick up Geneva at the airport?"

"Because."

"Because why?"

She sat on the second step and pressed her hands between her knees. "Because I'm still not sure what's appropriate, or where I belong in all this."

Hadn't he made his feelings clear? "Becca, we're in this together. All of it."

"I lost my reason for being here. Don't think I'm unaware my taking over for Mrs. Gallum is a sympathy job. Don't object. Yes, it's keeping me busy and yes, it's probably helping out in some small way . . ."

"Becca, come on."

"I'm not trying to play the victim here. I need to know my boundaries. Where do I fit? Am I overstepping my bounds if I rearrange the furniture or assume I'm included in the airport runs?"

"Becca . . ." He joined her on the step. Her distress reverberated in his belly.

"I'm staying in what should be your house. You're paying for and living in a condo you don't need. Your mom is coming to visit for the first time since you discovered she was your mom but I'm here as if I own the place. You don't think that's a little convoluted?"

He laced his fingers through hers. "I'd like you there when I pick up my mom at the airport."

She looked up. Her expression lost its crimp. "Thank you. I'd like to be there."

He kissed her forehead, lingering until the furrows eased. Pears. She smelled like pears.

She leaned against his shoulder and nestled there. "What time do we have to leave for the airport?"

"Ten minutes ago."

"Oh."

Neither of them moved.

—⊗∞⊗—

"God is smiling on us today, Becca."

"Not that I doubt what you're saying, but traffic's not moving and—"

"Take a look at this."

Text alert. Flight delayed twenty minutes due to gate congestion.

"We're not going to be late, Becca. We'll get there early. Sweet."

"Did you remember your sign?"

"Backseat."

"Such a different trip for her this time."

"For all of us."

As if an announcer had said, "And now, a moment of silence to honor the memory of the incomparable Aurelia Hughes," conversation stilled.

Traffic inched forward, then busted loose. The airport exit loomed before either spoke again.

"God, thank You for this."

Becca squeaked. "Those were the exact words in my mind just now. Weird, huh?"

He negotiated the exit and took the familiar path toward Arrivals. "What did you mean by *this*?"

"What did *you* mean?"

"Everything."

"Me, too."

———

Isaac positioned himself at the foot of the escalator in the baggage claim area nearest Geneva's baggage carousel. Becca readied Isaac's camera phone to take the first of a fresh batch of family photos.

"Here she comes!" she said, nudging him.

"I see that."

"Isaac."

"What?"

"Your sign says WOW. That's true and all, but . . ."

He flipped it right side up. MOM.

Geneva must have seen the interchange. She descended the escalator laughing hysterically.

She embraced her son as if it were the first time they'd seen each other since a deployment overseas. Becca watched other passengers step around the reunion, some smiling, some chuckling, some swiping at a tear.

Becca clicked off a dozen photos and got the two to pose with the sign—both ways.

The baggage carousel clattered to life. Good son that he was, Isaac hoisted her luggage when it passed where they stood.

"Did you have to pay an overage fee for this one? It weighs a ton."

Geneva jostled him with her elbow. "It weighs exactly forty-nine pounds. I could have left your Christmas present at home, if you wanted it lighter."

He snapped the pull handle into position. "Can I get your carry-on, too?"

Becca stepped in. "I've got it." She hadn't been left out of the hugs. Her heart was light enough to hoist the forty-nine-pound bag, if necessary.

Isaac's mom rode up front with him. Conversation flowed much more smoothly than the traffic. They had so many shared memories, it wasn't like starting from scratch in their relationship. It was more like filling in a few holes. And enjoying each other without reservation, nothing between them.

"I've loved you since before you were born, Isaac. Longer than anyone but God," she said. "Please know you weren't adopted because I didn't want you. I think if it had been anyone but my sister who volunteered to take you, I couldn't have done it. But at the time, I was still making lousy choices and I knew it."

"You weren't a teenager," Isaac said.

"No. I was old enough to know better. You're making much wiser choices than I did." Geneva peeked into the backseat and winked at Becca when she said that.

Becca turned her attention to the Christmas decorations against a snowless beach atmosphere. What a turn her life had taken. She drew a deep breath just because she could. Relaxed into the seat because she had nothing to fear. Listened in as a mother and son got reacquainted. And cried a little for all they'd been through.

By the time Geneva descended the stairs after unpacking, Becca had a pasta salad and fresh fruit plated and on the little table in the sunroom. She lit the hurricane candle in the center of the table, poured fresh-squeezed lemonade into fat goblets, flicked the switch for the tiny Christmas lights with which she'd outlined the window frames, and opened a couple of the windows to the enchanting night air. Jasmine and another fragrance she couldn't pinpoint mixed like an expensive but delicate perfume.

"This is lovely," Geneva said.

Isaac entered the room on her heels. "We like to eat out here as often as we can. Our own private bistro." He surveyed the scene. "Becca, there are only two places set."

She backed up to the door through which they'd recently entered. "I have a novel I've been eager to get to. I'll eat in my room. Enjoy your evening."

"Becca, no."

She raised a hand palm out to stop Isaac's protest. She stepped back into the room long enough to give both of them a quick kiss on the cheek. "I'm so happy for you two."

The room she'd borrowed felt more like home than anything she'd known in a long time. She stood at the window with its view of the side yard, curious about the conversation taking place in the sunroom, but content to let it be.

The stars weren't as bright here as she was used to seeing on a clear night.

She kicked off her shoes and settled into her favorite chair. She clicked the remote that started the music. A mix of Aurelia's favorites. The cool pasta salad tasted refreshing. The novel captured her attention from the first page. She held the book in her left hand and her fork in her right. Nothing would ruffle her this evening.

Except the sharp, toe-curling scream.

Becca raced toward the sound and found its source in the sunroom.

"What's wrong?"

Geneva sat at the table with both hands clamped over her mouth.

"Is she choking?" Becca hoisted the woman out of her chair and positioned her clenched fists at the base of Geneva's diaphragm, or thereabouts.

"No, no! I'm not choking!" She flailed her arms in protest.

Becca dropped her hold and stared at a motionless Isaac, hands behind his back. She hadn't taken him for someone who'd freeze in an emergency.

"Well, I *was* choking," Geneva added. "But it's all . . . good."

"I heard someone scream. Wasn't that you?"

"Y-yes. Oh, Isaac, I'm so sorry. I've made a mess of it."

"No, Mom. It's okay."

"It is not. I'm so sorry."

What had come up in their conversation that had rattled Geneva so badly? Becca thought they were done with scream-worthy events for a while.

"Becca, sit down. Please?" Isaac indicated the chair he'd occupied.

"What's wrong?" Her mind tumbled with possibilities. Geneva was sick. Isaac was sick. She couldn't read the answer in either of their faces, but Geneva looked anything but disturbed.

Isaac bit his lower lip, then said, "I shared something with Mom, something I intended to share with you when the moment was right."

"No more secrets, Isaac." Becca realized how odd the words sounded coming from her. The old, familiar hollowness returned. One night. Couldn't she have had this one night of serenity?

"Then I guess the moment is now. Merry Christmas?" His eyebrows arched as he drew his hand from behind his back and opened his palm to her. The square-cut diamond sparkled like a moonlit ocean.

"One knee!" Geneva whispered behind her.

She obeyed, sinking to the floor on one knee.

"Not you, silly girl. Him!"

Becca reclaimed her chair while Isaac knelt.

"Becca, a rose by any other name—"

"Oh, for Pete's sake." Geneva huffed. Becca giggled, caught up in a ridiculous dream, but one she hoped to remember when she woke.

Isaac cleared his throat. "Becca, you've taught me so much about tenacity and contentment. You've opened my eyes to the idea that love doesn't always look like we think it will. You've reminded me how love changes things when it serves others. I can't imagine living the rest of my life without you. I don't know how I survived before I met you, except by God's grace. Would you bless me by becoming my wife so I can bless you the rest of your days?"

She didn't look at the ring. She couldn't tear her gaze from his eyes. He meant every word.

Becca placed her hands on the sides of his face and kissed his forehead. "You are the dearest man."

Isaac's shoulders sank. "That sounds like something my mother would say."

"She did. She's coaching me in whispers. Didn't you hear her?"

He leaned around Becca to lock gazes with Geneva, "Mom!"

Becca fought to keep her composure over Isaac's adorable discomfort. She snatched the ring from his hand and threaded it on her index finger to the first knuckle. "Is this for me?" How would he have known the ring that lived only in her dreams? A tear hovered in the corner of her eye, then followed the curve of her cheek as gravity tugged on it. "Would you give that speech again?"

Isaac clamped his hands around hers, the ring still showing. "Every day of your life, if you'd like to hear it."

"Need. Need to hear it."

Isaac held a hand to block his mother's view and kissed Becca with a tenderness she wasn't sure she'd ever known.

"Becca, you said one time you didn't know where you belonged. I thought you'd stolen my line. Turns out our answers are the same. Here. Right here." He slipped the ring onto the fourth finger of her left hand, then pressed that hand against his chest. "Here. Right here."

His pulse—strong and steady—beat so unlike Aurelia's thready, weak one, yet so *like* hers, too. Faithful. Inexpressibly kind. Not only caring what God thought but also living it. And loving her. Loving her in spite of everything.

"It's too soon, isn't it? Too crazy around here." He grasped the ring and slid it off her finger. Or attempted to do so. Becca stopped him and secured it where it belonged.

"Isaac, 'these waves sound like the womb of my beginnings.'"

"You're mocking me. I should never have told you about that poem."

"I'm not making fun of it, Isaac. I want it to be *our* song, not just yours. I thought I wanted a waveless life. I didn't realize the life is in the waves."

Geneva leaned over Becca's shoulder. "Son, I think that's a yes."

30

It's the perfect solution, Mom." Isaac poured a warm-up for her coffee. "Doesn't it make sense?"

Becca entered the living room, tucked a mammoth present behind the tree, and plugged in the lights.

"Woman after my own heart," his mom said. "Keep those Christmas lights on no matter how sunny it is."

Becca picked up a mug from the tray on the coffee table and held it out to Isaac. "If you're pouring . . ."

"First things first," he said, setting the carafe on the tray. "Good morning, my bride-to-be." He kissed her lips, her nose, and her forehead in a pattern he hoped would always be their tradition. She'd said the kiss on her forehead felt like a blessing. If he could help it, she'd know that blessing every day.

"I thought I recognized a familiar voice," she said, leaning into his embrace. "When did you get here?"

"About a half hour ago."

Geneva pointed toward the banana bread fanned out on a china plate. "I made the mistake of telling Isaac I'd brought banana bread from home. Guess he couldn't wait. Help yourself."

"Thanks."

Isaac sat down on one of the couches and motioned for Becca to join him. "I couldn't sleep."

"Already regretting your decision?" Becca asked, twirling the ring on her finger.

"Never. An idea kept me awake."

"Oh, here we go," she teased.

"It's about the condo."

His mom scooted to the forward edge of her armchair.

"I've been praying about it. I think it would be ideal for you, Mom."

Becca choked on her sip of coffee. "Wait a minute. Did you ask her if she wanted to move out here, Isaac? That's quite a life disruption."

His mom's face clouded. "I've longed to move here for almost thirty-five years."

The muscles across the back of his shoulders tightened. "Thirty-five years? Why didn't you?"

Her mouth twisted. Tears pooled.

Becca laid a hand on his knee. "Because of you, Isaac. So you and your adoptive family could have the best possible chance to bond without her interference."

"She's a smart cookie, Isaac," his mom said.

"All this time?" he said. "All this time you've wished you lived here?"

"Every . . . minute . . . of every . . . day. The ache didn't throb as much when I was married to Lyle, short-lived as that was."

He had so much to learn.

"She didn't abandon *you* all those years ago, Isaac. She abandoned herself *for* you. That's what love does." Becca put her arm around his waist and squeezed.

"All the more reason for her to move here now." He geared up for the objections sure to fly.

Becca reached for a piece of the fragrant bread. "You won't get an argument from me, but it's really her choice, isn't it?"

"You two should be planning your wedding, not worrying about me." His mom brushed invisible crumbs from her lap. "You're starting your own lives together. You don't need my interference now any more than you did thirty years ago, Isaac."

Isaac thought long enough to swallow another swig of coffee. "You don't like my condo?"

His mom cocked her head. "Two things. It's not on the beach. And there's no room to entertain grandchildren." She sat back with an air of finality.

Isaac felt Becca's fingers tighten on his knee.

"Mom, we haven't"—he looked at Becca's bemused face—"talked about children . . . yet."

Bemusement turned to what registered as apprehension. Chin down, eyebrows pinched. "I'd like children," Becca said, her words more sigh than statement.

"Me, too." The room narrowed to the small space that held the two of them. "Four?"

"Three is the number I had in mind. But, Isaac . . . ?"

He leaned his forehead to touch hers. "What?"

"Never mind. Timing's not right."

"Since when have we ever waited for that?"

She chuckled. He could feel her smile in the skin of her forehead.

"I was hoping—" Their identical sentences tumbled over each other, stirring another round of laughter. "You first," she said.

Isaac traced the line of her jaw with one finger. "I was hoping we could include adoption?"

She linked her fingers behind his neck. "Me, too."

"We're agreed then," his mom quipped, sealing her statement with applause. "Sell your guy-friendly condo and keep your eyes open for a beach cottage with room for four grandbabies to visit." She seemed so utterly pleased with herself. "Merry Christmas to me!"

His adoptive parents would have loved to be here now, Isaac thought. They would have enjoyed the conversation as much as any of them. A twinge of grief sobered the moment, but couldn't completely dampen the wonder of the contentment that rocked his soul like a mom would rock a newborn.

"To new beginnings."

"New beginnings."

Was it just her, or was the Christmas Eve service more poignant than it had ever been? Was the story of Love's sacrifice more meaningful than in years past? The week between Christmas and New Year's stretched like a garland of little joys linked together by the discovery that her heart had found where it could safely nest.

She raised her glass of sparkling cider with the rest of Isaac's friends who filled the living room, dining room, and spilled into the kitchen. "New beginnings."

"Guacamole!" someone shouted. Other voices joined in. "Guacamole! Guacamole! Guacamole!"

Becca angled toward Isaac's ear. "I thought I'd made enough. We're out of avocados."

"Oh, my bride," he said, squeezing her with one free arm. "It's a Hughes-and-friends tradition. Guacamole reminds us to face the New Year bravely because some things are even better after they've been pulverized."

His dark eyes danced with delight. His kiss landed lightly on her forehead. "And we know a few things about that, don't we?"

"Don't ever stop calling me your bride, okay?"

"Okay."

"Isaac?"

"Yes?"

"Guacamole to you."

He threw his head back and laughed until tears rolled down his cheeks. He never loosened his grip on her.

"I might just as well leave this here," Isaac said, holding the photo collage against a blank spot on the living room wall.

"You don't like it."

He rushed to correct her misunderstanding. "I love it, Becca. It means more to me than you'll know. I'm seeing these photos of me with Aunt— with my birth mom in a new light. She was always there. It took me until now to know that."

"But you want to leave it here?"

Isaac set the frame on the floor and propped it against the wall. "Maybe I assumed wrong." The Mojave masquerading as his throat refused to let him swallow. "We should have talked about this."

"About . . . ?"

"I assumed we wouldn't wait long to get married. I didn't stop to consider how much time it would take to plan the wedding, or if you were thinking a year-long engagement sounded better."

"No!" She shuddered as if she'd been eating raw limes. "A year? No. Please."

He could breathe again. "What kind of timeline did you have in mind?"

"We don't have to wait for the weather to get nice."

"True."

She continued swaddling the pieces of the nativity set in bubble wrap for storage. "But we don't want to rush into this unwisely."

"No. Of course not. So, next week is good for you?"

"Isaac!"

"Six months?"

"That's a long time." She swaddled more slowly, as if mimicking the passage of time.

"But probably wise for the planning and the premarital counseling Pastor will want to take us through." Isaac said the words but felt as if his teacher had just announced a timed test for math.

"Probably."

"We won't be able to get a reception hall anyplace nice at this late date as it is."

"Can I tell you something?" Her wistful expression melted his heart. "I'm not the kind of woman who wants a lavish wedding to create one memorable day. I understand why some women feel that way, but it isn't me. I'd rather we created a memorable life together."

"Have I told you lately that I love you?"

"About five minutes ago."

"Still true."

"Good."

Six months times thirty days give or take. A hundred and eighty nights without her. Six months stretched before them like the distance to the moon. Make that Saturn.

31

By the end of January, the challenges of the Hughes office no longer intimidated Becca. The role suited her. She enjoyed most of the phone conversations with customers. Isaac had built a strong network of connections and had propelled the Hughes reputation even further than anyone in the family would have imagined.

Her workday had stretches of quiet that allowed her to study the "This Way to a Healthy Marriage" material their pastor had assigned. Thanks to Ginger's help, she'd found her wedding dress in the first store they visited. Simple, but elegant. Exactly what she wanted. Isaac and Becca reserved the commute home for discussions about the guest list. Not complicated from Becca's side. Isaac's list of friends and contacts circled the globe.

Six months was none too long to plan a wedding. But although he didn't talk about it, Becca sensed Isaac found it as difficult as she did when it was time for him to leave the house so they could maintain their commitment to purity.

Becca started sleeping on the right side of the leather sleigh bed at night rather than sprawled in the middle, practicing for when she would share the space with her husband. The wedding still months away, she shoved her clothes to one side of the closet and moved her toiletries into one of the two drawers in the bathroom vanity.

Over lunch at the Asian restaurant where they'd shared their first meal, Isaac laid his heart bare.

"Take a look at this, Becca."

"What is it?" She scanned the slick brochure with pictures of children, the young faces searching for something they hadn't yet found. "An adoption agency?"

"One of the best."

"Isaac, no one can ever accuse you of procrastinating." She used her chopsticks to snag a piece of baby bok choy. "But this is speedy, even for you."

"Not now. Starting the conversation. Merely starting the conversation."

"You'd want to adopt first?"

He slurped hot-and-sour soup. "Are you opposed?"

"No. I guess I never thought about adopting first."

Isaac set his spoon aside and made a tent of his linked hands and forearms. "I'd want our child to know he—or she—was chosen because we loved him, that we didn't wait to find out whether or not we could have children on our own."

"International adoption or domestic?"

"This agency does both. What are your thoughts?"

Becca sipped oolong tea, the warmth of the cup helping compensate for the hyperactive air-conditioning. "I think life with you will be anything but boring."

He tilted his head, just like his mother did, then said, "It was, before I met you."

"Oh, Isaac. That's the worst pick-up line I've ever heard."

"But you kind of liked it, didn't you?"

"I plead the fifth." Time to change the subject.

"Any messages?" Isaac asked, rubbing the back of his neck with one hand. It had been one of those days.

"'Hi to you, too. How was your afternoon, Becca? Good. Thanks for asking.'"

"Sorry. I have a conference call at three."

"I know. I set it up for you."

"Right." He stopped by her desk, let out a breath as if he could expel the tension of his previous appointment, and started over. "You look great."

"Good move."

"How was your afternoon?"

"Lonely without you here."

Isaac's mind raced through options. "How do you look in a hard hat?"

"Excuse me?"

"I could start taking you with me to appointments on work sites. But you'd have to wear a hard hat."

"Think I'll stay here and do my nails."

"Very funny. Any messages?"

"Nothing that can't wait until after your conference call. I have it all set up for you. Your notes are to the right of your coffee cup. Fresh coffee, I might add. I don't get paid extra for making coffee, do I?"

"And that, my dear, is why I keep you around. You dropped my blood pressure by about fifty points in one minute flat. Thank you." He kissed her on the forehead and disappeared into his office.

"You owe me dinner!" she called after him.

"As long as it's low sodium," he called back. "Blood pressure." Work was fun again because of her. *Thank You, Lord.*

Life was fun for the first time because of him. *Thank You, Lord.*

Becca added another item to her list of things to discuss on the commute home. Photographer. She searched the Internet for the website of the young mom at church who'd started a home-based photography business.

The online gallery of her photography convinced Becca by the third photo. Beautiful. Artistic. Unpretentious. Simple but elegant. The woman captured the soul of each shot. Wedding moments. Newborns. Families. More newborns.

A new longing, one she'd forbidden until now, bloomed within her. A child. Someday. By this time next year, she could be carrying a child inside. Or a picture of one they wanted to adopt.

First things first. Wedding photos. She checked the photographer's fees. That would have bought a used truck and a corn crib back in Iowa. She had a feeling Isaac would say helping a new business get off the ground would be worth it. And she'd say, "Artist, Isaac. It might be her business, but she's an artist." And then he'd say—

"We're out of here." Isaac closed his office door and stood at the end of her desk.

"What?"

"Nelson was a no-show for the conference call. And he had the most invested. So, let's take off early."

"Don't tell my boss, okay?"

"Promise."

They drove to the Oceanside pier, grabbed fish tacos from their favorite food truck vendor, and walked as they ate. The length of the pier and back. Then again. Becca couldn't remember a day more beautiful since . . . since the last time they'd walked the pier.

"Wait until you see her photography, Isaac. We'll go online when we get home and—"

"I think you should set up an appointment for us."

"Really?"

"I agree with sending her our business. And if you like her work . . ."

"Can't even describe how much."

Isaac spread his hands as if signaling the runner was safe at home plate. "Done. You know my schedule as well as I do these days."

"You're welcome."

"Can we get a few shots of us now, prior to the wedding? I need something for my desk."

She nudged him with her elbow. "I work in the same office. I'm there with you every day."

"Please? I never knew how much it would mean to chronicle our lives in pictures."

"*Chronicle*? Big word of the day?"

He nudged her back. "Do you have a better entry?"

"*Delirious.*"

"Not bad. Use it in a sentence?"

She closed her eyes and leaned on his arm as she thought. "I'm deliriously happy and so grateful I met you. I thank God for you every day."

"That's two sentences."

"Ooh! You can count, too? How did I get so blessed?"

They walked in comfortable silence for a while. Becca didn't know where Isaac's thoughts ran, but hers swam in pools of inexpressible peace.

⁂

Isaac dropped his keys on the kitchen counter and sorted the junk mail from the legitimate while Becca booted up his laptop to show him the photography website.

"Hey, you've got mail," he said.

"I never get mail."

"It's addressed to you. To . . ."

Becca looked up from the screen. "To what?"

Something fierce growled inside him. He wanted to believe it was his protective nature. But it churned more like anger.

"Isaac? I don't like the look in your eyes. What is it? It's addressed to what?"

"Both your names."

She bounced from the barstool. "Cool. A catalog came the other day, too, addressed to Mrs. Isaac Hughes. A little premature, but I'll take it." She reached for the letter.

"It can wait until tomorrow, I'm sure. So, show me this 'amazing' photography."

"Isaac, cough it up."

He glanced at the return address. It could only mean trouble. She snatched the envelope before he could figure out a way to postpone the inevitable.

"Jayne Dennagee, in care of Becca Morrow," she read aloud, her voice flat, lifeless. "From . . ."

"Who is that guy?"

"My father's attorney."

She held the envelope and stared at the address. Then she set it on the island, still staring. Arms at her sides, she rubbed her hands on her slacks as if rubbing away the scent of the envelope.

Isaac's pulse pounded in his ears. Hers must have been off the charts. "Do you want me to open it?"

She shook her head no. Kept staring.

"What could it be?" He mentally paged through the options. None would bode well for Becca's sanity.

From behind, he wrapped his arms around her and leaned his cheek on her crown. "Father God, help us here." He couldn't think of anything else to pray. They swayed that way, probably his doing, for a few moments before Becca pulled away.

"I have to open it."

"Yes, hon."

"Don't go anywhere."

"I won't. Do you want to read it in the living room, sitting down?"

"It wouldn't help."

"No."

"Don't you go anywhere."

He rubbed her back in slow circles, like a parent trying to quiet a fretful child. "I said I wouldn't."

"Did you?"

The muscles of his heart ripped into fissures and canyons. *Hold it together, man. She needs you.*

He worked the muscles of her shoulders like a manager would a prizefighter.

"Isaac, you can stop that."

"It's okay."

"No, really. Please stop that. It's not helping."

He backed away. A step.

"I'm stronger than this." She stood straighter now.

"You are."

"Going in."

"Okay. I'm right here."

She picked up the envelope, slid her forefinger under the flap, and turned to Isaac. "Band-aid. Top drawer to the right of the sink."

"Band-aid?"

"I have a paper cut," she said, holding her finger aloft. "I don't think this is the kind of letter I want to bleed all over."

"One Band-aid. Coming right up." His fingers fumbled so badly trying to pull the two halves of the paper wrapping apart, she had to take the bandage from him and finish.

He tossed the discards while she read the opening lines. Silently.

"Did he . . . did he die in prison, Becca?" What else could it be?

"Worse," she said, her voice husky with emotion. "He's not dead. He's dying. And he's getting out."

Isaac held her hair while she retched into the powder room toilet.

"I'm sorry," she whimpered.

"Don't be sorry, honey."

She retched again. He turned his head to the side and closed his eyes. When she was finished, he helped her to her feet and wrung out a cool washcloth for her face. She leaned against the sink and caught her reflection in the mirror. "Yeah, that's what I thought I'd look like."

"It's going to be okay. This doesn't have to affect you. He'll be thousands of miles from here."

She gripped the sink with both hands. "His . . . lawyer . . . wants to know if I'll take care of him until he's . . . gone."

"Quick answer. No way in—"

"Yeah, see? That's the thing." She turned to face him. "Got any gum?"

"What? Sure." He pulled a plastic container from his pants pocket.

She eased past him into the hallway. He followed.

"Isaac, I think I'm supposed to say yes."

"You can't be serious!"

She sank onto their favorite couch in the living room. "That's what I said to myself, too. But I think I'm supposed to do it."

"There was obviously something hallucinogenic in your fish taco."

"We . . . we already had our big word of the day." She dissolved in tears. "I don't think I can do this."

He pulled her into a hug. "I know. I know. That's why you shouldn't even consider it."

"That's why I absolutely should."

"You're running a fever."

"That's my sunburn."

Isaac had an urge to call Pete for help. Or his mom.

"Hear me out."

"I will if you will." *Brilliant, dude.*

"One of the key reasons Dad and I disagreed about this—in addition to the fact that it was illegal—was that he didn't know how to *love* someone to death. But he was skilled at cutting the process short. He tried to ease their pain, yes. But he cheated them out of the kind of richness we knew with Aurelia toward the end. He didn't understand the value of letting God decide the length of our days."

"That's way more than two key reasons."

"The man can still count." She laced her fingers on top of her head and closed her eyes briefly. "The fact that it seems impossible for me makes me think it's exactly what God is calling me to do, something only He could do through me. Haven't we survived a few impossible situations recently?"

"All the more reason to take a breather from Crazytown, don't you think? You don't owe him anything, Becca."

"That's what makes it more of a gift. But it's not for him. I'm not that noble. It's for me. It's to prove something to myself, that I'm free from his power to ruin me."

Isaac prepared his list of comebacks for his turn.

"How awesome would it be to succeed in loving and caring for someone that unlovable, Isaac?"

She'd lost her mind. Or found it.

"We could get a really neurotic puppy, if you want a project, Becca."

She folded her legs underneath her. "I don't want a project. I don't need a project. But I need to do this."

"Even though the thought of it makes you vomit."

"I had to get it out of my system."

The mantel clock ticked an entire round without interrupting anything. It hadn't stopped since it started again the day of Aurelia's memorial service.

"What's he dying from?" Isaac asked.

"Cancer of the everything. It's there in the letter."

"How long does he have?"

She ran the washcloth over her mouth again. "Does it really matter?"

"We're getting married in less than five months, so yeah. It does."

She tucked both hands—crossed at the wrists—under her chin and rocked back and forth.

"This can't come between us, Becca."

She looked him in the eye then. "I don't want it to. Oh, Isaac."

They sat that way another long minute.

"Isaac, I'm not afraid of him anymore."

"You were a half hour ago in the kitchen."

"I wasn't afraid of him. I was afraid of what God might ask me to do. I think I saw it coming. It took me longer than I thought it would to want what God wants more than what's comfortable. Your turn."

"What?"

"You get a turn to be heard."

He stood. "I think it's pretty clear you've already made your choice."

He would have heard her footsteps if she'd followed him out of the room, through the kitchen, and out the door. But she didn't.

32

A ringing phone at two-thirty in the morning sounds far louder and more sinister than it does in the light of day. If Becca had been sleeping, it would have launched a nightmare. She answered, despite the name on the caller ID.

"Are you awake, Becca?"

"Yes."

"I saw your light."

She bolted upright. "Where are you?"

"In the driveway."

"What are you doing out there?"

"I left my keys on the counter in the kitchen."

She wiped her eyes and padded through the house. "Where have you been all this time? Without your keys?"

"Walking."

"Isaac."

"Okay, so I sat part of the time."

"Will you get in here?"

"The neighbors will talk."

She sighed. "Unlike you and me, they're asleep at the moment."

"Right. I'm ready to talk."

She unlocked the door to the man she loved with all her heart. "I'm ready to listen."

This would take coffee. Lots of coffee. She started a pot while he used the facilities. He kicked off his shoes and slumped onto one of the island stools when he returned. He looked like she felt. Miserable.

"Becca, we have to get married."

"We are. The third weekend in June. I'm pretty sure you have it on your calendar."

"We have to get married now. It's the only way this will work."

"The only way what will work?"

"Do you have any ibuprofen?" He tilted his neck to one side then the other. She heard the snaps and crackles from halfway across the room. He squirmed in his seat. "I've been wrestling with God and think my neck's out of joint."

"That's hip."

"This is definitely my neck." He pointed for emphasis.

She handed him a glass of water and two tablets from the cabinet above the sink. Child-proofed already, she thought. He downed the ibuprofen and the entire glass of water.

"I can't let you do this alone," he said. "And I can't help like I could if I lived here."

"Isaac, I never presumed to bring him into your home."

"Our home. Soon. Is next week good for you?"

"What are you talking about?"

"We can do a proper ceremony after he's . . . after he doesn't need you anymore. But if we're married, I can help, and I can . . . . I need to protect you. It's not that you aren't completely capable. It's—"

"I get it. You don't have to explain. I'd feel the same way if the roles were reversed."

"We'll get a rental hospital bed again and put it in the sunroom."

"Isaac, no. That was such a holy place."

He reached for the coffee mug she extended toward him. "And don't you hope it will be again?"

"I know better than to assume I can get through to my dad, or rather that God can get through to him. All I can hope to do is set the stage."

"So, that's what we'll do." Isaac adopted a mask of confidence.

"I really don't want to."

"I know. Me neither."

"Perfect."

"Yeah."

"From what it sounds like, he'll need a lot of care."

"Are you open to our hiring a nurse to help, too?"

All the physical care that was hemmed in tenderness for Aurelia loomed grotesque and nauseating as it related to what lay ahead in caring for her dad. She couldn't avoid it. But she'd have help. Probably paid for from their honeymoon fund.

Isaac took several chest-heaving breaths. "What do we have to do? Are there legal implications, paperwork? Where is he now? How would we get him here?"

The tightness around her heart loosened every moment she was in Isaac's presence. "If you'd asked me those questions a few months ago, I would have said I don't really care. Leave me out of this. He's not my father anymore." She angled her head back to keep the tears from accumulating. "But he is. Whether or not he deserves to be cared for with any measure of kindness isn't the issue. This is bigger than that."

"Come here."

He held her, infusing her with his own strength, as he always had, praying in her ear until her sobbing ceased. "You're a remarkable woman. I love you."

"You're a remarkable man, Isaac. I couldn't love you more than I do."

His kiss sealed their contract to forge ahead into a dark unknown, their short-term missions trip to what could be a hostile environment.

"Isaac?"

"Yes?"

"You need to go home now."

"I'm not sure I can sleep."

She caressed his strong face one last time. "You really, really"—she growled—"need to go home."

He nodded knowingly. "I do. Yes, I do."

She slid from his embrace and crossed the kitchen to turn off the coffeepot.

He grabbed his keys from the counter and gave her a parting kiss on the cheek. "I hope you get some sleep."

"Not a chance. See you in the morning."

"It is morning. It's almost three-thirty."

"See you in the real morning."

"We could skip work. I'm tight with the boss."

"You are the boss."

"All the better."

Becca pushed him toward the door. "Let's try to put in at least half a day, then maybe we should call your mom and get her praying. Oh, and we might mention that we're getting married next week, if we can swing it."

How could his smile flash so bright at that hour? "Good plan, my bride."

Becca hopped on one foot to Isaac's car when he picked her up in the morning, tugging at the shoe she hadn't had time to slide into before he arrived. She'd gotten her teeth brushed. Her hair would work for today, long enough now to make a decent clip-and-go casual look. After greeting him, she pulled down the visor and started on the makeup triage.

"Ugh." This would take more work than she imagined. Perky and an hour's sleep were counterintuitive.

"Having second thoughts?"

"About you? Never."

Isaac groaned. "About . . . your dad."

"Every other minute. But I always come back to knowing it's the right thing to do."

"You're remarkable."

"You've said that before." She didn't need much blush. The sun had taken care of that on the pier the day before. "But don't stop. It helps."

"I keep thinking about all you're having to sacrifice."

"Wouldn't be a gift if it didn't mean sacrifice. And I'm not alone in this. You're giving up a lot."

Isaac glanced at her then returned his attention to the morning traffic. "Would you think less of me if I was kind of excited about the idea that we don't have to wait until June to be together?"

"No. Would you think less of me," she asked, choosing her words carefully, "if I'm grieving a little over giving up having your mom here to walk me down the aisle to you?"

"I promise you that will happen one day."

"If I have you, I'm okay with waiting for the rest."

"Becca, you are re—"

"I know. I know. Remarkable. Keep your eyes on the road, please. We can't afford time for a trip to the ER."

The morning plodded along like an Amish workhorse. Her mind was a greyhound racer making good time around an oval track that always led her back to the starting gate.

Isaac encouraged her to call her father's attorney and talk to him directly. Easier said than done. His assistant assured her she'd give him the message. The phone turned into a grenade ready to explode if she bumped it.

Maybe her dad was too ill to make the trip. She'd avoided news about him, but assumed he was still in the Iowa facility where he'd been sent after sentencing. How much would an ambulance ride across country cost?

And what were the California laws for marriage licenses?

And what if he died before arrangements could be finalized?

And did she want to wear her wedding dress next week or save it for June . . . or whenever?

And how long would he be with them? Was he conscious enough to carry on a conversation? Would he? Had he changed?

And was it silly to want that photographer from church at the courthouse next week? She'd have her work cut out for her to make something artistic out of a five-minute wedding ceremony.

"Becca?" The intercom startled her.

"Yes, Mr. Hughes?"

"Nice. Professional. Are you busy?"

My mind is as busy as a hamster overdosing on energy drinks. "What do you need?"

"A minute with you. I've been reading in Isaiah . . ."

His "God-thing," as Mrs. Gallum would have described it.

"I think I found our theme verse for this next leg of our journey."

Becca warmed at the thought of her business-savvy almost-husband running to God's Word while her mind was kicking up dust on a greyhound track. Why hadn't she thought of that? "I'll be right in."

"By the way, the Humbold issues are finally resolved," he said as she entered the inner office.

"That was a long time coming."

"Took some careful negotiating. Doused a few fires. But it's done and done."

"Great. What a relief for you."

"Come see what I found."

She crossed to his desk, stood behind his chair, and looked over his shoulder at the well-worn Bible open beside his laptop. She had to lean close to read the small print. Isaac took advantage of the opportunity to grab her wrists and draw her arms around his neck.

"Verse one of Isaiah 43. Start right here," he said.

"'Don't fear, for I have redeemed you; I have called you by name; you are mine.'"

Isaac tightened his grip on her.

She leaned back a little and rested her chin on top of his head. Closing her eyes, she turned the words in her mind. God had called her by name. Isaac called her by her new name. She belonged to the God who redeems, and to Isaac.

"I hope it's okay," he said, "but I called in a favor. I used to golf with a justice of the peace. He's agreed to meet us at the pier Sunday afternoon if we can apply for the license before the close of business today."

"The pier?"

"Is that okay with you?"

"Perfect. What do we have to have in order to get the license? Do I have to be an official resident of California?"

"I have the website on my computer screen. No. Just a photo ID."

"Huh."

"Problem?"

"No. Curiosity. When I had my name legally changed, I applied for a passport. Don't ask me why. I had no plans to skip the country and certainly no plans to take a Mediterranean cruise or anything." She backed away from Isaac and sat on a free corner of his desk. "I felt . . . compelled . . . to get a passport. It cost me money I couldn't afford at the time. But it was that same kind of urging deep in my heart that I have now regarding my father's care. Who would have thought having a passport would expedite our getting married, since I'm still waiting to get a valid driver's license with my new name?"

Isaac pointed toward the ceiling—beyond the ceiling—with the look of a football player in the end zone, paying silent tribute to the One who got him there.

"Back home, there's a waiting time for a marriage license, I think."

"Not in California."

"That's providential for us. What else do we need?"

"The fee. That's it." Isaac scanned the computer screen. "Oh, this. 'Where each of your parents were born—city and state—and the names of your parents, including your mother's maiden name.'" Isaac sat back in his chair. "Becca."

"What?"

"No matter which of my moms they're talking about, I now know the answer to that question."

She squeezed his hand. What a tumble of joy and strain, bliss and grief. "Do we need to call for an appointment?"

He scanned the screen again. "Not necessary if you don't mind standing in line as much as two hours."

"I'll make the call." She ruffled his shampoo-model hair and headed for her own desk.

Even with the appointment, it took longer than expected to fill out the paperwork and start the process. They exited the government building and took a synchronized deep breath.

"Well, there's no turning back now," Isaac said.

"Not necessarily your most romantic line."

He tickled her ribs. "You don't think I should include it in the vows, then?"

"Vows." She stopped in her tracks. "Isaac, we need vows."

"I, for one, am going to need more sleep before I can form a coherent sentence."

"Sure," she said. "We have until Sunday afternoon to pull this off." Her face was a mix of tension and delight.

"Step at a time. Step at a time."

"Speaking of which . . ." The smartphone she'd finally agreed to purchase chimed.

"Becca, you need a ring tone with a little pizzaz."

"Isaac," she said, hand to her heart. "It's my dad's attorney."

He wrapped an arm around her and steered her to an out-of-the-way, unoccupied outdoor bench.

"Hello? Yes, I'm Becca Morrow. Yes,"—her eyes searched Isaac's for strength—"he's my father."

"Did you know he'd been moved to minimum security in Arizona, Becca?"

She slathered mayo on a ciabatta roll in prep for Ginger's assembly-line addition of roasted turkey, Vidalia onion jam, and provolone, then back to Becca for slices of heirloom tomatoes and lettuce. Their guys would be hungry when they finished putting together the hospital bed and its lift bar in the sunroom.

"I didn't want to know where he was."

"Understandable. So close, though. Makes the transfer here a lot simpler."

"Mmm hmm."

"They didn't pardon him, did they?"

"No. It happens sometimes that a prisoner is released because of a grave illness. Not often. Depends on a lot of things. The nature of the crime. The slickness of the lawyer. The personal bent of the judge."

Ginger slapped the tops of the ciabatta on the assembled sandwiches. "Mercy killing isn't considered severe?"

"I quote from a legal website I checked: 'The severity of murder far often outweighs the severity of an illness.' But not in this instance. His lawyer has some connections somewhere."

"He must."

"Dad was deemed 'no threat to society.' The papers say, 'released to his daughter's care.'"

Ginger slid a glass of iced tea toward Becca. She wiped her hands on a towel and took the tea with a nod of gratitude.

Ginger held hers, swirling the ice. "He'll arrive Monday?"

"Yes. By prison van. That picture seems so wrong."

"Becca, you and Isaac will only have one night alone together."

She was well aware of the timeline. Well aware.

"I thought you two would be able to steal away to La Jolla for a couple of nights at least."

"Not to be." She arranged a plate of grilled vegetables left over from the night before. "It's temporary, Ginger."

"Temporary can seem like a very long time."

"I can't mentally rush his death or I'll be making the same kind of choices he did, in a way. It's a thought I'll fight until the end, I suppose."

The end. Her dad's death. She was fairly certain he wasn't ready for it and convinced she had very little influence to change that.

33

He's wearing his golf clothes at our wedding," Becca whispered out of the side of her mouth.

Isaac countered, "And you're wearing a wedding dress on a fishing pier."

"*Touché.*"

"Justice Barnes had a brief window of time for this. He's doing us a favor."

She lowered her voice even further. "Don't get me wrong. I'm grateful. He looks cute in that hat."

"I thought you only had eyes for me."

Justice Barnes cleared his throat. "And if the bride and groom would approach?"

"The sunglasses. Nice touch, Becca."

"Ginger blinged them up for me. See?" She pointed to the tiny pearls her friend had hot-glued onto the temples.

"Which wedding do you think we'll remember most, Becca? This one or the real one?"

She tightened her grip on his arm. "This, my love, is as real as it gets."

A pier full of fishermen and tourists hooted and applauded for them when Justice Barnes finished the ceremony with, "That ought to do it."

Isaac and Becca didn't care that he'd stolen the line from a movie. They laughed through their first kiss as a married couple and most of the way down the pier.

Pete and Ginger, Tony, and the rest of the crew had spread a table before them in the presence of many seagulls. Tony, ever the enforcer, kept the birds at bay while the bride and groom filled their plates with strawberry crème cake topped with fresh, chocolate-dipped strawberries. Pete, the best man, prayed over the couple. His amen was followed by the crowd's hearty "Guacamole!" Not the New Year. Certainly a new phase of life. *Some things are better after they've been pulverized.*

Becca captured Isaac's face in her hands. "We're going to need all the guacamole wishes we can get!"

He took her hand and trotted toward the water's edge. The photographer waited for them there. "Isaac, my dress." Her protests must have been carried off on the breeze.

She kicked off her white flats. The photographer showed her how to catch up the skirt of her gown in one arm so the two could wade a few feet into the water.

"This is the shot I want," Isaac said as he leaned close, his pant legs rolled to the knees.

The surf broke around their calves as they posed for the camera. The photographer started to give directions but stopped when Isaac took her chin in his hands and kissed her lips, her nose, her forehead.

"You take my breath away," she said.

"You can borrow mine." He leaned his forehead into hers.

" 'The sound of these waves . . . ' "

"Uh huh."

" . . . is getting louder!" She grabbed his hand and her shoes and ran for higher ground as the sand where they'd stood was swallowed by the surf.

Their friends had disappeared. Food. Cars. People. A package sat on the picnic table with a note. "Time is short. Love is forever. Use both well."

The two drank in the message of the note. Isaac snatched up the package. "Do you want to open it in the car? We should probably get going."

"Probably should."

Becca settled into the passenger seat and fluffed her skirts around her. Isaac laid the package in her lap and started the engine.

The white embossed paper opened easily.

"What's the gift?" he asked.

She fought for control.

"Honey? My bride?"

"Chips and guacamole."

Isaac smiled. "Guess that's our supper."

"Couldn't be more meaningful."

"Oh contraire," he said, revealing his lack of fluency in French.

"Did you mean, '*Je suis d'accord*'? I agree?"

"Where did you learn French?"

"Misspent youth."

"No, I meant oh contraire."

"Or something like that. Where are we going? You missed the turn for home."

"Home will be there tomorrow and the next day and the next . . ."

She searched the unfamiliar landmarks, trying to get her bearings. "Where are you taking me?"

"My mom wants grandchildren, so . . ."

"Isaac!"

"So . . . I thought we might . . ."

"Isaac?"

" . . . not have to go any farther than this tonight."

He pulled into the valet area of a luxury hotel on the beach. She pounded the sand from her shoes while the bellman unloaded two small suitcases from the back of the car and Isaac tipped the valet. Within minutes, the bellman unlocked the door to the honeymoon suite. The balcony doors were open to a view of the ocean they'd just left.

After pointing out the features and amenities of the room, the bellman exited with a wide grin.

Isaac stored the guacamole in the refrigerator in the large, teak armoire while Becca moved to the balcony. The wideness of the ocean scene overwhelmed her, as it had the first time.

She hadn't taken more than a breath or two before Isaac wrapped his strong arms around her and joined her on appreciation's balcony.

"Our beginnings," he said.

She lost track of where her soul ended and his began in that moment. "Our beginnings."

"I guess I don't have to show you where everything is," she said when they carried their suitcases into Becca's—now their—room a little before noon on Monday. "Will you stop smiling like that?"

"Never." Isaac tugged on her sleeve and pulled her into another embrace. "Welcome home."

"You, too."

"I love what you've done with the place."

"I haven't done anything. This is how you left it."

"I know." He kissed her neck, then stopped himself. "We . . . have to . . . focus."

She took two steps away from him. "Yes. The marshal said they'd call when they were thirty minutes out."

"Okay. So, what would you like me to do?" He paused. "Other than that."

Her slow smile made his pulse race. "I think we're ready for him. The nurse is waiting for us to call her to help get him situated and to be apprised of the doctor's instructions. I don't know how much Dad can talk, how alert he is."

"The officials haven't told you much."

"Lots of red tape. Lots of misinformation and confusion. This isn't a common practice."

"For good reason." Isaac picked up the hanger with her sand-dusted gown. "Should I hang this in the closet or are you sending it out to the cleaners right away?"

"Can we keep it here a day or two?" Her eyes misted.

"As long as you want. But if it starts to smell like the inside of an oyster . . ."

"Got it."

He watched her compose herself. Who could do that as well as she could?

"I'm going to start a load of laundry. The week's been a little . . . guacamole-ish." She grabbed an armload of things from the hamper. "Do you have anything to add?"

"Most of it is still at the condo. I'll drag stuff over little by little."

"Oh! Your mom wanted you to call her and fill her in on the ceremony at the pier. Can you download the images the photographer sent? And if your mom asks about grandbabies . . ."

"I know. I know. Tell her they're on the way."

"Isaac."

"Adoption. What did you think I was talking about?"

Becca paused at the bedroom door. "Adoption is only one of the things that's going to have to wait."

34

The marshals arrived shortly after three. Any picture she had in her mind dissolved when she saw the gaunt figure of a person only faintly resembling the imposing man she knew as her father. The combination prison van/ambulance couldn't have made for a comfortable trip. His colorless lips were pursed unnaturally, his eyes blank, his body prone to random jerks and tremors.

He looked at Becca once, moving only his eyes, then not again while they maneuvered the gurney through the front entrance, in a solemn, silent procession down the hall, and into the room Aurelia and her God had made holy.

Bertram Dennagee glanced around the room and squinted his eyes.

"Too bright, Dad?" The word stuck in Becca's throat like a sideways fish bone.

"*Lovers of darkness rather than lovers of light,*" she thought, remembering a passage of Scripture she hadn't understood as clearly as she did now. "Let me close the shutters for you."

Isaac helped with the transfer, but his body language told Becca he couldn't have been less comfortable. What had she done to him? This was her burden to bear. He'd been roped in by association.

The home-health-care nurse—Cora Leeds—arrived before the transfer from gurney to hospital bed was complete. She reviewed the files one of the marshals handed her. "Are you the daughter?" she asked Becca.

"Yes."

Cora stood near Becca with her back to Bertram's bed and spoke softly. "It won't be long. I'm so sorry."

"How much time do we have?"

The nurse shrugged. "I'm surprised he survived the trip, frankly. A lot of rigamarole for what could be only a few weeks. Maybe a month."

Becca drew Cora into the hall. "You do understand why he was in prison? I thought it only fair for you to know."

"I'm a nurse, not a judge. That's not up to me."

Becca was once good at it. Somewhere along the way, she had lost her judging touch. "We're glad you're here."

"Met your fiancé in the entry. Nice guy."

"He's my husband." The word soothed the tension in Becca's throat. "Another name change. I'm Becca Hughes now."

Cora Leeds wouldn't understand the reference. It didn't matter. They could swap stories some other time.

"Well, I have some work to do in there," Cora said, tapping the file in her hands.

"And the marshals said I have paperwork to sign."

"Nice to meet you."

"You, too. Thanks for any help you can give us."

Becca repeated the statement to someone with more clout. *Lord, thanks for any help You can give us. We're going to need it.*

She followed Cora into the sunroom, which already smelled like a decomposing man. Isaac leaned over the bed and said, a little too loudly, "Welcome to our home, Bertram."

Her father's mouth moved. No sound came out, but he distinctly mouthed, "Thank you."

Isaac pressed his crossed palms to the back of his neck. "I have to go to work tomorrow, Becca."

"I know." She closed the door to their room and locked it.

"He can't move. You're safe in here."

She reached to unlock the door, but left it as it was. "Just tonight?"

"Doesn't bother me."

She flicked the switch on the monitor, not sure what good it would do if her father couldn't speak. But she'd hear if he fell or . . .

"That, on the other hand, will bother me." Isaac noted.

"We could get him a call button, like they have in hospitals?"

Isaac tossed his shirt in the hamper. "Might be something higher tech than that available now. I wish we could afford around-the-clock nursing care for him. For your sake."

"Are you going to be okay at the office without me?" Was *she* going to be okay with that?

"Not even a little bit. I'll work as much as I can from home."

Her breath came easier. "And I'll have stretches of time when I can do office work, too. Could we get phone calls routed here?"

"Let's wait to see how involved this is. Give it a couple of days."

She wrapped her arms around his waist and laid her head on his chest. "Thanks for this." ·

"I have to tell you he makes me feel a little squirmy." Isaac shuddered to illustrate his point.

"So it's not just me."

He stroked her sun-streaked hair. "Want to read for a while? Watch television?"

Becca didn't raise her head. "I want to curl beside you and listen to your heartbeat all night long."

Why?

He clearly mouthed the word *why* when Becca shaved her father's whiskers the next morning. She took it slowly, carefully scraping the razor through the shaving cream as she learned the contours of his face. "Because they brought you here a little scruffy-looking, Dad."

He shook his head. *Why?*

"Because you needed a place to go."

Why you? He pointed at her with a frail, tremulous hand.

It wasn't an unfamiliar question. She'd been asking it herself since the letter came from his attorney.

"Because I'm all you have." She wiped the disposable razor on the towel in her lap. "And because we have a lot to talk about."

He turned his head away from her. She'd have to change the pillowcase and his hospital gown. Both were smeared with shaving cream.

"Can you logroll, Dad? I need to put a fresh pad underneath you."

He didn't answer or move for a long moment. Then he reached for the far railing and pulled himself onto his side. She used her shoulder to hold him in that position while she slid the used pad from underneath him and slid another into place. Her free hand could just reach the basin of warm water and the washcloth floating in it. She squeezed the excess water and gently washed his back and bottom. He was shaking hard when she lowered him onto the new, soft pad.

"There," she said. "We lived through the first time."

They may have lived through it, but they were both crying.

"Do you prefer to sip through a straw?"

He nodded.

"I'll get you some from the kitchen when we're done getting you prettied up for Cora."

His eyebrows asked, "Who?"

"Your nurse. You met her yesterday afternoon briefly."

His eyebrows relaxed.

"She'll be here four hours every day. She knows more about the medical care you need."

He rubbed his thumb and fingertips together.

"We're taking care of the money end."

His hand dropped to the bed as if the ligaments had given out.

He pointed to the diamond on her left hand.

"Yes, Dad. Isaac and I are married."

How long?

Why did that question choke her? "Two days."

He pursed his lips again in that prune-like way and stared at the ceiling.

He cooperated very little with the rest of his morning routine: teeth brushing, changing his gown, brushing his hair. He needed his hair washed. Some other day. She rubbed lotion on his feet and legs. Even the gentlest touch made him flinch.

"I'll be back with your breakfast in a few minutes."

He shook his head no.

"Sorry, Dad, but everybody eats in this house. We'll find something you like. Might take us a few tries."

She tucked the lightweight blanket under his arms and made sure the guardrails were locked in place. The basin in hand and towel over her arm, she left him lying there in a room with all windows and no light.

Becca draped herself over the kitchen island and let her cheek soak in the coolness of the granite. She'd been at this task an hour and was emotionally spent. What did he like to eat? Think.

She poached an egg and made a single slice of toast. Milk was hard to digest, she'd read. Orange juice, too acidic. She made a cup of weak tea. Did he even drink tea? She'd soon find out.

The tray chattered in her hands as she carried it down the hall to the sunroom.

"Can you feed yourself?"

No, he mouthed. He raised his hand and showed her an inch of space between his thumb and index finger. *A little.*

She dipped a triangle of toast in the egg yolk and held it to his mouth. One second. Two. He opened his mouth and bit off the corner. Two bites later he'd had enough. She wondered if the act of eating exhausted him. He couldn't feel full after that little. He sipped the tea through a straw.

"More?"

One nod.

"I didn't know if you would like tea." The fact that she was pleased reflected in his face.

Hurts. To. Talk. This time a gravelly, coarse, airy sound accompanied the forms his lips made.

"Then don't try to talk, Dad. We're doing fine so far."

Not. Doing. Fine! If a whisper could be a shout, his was. *You. Need. To. Know.* His face contorted with the effort.

"Know what?"

How. Sorry.

His eyes pinched tight, he said no more. An invisible pain shook his body. She waited, laid a hand on his frail arm, then left the room after the shaking stopped and his breathing fell into slumber mode.

As she should have years earlier, she stood at the door and prayed for peace for his soul.

35

He's sleeping more than I thought he would. I'm not sure we need Cora, Isaac." Becca curled up next to him on the sofa. He set his laptop aside and tucked her head under his chin.

Isaac fought for the right thing to say. "Do you think that's a bad thing for him to sleep so much?"

"I think it's the only thing that keeps the pain at bay. He flinches even in his sleep. In that way, and that way only, he reminds me of Aurelia."

Isaac smoothed the creases in her forehead, stirring the faint scent of ripe pears. "Why would you want to get rid of Cora?"

"The money. And when she's here, she doesn't talk to him or anything. She tends to her responsibilities and then sits and knits or reads." She sat up. "Not that it's wrong for her to do that. We knew she wouldn't have to be busy the whole time."

"Save some of the ugly work for her. She can do his bath, brush his teeth, shave him."

"Cut his toenails."

"Exactly." Isaac laid her head against his chest again. She popped back up.

"That doesn't seem right."

"Becca, she's hired to do those things."

"I'm not talking about division of labor. It seems like my humbling myself to do the jobs no one wants to do is part of my . . . my assignment." Her eyes pled for him to understand.

"From God."

"Yes. From God."

"Like Jesus touching the lepers."

"Kind of."

"Or me rubbing your feet *before* you've had a shower."

She pinched his stomach. "Isaac."

"Ow!"

"Or me making cheesecake today and keeping it a secret until this moment so you wouldn't be tempted to eat more than one slice before bedtime."

Isaac sat upright. "You made cheesecake?"

"Let's use another example."

"Becca, you made cheesecake?"

He beat her to the kitchen, but only by a few feet. He snatched two forks from the drawer and had two small plates waiting on the island when she retrieved the cheesecake from the fridge.

"Coffee, too?" she asked. "I have decaf brewed."

"Awesome. Yes. Thanks. And someday I will make all this up to you."

"All what?" She sliced into the creamy dessert and slid a generous slab onto his plate. A small one for herself.

"All the sacrifices you've had to make. All you've—" His phone buzzed. "It's Mom."

"Ooh! Let me talk to her when you're done, okay?"

"Mom? I love you but you have to know I'm going to eat cheesecake while you talk. No debate. I'll chew quietly."

His mom's laughter warmed him. "Cheesecake, huh? I'll be right there."

"Becca made it."

"Married life is rough, isn't it? How's she doing?"

Isaac looked at his wife, gazing at him as she devoured her own dessert.

"It's hard. But she's amazing."

"Well, we both knew that."

He winked at Becca and whispered, "She likes you."

"I may have someone interested in buying my business, Isaac."

"Really? How interested?" He watched Becca perk up at his end of the conversation.

"Coming tomorrow to scope things out. I've been working like fury to make sure the books are all in order so the business presents well. Any leads on my grandparent cottage?"

"No, Mom. No grandkids yet."

Becca threw her napkin at him. "She did not ask that."

"I've been watching the listings every day. Nothing suitable that's also reasonably priced. We should find something in this market, though. Becca and I talked about you staying with us for a while until you find something if your business sells."

"Oh, that's all you two need."

"We'd love to have you." He nodded in Becca's direction. She nodded in concert.

"We'll see. I'd like to talk to Becca for a few minutes if she has time. But first I have something for you."

"What's that?"

"Becca's come through kind of a barren time in her life, wouldn't you say?"

"That's one word for it."

"Do you know what I found to be the sweetest verses in the Bible about the Isaac you were named after?"

"No."

"This is the first. It's at the end of Genesis 24. 'Isaac brought Rebekah into his mother Sarah's tent. He married Rebekah and loved her. So Isaac found comfort after his mother's death.'"

"You're choking me up here, Mom."

"And here's the second, the one I hope you latch onto. The next chapter. The Bible says Isaac prayed to the Lord for his wife, since she was barren. And the Lord was moved by his prayer."

Isaac set his fork on his plate.

"Are you there?"

"I'm here, Mom."

"God is moved by your prayers for your wife. I think the biblical Isaac's shining moment was right then. He saw his wife's pain and he committed to pray for her. You don't happen to see any parallels, do you?"

"I already do pray for her, all the time." He noted Becca's movement—hand to her heart.

"I'm sure you do."

"But I needed the reminder that no matter what else I do as her husband, those are my shining moments."

"You're such a quick study. Now, put her on the phone, would you?"

"Mom?"

"Yes?"

"I love you so much."

"I'm glad we finally found each other. I love you, too."

He handed Becca the phone. She held it away from her and asked, "Would you go check on Dad? Please?"

"Sure. Do I need to take him anything?"

"Just see if he's doing okay. He didn't eat much. He might be hungry. Then again . . ."

"I'll take care of it."

"Thank you. I mean that."

His mom's voice called through the phone, "I can hear you two kissing, just so you know."

⸻

The fire flickered low. Becca could hear the air conditioning unit kick on. They'd waste a little electricity tonight for the privilege of having the ambiance of a fire in the fireplace. Ginger's orders. It was the one-month anniversary of their wedding. Ginger and Pete insisted they celebrate with a quiet meal for just the two of them with no responsibilities. But Becca's dad's health flickered like the fire. All Becca and Isaac would agree to was locking themselves in their suite around the corner from the sunroom.

The table between the two armchairs was set with a linen tablecloth, china, fancy silverware, goblets of Isaac's current favorite—sparkling pear juice, and Mediterranean pizza—Becca's favorite.

Light jazz stayed just far enough offstage to support but not interfere with conversation.

Pete and Ginger had dragged two of the living room chairs into the sunroom and alternated taking care of Bertram's needs and working on their taxes.

Becca and Isaac were free to enjoy a night off, a night focused on each other.

Isaac finished the last of the pizza crust on his plate and drained his goblet. "More?" he offered her as he poured himself another glass.

"Thanks. Yes."

They both leaned back against the luxurious softness of the leather chairs.

"Are you ready to talk about it yet?"

Becca kept her eyes closed. "Talk about what?" Which of the million things on their minds did he mean?

"The details of what sent your father to prison. And how they affected you."

A long-ago ache thrummed in her chest. An ache, not a wound. A spot where a wound used to be.

"You don't have to tell me if you don't want to. Someday I hope you will feel safe enough with me to—"

"I feel safe enough with you now. Weak is the new strong, as they say."

His deep, inviting eyes questioned her.

"The verse? 'When I am weak, then I am strong.' I had to give up my old method of trying to manufacture strength to endure this, thinking I could run away from what he'd done and how I felt about it."

"No one blames you for that." His voice poured like warm caramel sauce.

She sipped from the goblet then watched as the bubbles sparkled in the light from the fire. "Fake strength shatters pretty easily. And maintaining it is exhausting. I tried to hold my dad accountable for his actions. That wasn't my job. His reputation dogged me, true. But some of it was the result of my own imagination."

Her throat tightened, but with grief this time, not fear or guilt.

Their one-month anniversary, with a lifetime stretching before them like an ocean spilling over the horizon.

She blinked back tears. "I think he had to disengage from any faith connection he'd had, which wasn't much, because if he'd heard God's voice, he would have to answer to Him." She hadn't spelled it out, even to herself, until this moment in the presence of someone who loved her forever.

Silence considered her words.

"So," Isaac said after a long pause, "you sympathize with him?"

"I don't agree with what he did. But I now know what it feels like to agonize with someone else in pain and long to trade places because of love, or long to have a legitimate, God-honoring way to relieve their suffering. I think if my parents had known they could trust God with the outcome and with the path to get there, they would have waited on His timing. And, horrific as it might have been at the end, the glory a nanosecond later would have swept all that away into oblivion. I wish they'd known."

Absently, he played with her fingers. "I hated seeing my mom in pain. Hated it."

"I know."

"She fought so hard." His voice cracked.

Her heart broke.

"They haven't set a date for Riggo's trial yet." Isaac's voice seemed to stabilize in the discussion of the timeline.

"It'll seem as if it takes forever," she said. "Riggo didn't know it, but he played a role in my ability to look at my father through different eyes."

"Riggo makes my skin crawl."

"Mine, too. But in the pharmacy that day, he said my dad wouldn't mentor him. That was before Dad was imprisoned."

"So?"

"If my father had wanted to leave a legacy, if he'd wanted to trumpet a cause of mercy killings, he would have jumped at the chance to mentor an eager student." It wouldn't ever feel right, but it might not always feel raw. She closed her eyes and pressed into what she knew for sure—that God's wisdom would always outshine her own. "Can we change the subject, Isaac?"

"Sure."

A long moment passed. The world spun. People somewhere beyond the doors of their home were leading ordinary lives.

"Your men's group is such a blessing to you."

"Love those guys."

"I'd like to open our home to an accountability group like that for women." She hardly recognized herself. Intentionally making strides to get to know people better? To build relationships?

Isaac sat upright in his chair. "Great idea. We have the room for it."

"Not right away, with my dad here. Maybe in the fall."

"Love it."

"But . . ."

"What is it?"

"That would mean the men would have to babysit the kids. Think that will be a problem?"

"Not with this group. Kids? Are you trying to tell me something?"

She pushed against his arm. "Isaac, you're as relentless as your mother."

36

How they'd passed the two-month mark, Becca didn't know. Her father weakened, but by millimeters each day. He didn't rally. Nothing that positive. A slow fade.

"Dad, I'm going to start having my morning focus time in here with you, if that's okay." Becca peeked through the closed shutters as she spoke, not wanting to see whether he agreed or disagreed with her plan. The garden vibrated with color. A few things needed trimming. She'd get to that after Cora relieved her at ten.

"We always have a little time between getting you ready for the day and the nurse arriving." She turned and busied herself with checking the level in the fluid bag that hung near floor-level from his bed. She lifted his head and flipped his pillow to the cool side. "It helps me get a better start to my day if I take time to read something from God's Word and"—she watched his eyes now for a flicker of disapproval—"pray." Nothing. No reaction.

"Want some aftershave this morning? I borrowed some from Isaac's medicine cabinet."

He shook his head no.

So he was alert. Still aware.

She pulled a straight chair to a spot near the head of the bed. "I've been reading in the book of John." His stare widened. She laid her small Bible—open—on his bed, with its back resting on the side of his ribs.

He jerked.

"Does that hurt, Dad?" She reached to move it, but he mouthed *No*.

With the Bible resting against his heart like that, she began to read.

The story of Jesus preparing His followers for the time when He wouldn't be with them anymore. She hadn't planned it. The spot was where she'd finished reading the day before.

"'Jesus knew that his time had come to leave this world and go to the Father. Having loved his own who were in the world, he loved them fully.'"

She stole a glance at his face out of the corner of her eye. Immovable.

She skipped ahead a few verses. "'He got up from the table and took off his robes. Picking up a linen towel, he tied it around his waist.'" Becca hesitated. Was this the best passage for either one of them?

"'Then he poured water into a washbasin and began to wash the disciples' feet, drying them with the towel he was wearing.'"

Her father's hand lifted from the thin sheet. He pointed to the page and then to her. *You*, he mouthed.

Oh, Daddy!

She swallowed back tears. Skipped ahead a few more verses. "'Jesus replied, "Unless I wash you, you won't have a place with me."'"

Maybe something from the Psalms would be more appropriate. She flipped the crisp pages back, back. He laid his hand over hers on the book and squirmed for her attention.

She'd clearly agitated him. Not her intention at all.

His mouth worked to form the words, his eyes wild with the inexpressible.

Help. Me. Die.

She shook off his hand and grabbed her Bible from its resting place against him. "I won't do that." Her chair scraped against the hardwood as she backed it away from the bed. She pressed her hand to her racing heart, fully aware it must have looked as if she were pledging allegiance. In a way, she was. Allegiance to the God she trusted with her life . . . and his.

His head shook from side to side. He lifted his hand and let it drop to the bed, then lifted and dropped.

"What is it, Dad? I won't help you—"

His hoarse growl forced out a word, and another.

Help. Me. Die. At. Peace. He tapped his nearly hollow chest then pointed to the Bible she clung to. The movement exhausted him. She watched him fight to swallow, his face twisted in pain.

She stroked his forehead until it smoothed. She planted a featherweight blessing kiss just above the crease between his eyes. His hair smelled like her pear shampoo mingled with the sweat of pain.

"What do you need, Daddy?"

He opened his eyes and turned them to her. Scrolls of dialogue they'd never shared poured out of them. She couldn't read a word. Then he turned his head to face the ceiling and beyond. *For. Give. Ness.*

Forgiveness was his final word.

He still nodded. Could squeeze a hand. Tried to mouth something but couldn't succeed after the exertion of expressing what had been building for years. But he could no longer even whisper a word.

The pattern of days remained, but the air held an intimate vibrancy to it. Even Cora commented that it felt different in the room.

On his way to view a beach property that might work for his mom, Isaac stopped at the house around noon a week and a half later.

"I miss our lunches together, Becca."

She dished up three plates of leftover enchiladas—one for Isaac, one for herself, and one for Cora, who reinforced the decision Bertram and his doctor had made not to introduce a feeding tube when it became necessary. And it had. "I do, too. I don't have much appetite, but I miss being with you."

They spoke in hushed tones. The grandfather clock in the hall had dampened its ticking. The whole house sensed time was short.

"Where were you reading this morning?"

"John fourteen. His facial muscles can't form a smile anymore. I know that. But I could have sworn that's what I saw. We've been skipping around. A little of the Psalms. Something from Isaiah. I read him those verses from Genesis about Isaac praying for his wife."

Isaac drew her onto his lap. She balanced with one hand against the kitchen island.

"This isn't how I pictured our marriage would start," he said.

"I didn't dare dream I could ever be married to someone like you," she said. "So it seems perfectly normal to me."

They shared a knowing that sustained them and a sense of humor that made life easier to swallow. *Guacamole.* For the pulverized moments.

Becca laid her head against Isaac's chest, her favorite position, aware she'd have to microwave Cora's enchiladas to get them hot again.

Cora stepped around the corner into the kitchen. "Oh, you're both here. Good. You'll want to be with him for this."

Isaac and Becca took up stations on either side of the bed. Bertram's breathing was even shallower than it had been the past week. His tremors were gone. No flinching. No jerking with pain.

Cora pointed to a spot on his neck where his pulse was visible. "Watch," she said. She grabbed her knitting and headed for the door. "You belong here. I'll be in the kitchen. Call me when he's gone."

You belong here.

Becca let the truth of those words swirl around and through her. All her belongings, all her longings, huddled in that room, waiting for God to have the final say, waiting for death to meet its match, waiting for three lives to start fresh. And if she was right, a fourth. She pressed one palm low against her belly and rested the other on her father's forehead.

Isaac prayed aloud, a sweet prayer about going home. Becca was sure her voice wouldn't hold out, but whispered, "Daddy, see what you would have missed?"

The pulse in his neck weakened. The beats came too far apart. His breaths didn't register. All that moved was the small, faint bump of another heartbeat. Then there were none.

Isaac moved to her side of the bed and held her. He did that so well. She sobbed, tight-throated, silently except for the sniffs to snatch another breath.

After a few moments, Isaac led her away from the bed to the windows. He cupped her hand in his. Together they opened the shutters and let in the light.

Discussion Questions

1. Have you known someone like Jayne, born to a couple who didn't want to have children? Did the parents change their minds? How did their initial reticence resolve: with unconditional love or with soul-raking disinterest?

2. Some might say Bertram Denagee perpetuated his "community service" acts to legitimize or even ennoble what he'd done to Jayne's mother. What do you think resided at the core of his actions? fear? pain? selfishness? something more sinister?

3. Jayne bore a lumbering, awkward guilt burden for reporting her father's crime. Why do you think it was especially difficult for her to maneuver around that guilt?

4. How do you explain Becca's exceptional connection with Aurelia? What made Becca the caregiver Aurelia needed?

5. Is there a location or home or setting that calls to you, like water did to Becca? If so, where? Why? For Becca, the vastness of the sea spoke not of her smallness, but of her connection to something larger than herself, as if the waves were a heartbeat, a "tupping" that resonated deep within her. Where is that spot for you?

6. Becca made an incredibly difficult choice near the end of the story. What freed her to make that decision? Would you have made the same choice?

7. "Love is intensely sweet, even when crumpled." Do you agree with that statement? About which character in *All My Belongings* do you think it best applies?

8. Becca described Geneva's faith as a "sustaining" faith. How would you describe what that means?

9. The same heat that scorches vegetables makes a rich, deeply intense, and flavorful reduction sauce. How did the hardships in Becca's life show up as a rich reduction rather than a scorched, blackened, unusable pile of ashes?

10. Becca didn't long for a change of climate, a town that would accept her, a house she could call her own. It was much deeper than that—a core need. The need to belong. She grew into a whole person on her journey. When in the story was it most evident to you that her place to belong was an intangible but more real than any flesh-and-bone or wood-and-cement or waves-and-shoreline creation?

Want to learn more about Cynthia Ruchti
and check out other great fiction from
Abingdon Press?

Check out our website at
www.AbingdonPress.com
to read interviews with your favorite authors,
find tips for starting a reading group,
and stay posted on what new titles are on the horizon.

Be sure to visit Cynthia online!

www.cynthiaruchti.com